WHERE WE FOUND OUR
Heart

NATASHA BISHOP

WHERE WE FOUND OUR

Heart

CHAPTER
One

Nina

LOOK AROUND THE WEDDING VENUE AND FEEL A SENSE OF CALM FOR the first time in months. Everything has come together beautifully. The color theme is white and gold. It's both whimsical and regal at the same time. White draping across the entire ceiling makes the venue seem endless. The hydrangeas at each table stand tall and command attention. The gold accents are subtle, not ostentatious at all, yet emit power all the same.

The bride, my best friend Ciara, is wearing a gorgeous A-line V-neck floor-length gown. The bodice fits her like a glove while the bottom flares out a bit to give a princess vibe. The whole dress is covered in a stunning gold lace. The intricate details of her bright red phoenix tattoo, spanning the entire length of her arm, accentuate her beauty and make her dress pop against her almond-colored skin.

I remember being with her, her mom, and our friends when she found the dress. We all cried at how beautiful she looked. Until today, that was the last time I cried tears of joy. The tears I cried that day were beautiful. I was proud to let them fall and give them over to Ciara's happiness.

The tears I cried mere weeks later and every day after were ugly and angry. Full of pain and loss. If I could go back to Ciara's wedding dress shopping day, I'd appreciate those tears a hell of a lot more. We knew her soon to be husband, Lincoln, would lose his shit when he saw her in it, and he did. The look on his face when he saw her walking toward him was enough to bring anyone to their knees. The look of the man behind him, watching his brother with pride, is one I tried and failed to ignore.

I'm staring out at the dessert table when I feel a tap on my shoulder by a tiny hand. I turn around and look at my sister, Jada. She looks adorable in her light pink floor-length dress. She insisted on getting a long dress to match me. She's tripped over it four times tonight, but she's so damn cute. She looks so much like our mom—it's why I call her Mini—it almost hurts to look at her.

"Nina, ShaSha said CiCi and Linc are going on a honeymoon. What's that?" I laugh every time she calls my other best friend, Sasha, "ShaSha" because she can't seem to pronounce Sasha.

"A honeymoon is a trip that couples take to celebrate their wedding alone." Her face drops at the word "trip" and I curse myself.

"Are they going to take a train?" she asks, frantic.

"No, Mini. They're going to take a plane, but they'll be okay, I promise." It's a tricky thing. Because I can't actually promise that. I shouldn't say that. But I have to give this innocent little girl some peace of mind.

"Okay, if you're sure." I look up at my brother, Logan, and though he's looking down at his lap, I know it pains him to listen to our conversation right now. It's been four months, and I still don't know how to properly explain to her that a vacation doesn't mean a death sentence.

Our parents were on their way to New Orleans for an anniversary trip when their train derailed, and they were killed in the crash. Now I'm the sole guardian to my fourteen-year-old brother and six-year-old sister, and I have no idea what I'm doing. I used to babysit my siblings a lot because my parents often acted like they didn't have minors to raise and took off on vacations frequently. But babysitting for a few days and being completely responsible for shaping them into well-rounded people ready to enter the world is completely different. And let's face it, I have an uphill battle here. I'm left trying to undo the damage our parents have caused while trying not to fuck them up any more. Thanks, Mom and Dad. I hope you're having a great permanent vacation wherever the fuck you are. Ugh. I don't want to be mad at them. That's not fair or right.

I'm pulled back to reality when Ciara approaches our table.

"Hey, gorgeous." I turn around and give her a huge hug. She asks Logan and Jada if they'd be okay if I step outside with her for a minute. Jada looks nervous at the thought of me being out of her sight. She's become a permanent attachment at my side since our parents passed, and I know it's not healthy, but honestly I think the only reason I haven't had a mental breakdown yet is because she's always with me. Logan just nods, and I drown in his silence. I miss my brother. He's always been quiet, but he had a charming personality with the people he loves the most. That boy is nowhere to be found right now.

I follow Ciara out to the venue's patio, and she wastes no time diving in. "How are you doing?"

Nope. Not going there. Not today. Not tomorrow. Maybe not ever. "Uh-uh. No you don't. Today is your day; you don't need to check on me."

She levels me with a hard stare. "You are my sister, Nina. I don't just push you to the side." And this is why I love her. We've only known each other for a year and a half, but I've never met anyone as selfless as she is, always putting everyone above herself. But she's done enough of that for a lifetime. She's earned the right to be blissed out of her mind with happiness today. I'm not going to drag her down with me. My misery does not want company.

"I'm fine, really."

"Okay, sure. But I have a surprise for you anyway." Who gets someone else a surprise on their wedding day? I don't respond; I just raise my brows in question. "Sasha is going to keep Logan and Jada for the weekend so that you can have some time to decompress."

"What? No. No. I can't do that. Jada will freak out."

She shakes her head adamantly. "We talked it through with her earlier

3

today, and she's excited to hang out with Nevaeh. Reggie and Michael are gonna bring Malcolm and Niecy by too, so I think she'll be distracted enough. If it gets to be too much for her, you can cut your weekend short, but you deserve to try. We are going to get you all through this. Together. Take the break, Nina." Nevaeh is Sasha's daughter. She's Jada's age, and they always have a good time whenever they hang out. Reggie is Sasha's sister. She and her husband, Michael, have two kids, Malcolm and Niecy, who are older than Jada and Nevaeh. Niecy is thirteen and Malcolm is ten, so they'll probably spend most of their time with Logan, if he doesn't crawl deep inside a book and shut out the world.

The idea of having a weekend to myself sounds nice. I'm a speeding car headed straight for a brick wall. I just need someone to hit the brakes for a moment. But can I do that? What would I even do with a weekend to myself? I've been part of a trio every day for four months. I don't understand the meaning of privacy anymore.

I feel him before I see him. I look up and there he is. Isaiah Cole. He's the guy I want nothing to do with and yet I can't seem to stop thinking about him. He also happens to be Ciara's brother-in-law now. He's looking right at me, and I can't tell what he's thinking but I don't have time to decipher his mood today. He's so hot and cold, I can't get comfortable. But part of me just wants to take a bite out of him. *Jesus.*

I realize too late that Ciara has seen the exchange between us. I'm not stepping on that landmine yet so I give her the answer she's looking for instead. "Okay, okay. I'll do it. Thank you, Ci. Really." I squeeze her shoulder and head back inside.

Long after the wedding is over and the kids are with Sasha and Carter, I'm sitting on my couch wondering what the fuck I'm going to do with this newfound weekend of freedom. I've been forbidden from seeing the kids—unless Jada can't cope—and from going to the bar I manage, Neon

4

Nights. Who the fuck am I if I'm not watching the kids or running that bar?

You're a woman with needs that haven't been met in quite some time.

I feel like that meme of Kermit with the hoodie on.

The non-hoodie version of me is saying, "Spend the weekend coping with your feelings. There's plenty of housework you can do. There are a lot of healthy ways you can spend your time."

While the hoodie version of me is screaming, "Sex is healthy. Go to Isaiah's place in this sexy-ass bridesmaid dress and fuck his brains out like you've wanted to do for over a year."

I look myself over in the mirror. This dress really is beautiful. It's gold and looks amazing against my chestnut skin. It's mermaid style and hugs to my round hips like a second skin. I know I saw Isaiah checking out my ass at least once tonight. And he looked like a damn GQ model in his suit. Part of me knew I was going to do this. It's why I haven't taken the dress off yet. Yeah, okay. Decision made. I strap my heels back on and head out before rational thought can take over.

The whole ride over to Isaiah's, I'm a hot mess. I debate turning around about a hundred different times, but the hoodie version of me keeps her foot firmly planted on the gas. I've been to Isaiah's house exactly three times before. I dropped Sasha off there once after we'd gone to brunch because she didn't want Carter to see how drunk she'd gotten and tease her. He hosted Nevaeh's birthday party last year. It was not adorable at all. My ovaries did not almost explode. Nope, not at all. And Ciara and Lincoln's engagement party was held at Isaiah's house. I never understood why a single man in his twenties chose to buy a single-family home in the burbs. To each his own I guess. I loved my apartment in the city, but now that I've got two kids to raise, I'm a fellow suburbanite.

I spend an embarrassing amount of time outside of his door debating how many knocks makes me look casual and not like I'm desperate for sex. Even though I'm very desperate for sex. Three knocks then silence. That's my limit. I won't knock again. It seems three is the magic number because it doesn't take long to hear the lock to the door clicking.

This man has the audacity to answer the door in the men's equivalent of lingerie—grey sweatpants and no shirt. I do what I hope to God is a subtle drool check because I am Nina Fucking Williams and I'll be damned if I let a man see me drooling over him. Even if he is too sexy to be real.

He leans against his door with a knowing smirk, and I make it my mission to wipe it right off his face. "How you doing, Nina?"

Okay, we're off to a good start. Since I met Isaiah he's given me whiplash. One minute he flirts with me and gives me all his attention, the next he barely acknowledges my existence. And having a serious conversation without him defaulting to flirtation or jokes is like pulling teeth. I have no time for games which is why I said I'd never date him, but I'm not exactly here to date him, now am I? He's starting off by addressing me like Joey from *Friends,* so I'm guessing he's in a flirty mood.

"Am I Rachel or Phoebe?" He just smiles and steps aside so I can come in.

"Definitely Phoebe. That fits you. Kind of like how that dress fits you."

"Perfectly, you mean?"

That gets a real laugh out of him. "I always love your modesty."

"Modesty is overrated. We both know I look fine as fuck in this dress." His eyes trail down my body, and I resist the urge to shiver under his gaze. I wait for his eyes to lock with mine, and when they do, I hold my stare, daring him to make the next move.

"You do. It would probably look even better on the floor." Now he's speaking my language.

"My thoughts exactly." His eyebrows rise at that. Yeah, I'm not here to play games tonight.

"Shit. I've never loved weddings more than I do in this moment."

"Look, you and I have been doing this dance for too long now. The kids are at Sasha's for the weekend against my will, so I can do anything I want to do, and I want to do you." His eyes soften at the mention of my siblings. That's exactly what I don't want. I need to lock up the sympathy and get the heat back in his eyes. I mean, Jesus, didn't he hear the part where I said I wanted to do him? Focus, man. I swish my hips as I get closer to him, and his eyes follow the movement.

Bingo.

"Nina, you don't have to explain. If you have needs, I'm more than capable of taking care of them for you."

"Then stop talking and get over here." He closes the distance between us in a second and pulls me in for a heated kiss. This kiss is full of passion and promises of what's to come, and I immediately feel the heat in my core. I want to lift my leg up to his waist, but this damn dress is preventing that. I did not think this through well enough. He reads my mind, though, and spins me around to unzip the dress, following the zipper with his tongue. Holy shit. I step out of the dress, and his eyes are hooded with desire, staring at me in nothing but my sheer bra, panties, and garters.

"Fuck. You are gorgeous."

His words have me feeling bold. "Needy over here, Isaiah. What are you gonna do about it?" He growls and lifts me up with ease then walks us down the hall to his bedroom.

He follows me down to the bed before lifting my legs over his shoulders and kissing up my legs from my ankles to the place where I need him most. He blows a breath against my panties, and I'm already about to lose it.

I have dreamed of this moment several times. We've been treading the waters of this sexual tension for over a year now, and it's finally pulling us under its waves. I've never wanted to drown more in my life.

"Shit, Isaiah." He taps my hips, and I instantly lift so he can pull my panties down. He continues kissing my inner thighs. A bite here, a nibble there. He's teasing me, but never giving me the pressure I need. I'm going to kill him.

"Isaiah?"

"Yes?" He drags out the word.

"If you don't eat my pussy soon I'm gonna finish without you."

He throws his head back in laughter. "Hmm, I'm tempted to keep teasing you until you beg for it."

Ha! Yeah, okay. That's not even in my vocabulary. I glide my hand down my chest until I reach my folds. I want him to touch me, but watching him watch me touch myself is getting me going all the same. I make a show of pleasuring myself until I hear him curse and slap my hand away.

"That's what I thought." I feel vindicated until he finally licks up my center and then all thoughts leave me. His tongue is the stuff dreams are made of. All his teasing is over with. He dips two fingers inside of me, spreading me wider. His free hand squeezes my ass, pulling me closer to his mouth. I moan his name loudly when he thrusts his fingers deeper inside me. He sucks my clit so hard I don't even have a moment to breathe before my orgasm hits me like a freight train.

What the fuck? I may not have been fully prepared for Isaiah Cole but damn if I'm turning back now.

My legs are shaking, and he caresses them while climbing up my body to reach my lips. He crushes his mouth to mine, and I taste myself on his tongue. I grab the band of his sweatpants and pull him down to completely cover me. He leans back up to pull his pants and briefs down. His erection bobs free. *Holy shit.*

I should've known. I should've seen this coming, but I really was not prepared for this man tonight.

That thing is a weapon.

A weapon of mass orgasms.

He has what I like to call "Special Occasion Dick" or SOD. A dick so big it's not meant to be experienced on a regular basis because it will rearrange your fucking organs. I've only experienced it once in my lifetime. You don't find them in the wild—otherwise known as the streets of Austin—often. It's only meant for a special occasion—like a birthday, or a promotion, or a recovery from a shitty breakup, or your parents dying and your first weekend alone without your siblings. *Eww.* That's incredibly morbid. *Buck the fuck up, Nina.*

I hear the crinkle of a condom wrapper and watch as he sheaths himself, never taking his eyes off me.

"I've been waiting a long time for this moment," he confesses. He leans down and bites my neck then immediately cools it with his tongue. He continues that trail down to my shoulder, making it impossible to think straight.

"You're the one who's been playing games for the last year. You're so hot and cold I can't tell which way is up." He sobers for a moment at that statement but immediately morphs his face back into that schoolboy smirk.

He starts singing—well, it's more like talking in a slightly higher pitch, but I can tell it's supposed to resemble singing—something. I recognize the lyrics but I can't quite make out the song. Hot? Cold? Up? Down? What? Wait, is that… "Are…are you singing Katy Perry at me?" That is definitely Katy Perry that I just heard. He's full of all kinds of surprises.

"I didn't turn any music on, so I thought I'd set the mood." I look back down at that fucking python between his legs, and I don't know if I want to laugh at his dumbass behavior or yelp in anticipation. He kisses me breathless before entering me in one hard thrust, and the yelp wins.

"Are you okay?"

My pussy clenches at his words, and I feel him shudder inside me. "Yes. Move." He thrusts again and I match his pace.

He continues singing about wrong and right and black and white.

I let out some mix between a laugh and a moan. "Are you seriously still singing that fucking song?"

He seems to come out of a daze in that moment, shaking his head slightly. "It honestly just slipped out. I'm trying to focus on not coming early. You feel so good."

He lifts one of my legs so he's stroking me deeper. He's devouring me with his eyes. My back is arched, my hands tracing my puckered nipples. I take a moment to admire the body of this man. He's got the body of a swimmer. His shoulders are broad. The veins in his forearms stand out. The abs on his torso are defined, hard-earned. The deep V on his sides is begging for my tongue. There's a sheen of sweat covering his chest. I follow the path of a bead from the top of his strong pec all the way down to the place where our bodies become one. I never want this to end.

I wrap my arms around his neck and pull him down to me for another kiss. I push my hips upward and place my hand on his chest until he falls back. Grabbing his shoulders, I force him to sit against his headboard. I straddle his hips, and he lines himself up to my entrance. I slowly sink back down his shaft, and it draws a guttural groan from the both of us.

"Fuuuuuck," he cries out.

I rock my hips forward, taking what I need from him. His lips are parted, and his breath is shaky. He's watching me with fire in his eyes. I feel powerful under his gaze. He grips my hips so tight it may leave bruises, but I don't care. I need it all. He thrusts forward, hitting me right where I need him. I can't hold eye contact anymore. I throw my head back and moan. He takes advantage of my exposed throat and licks a trail from the swells of my breasts to the erogenous zone behind my ear.

"Oh fuck, I'm coming," I announce before I come apart.

"Thank fuck," he cries out before pumping another two times and spilling his release.

I let out a deep exhale. "Holy shit. SOD for the win."

His eyes crinkle with amusement and confusion. "What the hell is SOD?" he asks.

"Special Occasion Dick." I explain to him what the term means, and he lets out a deep bark of laughter that's like music to my ears. He kisses my forehead before going to the bathroom to dispose of the condom.

I'm on cloud nine right now, but I also have no idea what comes next. I don't want a perfect night to be ruined by him awkwardly trying to get rid of me when he comes back. I got what I came here for, so it's time to get the fuck out. Maybe now I can focus on housework.

"Where are you going?" he asks when he sees me snapping my bra back into place.

"Umm…I was just going to—"

He cuts me off. "I don't think so, Phoebe. That was just a warm-up. Tonight's still a special occasion, isn't it?"

Welp. That housework can go fuck itself. I unclasp my bra again.

The next morning, I am deliciously sore. This was exactly what I needed. Isaiah is back in his room getting dressed while I'm in his kitchen making coffee.

Even though most of our hours were spent exploring each other's bodies, we also spent a lot of time talking and laughing. It's hard to reconcile the Isaiah who doesn't take shit seriously with the Isaiah who senses exactly what you need and delivers. I feel like I can finally catch my breath when I'm with him. That's a dangerous feeling. I don't want to accept this ventilator I've been given, because when I'm forced to breathe on my own I may fail.

The handle on Isaiah's door turns, and my head snaps in that direction, wondering who the hell is about to walk in here. I'm dressed, so I'm not worried about that. But I am in my bridesmaid dress from last night so there will be no mistaking what went down here. A gorgeous black girl walks in and stares at me like I've broken into her home.

She can't be taller than five feet, four inches and I'm five feet, eight inches—six feet with my heels on—but she sizes me up in a way that makes me feel more naked in my dress than I was with Isaiah last night.

"Hi. You're cute. I guess you're why Isaiah didn't answer my call last night. Figures. You done yet?" Her tone is so flippant, like she and Isaiah have some sort of open relationship and he has a revolving door of women coming out of his house.

I'm not foolish enough to think that just because we had sex that means we were going to be anything serious. But damn, I just feel cheap now.

I chug the rest of my coffee because I'm not one to waste caffeine. I leave the mug on the counter because fuck him, and I walk toward the woman who brought my fantasy crashing down around me.

"Yeah, I'm beyond done. Have fun." I walk out with what's left of my dignity and run home to lick yet another wound.

CHAPTER
Two

Nina
(Two months later)

"LUNCH?"

"Got it."

"Did you pick your snacks for today?"

"Umm…yes," Jada lies while running over to peruse our snack cabinet where she chooses a pack of Pringles and over to the fridge to grab a pack of apple slices. I pack Jada's lunch for her, but I let her pick her own snacks so long as she picks one snack from the junk cabinet and one from the healthy snacks. It seems to be working, so that's one guardian win. I'll take whatever I can get.

The kids have been back in school for a month, and I'm finally starting to get their routines down. Elementary school for Jada starts at seven forty-five a.m. while high school for Logan starts at nine a.m. While I'm getting Jada ready in the mornings, Logan is usually lounging about reading or still sleeping until I get back home from drop-off and start the process all over again with him before he catches the bus. By the time they're both out of the house, I'm usually on my second cup of coffee and debating having a third with a shot of whiskey in it.

"Backpack?" I continue my daily checklist with Jada.

"Yep."

"Homework?"

She taps her finger on the kitchen table so I know whatever she's about to say is a lie. "I didn't have any homework."

"Not even spelling?"

"Umm…" As I said, kids are shit liars, which works in my favor this time, so I won't complain. I have to remember to double-check her homework at night. Or do I? Is this one of those times when I'm supposed to let her learn on her own the hard way? It's far too early to try to navigate yet another fork in the parenting road. A spiked latte will definitely be needed today.

"Jada…" I deploy the "mom" voice—who knew I was even capable of that? It's been a godsend since I discovered it.

Jada cracks under the force of the "mom" voice. Works every time. "Okay, I forgot spelling. I'm sorry."

"Well, you're the one who has to explain to your teacher why you don't have it done, so have fun with that. And you can put the Pringles back and grab carrots instead today." There, that's a valid punishment, right? You don't do your homework and lie about it, you get veggies instead of chips?

"Eww, I don't like carrots."

"Me either, kid, but I didn't forget to do my homework so get to switching." She huffs but doesn't argue. I'll take that as a win today.

I yell upstairs to Logan and wait until I hear his footsteps pad into the bathroom and close the door. Good, he's up.

I turn back to Jada. "Alright, Mini. Grab your stool and wash your plate and fork." Our parents never let me use the dishwasher growing up because in their words, I was the dishwasher. I've kept that tradition alive, so Jada has her very own step stool that allows her to reach the sink and wash her dishes. Another guardian win? I can't say I'm a better person for having washed all those dishes in my childhood, but it does teach some responsibility so let's go with it.

In the car on the way to drop off Jada at school, I'm trying to remember what I have to do when I get to the bar later. I swear there's something I'm forgetting. I mean, I'm always forgetting something these days.

"Hey, Nina?"

"What's up?"

"I don't have my gymnastics stuff."

"Gymnastics is tomorrow."

"No, it's Wednesday. Gymnastics is today. Therapy is tomorrow."

Oh fuck. I thought today was Tuesday. What the hell did I do yesterday?

"Right. Okay, well, I'll drop it off for you later, okay?"

Jada claps with excitement. I really need to start writing my daily checklists down.

The rest of the morning proceeds without too many fuckups. I dropped off Jada's gymnastics gear. I put laundry away, including Jada's favorite blanket which I misplaced last week and lied to her about. I now know it's Wednesday and not Tuesday, so I've mentally documented that Jada has gymnastics after school and her teammate's mom will drop her off at home when they are done. Logan has robotics club after school, and his friend's mom will be dropping him off.

I end up skipping my third cup of coffee at home, but I do text Ciara and ask her to pick me up a latte from Sasha's before coming to Neon today. I open my closet in search of today's outfit, which for me means a pair of jeans and a graphic tee. I basically have the fashion sense of a nineties middle schooler on most days. I've been wearing graphic tees damn near every day for as long as I can remember. It's how I project my mood to the world without actually saying it. Not that anybody picks up on that. They either like my shirts or they don't, but no one realizes I'm trying to say something with them. I really can't remember why I started treating my clothes like a mood ring. If I dig deep I'm sure it has something to do with the fact that I always felt like I had to keep my emotions close to my chest because my parents weren't equipped to deal with them. So I let them out in another way. But I choose not to dig deep right now.

If I'm feeling like a sassy bitch, I might throw on a *Golden Girls* or *The*

Office tee. If I'm in a fighting mood and I want to dare somebody to test my gangster, I'll probably throw on an N.W.A. tee. If I'm feeling like I can do anything, I'll probably wear an Avengers tee. I don't wear a lot of Avengers tees these days.

Today I'm feeling a little frazzled and like I'm running all over the place, so I throw on my *Mario Kart* long sleeve shirt with a pair of ripped jeans and my black Converse. How many hours until I can nap? Nap. That's funny.

"Your fairy godmother has arrived," Ciara announces when she walks into Neon with my piping hot latte.

"I could kiss you."

"Lay it on me." She puckers her lips at me, and I just throw an olive at her while I pour a shot of whiskey into my latte. Do not judge me; I said I was going to do it.

Ciara eyes me dumping my shot into my cup and smirks. "Crazy morning, huh?"

"Aren't they all?"

She comes around to my side of the bar and starts on inventory while I continue running through our orders. "How's the kids' therapy going?"

"It's fine. They seem to like Dr. Reynolds, so that's good." Ciara got me the recommendation for Dr. Reynolds from her own therapist. Ciara went through a lot a few years ago. She moved from Baltimore, Maryland to Austin, Texas in an attempt to run from a stalker who made her life hell. She ended up meeting and falling in love with fine-ass fireman Lincoln Cole along the way, who happens to be the brother of my other best friend, Sasha, and the man who dickmatized me for a hot minute, Isaiah. Ciara saw a therapist throughout all of that. She insists that at times her sessions were the only thing keeping her sane.

Ciara has been encouraging me to see a therapist as well, and I'm not opposed to it, but I just feel like I have enough on my plate as it is. I'm more focused on the kids and making sure they're coping.

"That's good. And just so you know Dr. Laver is still accepting new patients, or she can recommend another therapist if you don't want to see the same person as me."

"I know, Ci."

She throws her hands up. "Okay, okay, I won't nag anymore. Today. So what are you going to do Friday?" Dr. Reynolds suggested that I have Jada and Logan do a sleepover once every week to try to assist Jada with her separation anxiety and to help coax Logan back out of his shell. So every Friday I ship them out. Usually they stay with Sasha, Carter, and Nevaeh, but sometimes Jada goes to a gymnastics teammate's house and Logan goes to spend the night with his friend from robotics club.

Friday is by far the worst day of the week. I miss my alone time, yes, but I find that I miss the kids more when they're not around. I also find that I hate being alone with my thoughts. Hmm.

"Movie marathon."

"Ooh. What's on the docket this week?"

"Well, I'm thinking my theme will either be Black Classics: *Boyz N the Hood, New Jack City, Coming to America, Poetic Justice,* and *Love Jones* or Action Classics: *Kill Bill, Die Hard, John Wick, Goldfinger,* and *Equalizer.*"

"Oooh, black classics for sure. I'm definitely in the mood for some *New Jack City.*"

"You're more than welcome to join me. You just have to hop off your husband's dick long enough."

She throws her head back in laughter. "Alright, alright, it's not like I neglect you! But it's good dick so what do you want from me?" Believe me, if it's anything like his brother's dick, I get it.

Nope! We are not thinking about that manwhore. We had our fun. It's time to move on.

"Yeah, yeah. Really, what I need to do this weekend is work on ideas for the kids' rooms."

She cringes. "Yeah…I don't want to speak ill of the dead, but why the hell would your parents have had Logan and Jada sharing a room?"

I can't be upset with Ciara for her comment. I find myself talking shit about my parents in my head more often than not these days. I gave up my apartment after they died and moved into their house to take care of Logan and Jada. I didn't realize my parents had them sharing a room even though the house has three bedrooms. The kids never told me, probably because they knew I'd yell at our parents about it and they still wouldn't listen to me. I didn't spend much time in the house. Usually I brought them back to my place with me when our parents left on yet another trip. I'm regretting that now because I feel like I missed so much. The kids needed me more than I ever realized. I feel like I let them down.

I still can't wrap my head around the fact that my parents thought it was a better idea to have a fourteen-year-old boy and a six-year-old girl share a bedroom and use the third bedroom as Mom's craft room. A fucking craft room. She barely ever finished any crafts, she and Dad were gone so often.

"Girl, I have no idea. #Craftingislife? Who the fuck knows what was running through their minds half the time, but it sure wasn't parenting."

"Let me know if you need any help clearing stuff out or reorganizing. We'll get Linc and the Band of Fools up there real quick." She's referring to Lincoln's best friends Kai, Dominic, Shane, and of course Isaiah. They're ridiculously good-looking and an unlikely group of friends, but they're incredibly loyal to each other. Apparently there's some wild story behind how they met, but they refuse to share it with anyone. Ciara told me they vowed not to tell anyone until they're all in love, married, and settled down. Idiots.

I definitely don't want Isaiah in my house, but I'm not going to exclude him from the invite and let him know I'm bothered by him, so I just won't have any of them help. At least not right now.

"Thanks, boo. I'll let you know."

The rest of the day flies by and not in a pleasant way. Jada is upset with me because she's somehow discovered my lie about her favorite blanket. She's also neglected to tell me until tonight that she's supposed to bring brownies in for her entire class tomorrow. So I'll be spending my night with my KitchenAid instead of a glass of wine. Logan is even quieter than usual if that's even possible. He claims it's because things didn't go according to plan in robotics club today, but I don't know if that's the full truth. I slipped on a spilled drink tonight and hurt my damn knee. I was accosted by one of my regulars who wanted to ask me all about my dead parents. I was also referred to as a "hoity-toity-ass bitch" by a drunk patron when I refused to serve him another drink. It was six p.m., ladies and gentlemen.

In short, I'm exhausted. Physically, mentally, emotionally, spiritually. In all the ways.

Today is officially over. I can't take any more today.

I step in the kids' room, and Jada is cuddling with her blanket while Logan is reading. I crouch by Jada's bedside. "Hey, Mini."

"Hi, Nina. I'm not mad at you anymore."

"Oh really?"

"Yeah. Logan said you didn't mean to hurt my feelings. He said sometimes adults lie to make kids feel better." Logan doesn't acknowledge the statement, he just flips his page very loudly. I'm so honored to be his sister. I realize he's been more of a father to Jada than our father ever was. He's been shouldering a lot of responsibility for way too long. It's time for him to just be a kid.

"He's right. Sometimes adults do lie to make kids feel better, but I'm going to try to do better with that. We're a team."

"I love you, Nina."

"I love you too, Mini. Did you do your homework tonight?"

"I did, I swear it." I kiss her on the forehead.

I move over to Logan's bedside and whisper, "My hero." He doesn't comment, but he blushes slightly.

"What are you reading tonight?"

He holds the book up toward me as he answers, "Lord of the Flies."

"Hmm, maybe I should get myself a conch to call family meetings with." He looks up and smirks at me, acknowledging my book reference.

"I'm halfway through the book, but I know enough to know we don't wanna be like these boys." A tear springs to my eye against my will. That's the first joke Logan's cracked in a while. I wipe it away before he sees it and freaks out.

"Definitely not, but they were on the right track with their first two policies."

"To have fun and to survive?"

"Exactly."

He sobers. "I don't think we're doing that well with the first one." I hate this. He's absolutely right. It's been a while since we've just had fun without guilt or sadness creeping its way in.

"We'll have to work on it then." He nods in agreement before returning to his book. I kiss his forehead and stand up. "Don't stay up too late, kid." I make my way to the door when Logan calls my name, and I turn back to him.

"We're doing fine with the second policy, though. Because of you." I wink at him and close the door when I leave.

I turn my shower on as hot as it will go and step in. I let the water run down my body for a full three minutes before the tears finally fall. I spend the rest of my shower letting my sobs drain me dry.

CHAPTER
Three

Nina

I LOVE HALLOWEEN.

I love the costumes, the movies, the decorations, the parties. Everything.

When I was a kid, I would put my all into my costume. My parents weren't into trick-or-treating, so I'd go with friends. I'd organize the kids in my neighborhood so we'd have coordinating outfits. We'd be anything from the kids from *Proud Family* to the Spice Girls to the Power Rangers. When I was a teenager, I would go to all the parties and I'd marathon all the scary movies, waiting for trick-or-treaters to come by. When I was in college, I'd go to bar crawls and participate in all the costume contests. When I became the manager at Neon Nights, I dedicated myself to transforming the bar into my patrons' greatest nightmares every year.

So I should be fully invested in this year's themed decorations for Neon Nights, but instead I feel like complete shit.

For the past few days I've been sick as a dog. I've been nauseous as hell, really dizzy, and had a migraine that just won't quit.

I've been running around making sure we'll have all of the decorations for the bar ready in a few weeks and ensuring I have the costumes ready for me and the kids. This year we're doing a *Beetlejuice* theme. The bar is going to look just like the netherworld from the movie. The kids are going to match the theme with me. Logan is going to dress up as Beetlejuice, and he's been put on notice by Jada that the green wig is nonnegotiable. Jada is going to be our very own Lydia, and she's been practicing her performance of "Jump in the Line" since we decided on the theme months ago. I'm going to be Barbara, complete with the open-mouthed mask and all.

It's not lost on me how Barbara and Adam meet their untimely end in that movie. When I showed the movie to Jada for the first time, I conveniently skipped over the part where the husband and wife drive their car off a bridge and told her the DVD messed up. I know I said I'd work on the adult lies but that in itself was a damn lie. Sorry not sorry. I have to do what I have to do to protect them.

I'm at Neon with Ciara and two of my other bartenders, Julie and Lindsay. Lindsay is one of the sweetest girls in existence. She's been working with me for three and a half years now, and she always has a good attitude. She's all of five feet tall, and her blonde hair bounces against her shoulders when she walks. Julie could easily be a supermodel. She's five feet ten with long, dark hair and amber eyes and sharp cheekbones. She's been working here for a year, and her sharp tongue balances out Lindsay's bubbliness perfectly. The three women have all really stepped up since everything happened. I can no longer stay until closing every night because I've got two kids at home, so they handle all the closing shifts. I come to work in the mornings when the kids are at school to handle the lunch crowd and all the administrative tasks. Sometimes I stay to help with the beginning of the dinner rush if the kids have after-school activities or if Logan agrees to watch Jada. Other days, I leave in time to pick up the kids from school. I'm grateful to have these amazing women by my side. I tune back in to the conversation with Ciara right as she says, "I can't wait to see Jada as Lydia. I'm surprised she's so into the goth costume. She's such a ray of sunshine."

"I know. She loves the movie. I was nervous about showing it to her but it worked out. She won't stop singing that damn song either, so be prepared to hear it next time you come over." Then I ask, "Wait, what are you gonna be this year?"

"Linc and I are gonna be Daenerys Targaryen and Khal Drogo." She laughs almost to herself. I don't think I want to know the story behind this costume choice.

"Not Daenerys and Jon Snow?"

She scoffs. "Jon Snow is cute, but Khal Drogo was a MAN. And I'm not a nephew fucker."

Can't argue with that.

"Makes sense. Have you talked to Sasha? She's excited about her costume." I inject that statement with all the sarcasm I can muster in my current state.

She snorts. "I'd be hurt too if I had to dress like a little boy with a Dorito shaped head."

I want to laugh at that, but I'm honestly too tired. "It's supposed to be shaped like the letter P. P for Phineas." Sasha's daughter, Nevaeh, begged her and her dad, Carter, to dress up as the cartoon characters Phineas and Ferb this year while she dresses as Perry the Platypus.

"Okay, and that's fine but is it or is it not also shaped like a Dorito?" She folds her arms across her chest as if her logic couldn't be broken down.

"I can't even with your dumb ass today."

"You love me. And oh! Did I tell you what Reggie and fam are dressing as?"

"No, who?"

"The Golden Girls!" Oh my God, if I had the energy I'd be on the floor laughing right now.

"Please tell me this was Malcolm's idea."

Malcolm developed a deep appreciation for *The Golden Girls* since Ciara told him about it during a game of TV tag. I find it hilarious imagining a ten-year-old being tuned into four old bitties being sassy and fabulous, but I fully support it. Ciara proceeds to tell me how a friend has been making fun of Malcolm for liking the show so much and dared him to dress up as one of them, so he roped the whole family into it. My kind of kid. He's going to be Sophia because in his words, she's the Greatest of All Time, what is called the GOAT. He's not wrong. Even though I'm more of a Dorothy bitch myself. Apparently, Reggie is going as Blanche, Niecy as Dorothy, and Michael as Rose. I would pay good money to see this.

We continue talking shit and getting the bar ready for tonight. Even though I'm tired as hell, I'm holding on just fine. That is, until I smell something disgusting. Something nasty and rancid. I sniff the air looking for the culprit, fully expecting to find a rotting corpse I somehow missed. I turn around and see Lindsay stuffing her face.

"What the fuck is that?" I ask, harsher than I intend.

She pauses. "A hot dog. I was starving, so I went around the corner and got a chili-cheese dog with onions. Wanna bite?" She holds out the hot dog to me, and my stomach flips. Oh God.

I take off and barely make it to the bathroom in time to lose my breakfast. I don't know how long my head is in the toilet before Ciara shows up to rub my back and hand me paper towels.

"You've been sick for a few days now. What's going on with you?"

I don't have the energy to look up at her, but I hear the concern in her voice. "I don't know. I guess I got a nasty stomach bug."

"Well, what else is going on?"

"Nauseous all the time. Dizzy spells. Headaches." I'm trying to think if there's anything I'm leaving out when Ciara grabs my damn breast and it hurts like hell. "Ouch! What did you grab my titty for?"

"Are they tender? Do they hurt?"

"I mean, yeah, I guess." Not sure where she's going with this, being as anyone's titties would hurt if someone grabbed and pinched them out of nowhere.

She rubs her palms against her legs as if nervous to speak next. "Yeah… it's just that I noticed your boobs were getting a little bigger, and now you're saying you're nauseous, dizzy, tired, and have headaches. You know what that sounds like, right?"

What the fuck?

"I'm not pregnant, Ci."

"Are you sure? Your symptoms are spot on, boo. When was your last period?"

"I just had it…"

Wait. I didn't just have it. I've been so ridiculously busy with everything that I didn't even notice I haven't had my period in…two months. I've always been irregular but to not get them at all, well, that's a problem.

Shit.

Shit.

Shit.

"Voldemort. Voldemort. Voldemort," I chant.

Ciara tilts her head in confusion. "Umm, what?"

"I'm hoping if I say his name he'll show up."

"And I say again…what?"

"I call my period Voldemort because he's an evil bitch whose name shall not be spoken or else he'll appear."

Her eyes crinkle in laughter as she points her finger at me. "Okay, that's fucking genius. I'm stealing that."

"Feel free. Right now I'm going to continue my chant because I actually want that evil bitch to show up."

She grabs my hand and stares deep into my eyes. The air suddenly feels thinner. "When was your last period, Nina?"

"Two months ago."

She gulps. "So…hypothetically speaking, if you were pregnant, who would the father be?"

My turn to gulp. I never told Ciara or anyone else about my hookup with Isaiah. I wanted to forget about the whole thing.

I look down at where she's holding my hand—thankful for some sort of connection to reality—then I spill the whole story about the night I spent with Isaiah and how it ended. She doesn't look the least bit surprised which has me wondering if maybe Isaiah didn't abide by the same vow of silence I did.

"Say something."

"I mean, I'm just not shocked. You and Isaiah had this weird sexual tension going on for a while. I was wondering if you were ever gonna act on it. I'm a little surprised about the girl who showed up though. I don't think he's dating anyone seriously enough for them to have a key."

"Well, we did and she did. It doesn't matter anyway."

"Right. Let's focus. We need to get you a test."

A test. A pregnancy test. This is really where I'm at in life right now?

"Nina. Are you okay?" No. I'm not okay at all. I'm still that car speeding toward the brick wall and no one has yet hit the brakes. If anything, they've pushed the accelerator down to the ground now.

Hit the brakes. Hit the fucking brakes.

"Mhm." I wash my hands and sprint out of the bathroom, returning to my original task and tuning everyone out.

"Hey," Ciara whisper shouts to bring me back to reality a few minutes later. When I look up, her brows are furrowed in worry.

"What's up?"

"I ran out and got you a test. I can come with you to the bathroom if you want." I snatch the test box off the bar and throw it in my bag. I have no idea how long I've been zoned out, focusing on inventory. Long enough for Ciara to slip away and buy me a pregnancy test. Isn't it funny how our minds can just block out bits of time like that?

"Thank you. I just…I can't with this right now. It's a stomach bug. It has to be."

"Nina."

I cut her off. "We used condoms and I'm on the pill." I'm speaking more to myself than her because I'm still trying to wrap my brain around the fact that I've lived thirty years without so much as a pregnancy scare and now here I am, after using every precaution, potentially, most likely, pregnant by the most complicated one-night stand in history.

"And that really fucking sucks and I'd be wanting to sue pharmaceutical companies everywhere right now if I were you, but you can't run away from this. It's not going away. The sooner you find out the truth, the sooner you can make a plan. You're not alone. I'm right here with you."

"And I appreciate that. But I'm not willing to accept that right now. And I know what you're gonna say. I know it's an irresponsible choice. But I am seconds away from breaking, okay? I haven't slept in days. My parents are dead and I don't know how to really process that. My siblings are looking to me to guide them, and I just hope I'm not guiding them right into the same fucking ditch I've been buried in for months. If I try to pile another thing on top of this delicate pile, it's all going to come crashing down and I just can't right now. So I'm not taking this test. I'm going to leave this bar and hope that even though I'm being an irrational bitch toward you right now that you'll take over for me. I'm going to go home and pull my shit together before I have to pick up the kids and have to put on my brave face again. Is that okay?" I look at her, expecting to see disappointment in her eyes, but I see nothing but understanding there. She just nods, and I don't say another word. I walk out with my head held high.

I've done everything to avoid this moment. I took the kids to and from therapy. I cooked dinner. I ordered another decoration for the bar and another piece of Logan's costume. I reorganized the kitchen. Now Jada has Logan wrapped up in a game of Uno, and there's nothing left for me to do but put my big-girl panties on and get in that bathroom.

I grab my bag and shut the master bathroom door behind me.

I am Nina Fucking Williams and I can do this. I have to do this.

Three minutes later my fate is sealed.

Pregnant.

Holy. Shit.

What the fuck am I going to do? A baby? On top of everything going on in my life? Am I good enough to be someone's mother? I don't think I'm good enough for Logan and Jada but they're stuck with me. This baby isn't. Am I the right choice for him or her? I...

I don't complete that thought because Logan yells up the stairs that someone is at the door.

I somehow put one foot in front of the other and make my way to the front door. Ciara Jeffries-Cole is standing in front of me, arms out.

"What are you...?" I stop when I see Lincoln walk up behind her, smiling.

Ciara pulls me in for a hug and whispers, "He doesn't know anything." She steps back and takes her voice back up to its normal tone. "We wanted to have an impromptu game night with the kiddos." Lincoln holds up his hands to reveal he's carrying a bunch of snacks and Monopoly.

They come in, and Jada looks excited to have more victims for her next game play while Logan looks pained to be away from his book for even longer.

Ciara catches my attention and throws her eyes toward the stairs before turning back to Lincoln. "Linc, can you get everything set up? I just need to go upstairs with Nina so I can get that shirt she's been telling me I could borrow for weeks and she keeps forgetting."

He raises his brows at that but smiles nonetheless. "Whatever you say, Angel. Jada's about to lose to me in Uno first anyway."

Jada's hands fly to her hips. "Hey! I am not gonna lose!"

Lincoln chuckles then drops a chaste kiss on Ciara's lips before allowing Jada to drag him over to the living room where the Uno cards are. Ciara pinches my arm and leads me upstairs.

"What are you doing here?" I ask once we get to my bedroom.

"I figured you might need that support system after all."

Tears spring to my eyes. She hit the brakes for me. I can feel the car slowing down. She holds her arms out again. I fall into them and allow myself to break.

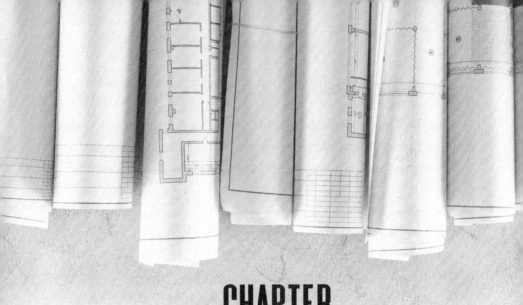

CHAPTER
Four

Isaiah

"**C**OLE, ARE YOU GONNA HAVE THOSE PLANS DRAWN UP BY THIS afternoon?"

I look up at my colleague Carl Boone. He's a good four inches shorter than I am. He's got a round belly, courtesy of all the beer he consumes on a regular basis. He's got a small bald spot on the back of his head. It's so small you may not even notice it at first, but once you do your eyes will keep going back to it like it's a tiny glitch in the matrix. "Which plans? The Gardner building or the Mayflower house?"

"Gardner building." He puffs his chest out slightly, thinking he's got me. He couldn't be more wrong.

"Trick question. I finished them both. I'll be presenting them in today's meeting."

He visibly deflates and shakes his head with laughter. "Son of a bitch. One of these days, I'm gonna trip you up, man." He does this every week. Tries to trip me up before our staff meetings to see if I'm on deadline or not. He's not an asshole though. He doesn't do it to try to make me look like a fool. I honestly think it's his way of forging some sort of friendship. He's not the most social guy. I think our weekly banter is his only form of entertainment. I'm always putting on a show anyway, why not another one for good ol' Boone here?

"One does not simply trip up a legend, Boone." He chuckles as he walks back to his desk.

I'm an architect at A. Paterson Architects. I've only been at the firm for five years, but the owner, Alan Paterson, took an interest in my career early on and became my mentor. I've been given some pretty senior projects ever since.

In today's meeting, I'm presenting the blueprints for both a Colonial style home and a commercial bank building. I started off focusing primarily on residential architecture, but I've been doing more commercial projects as of late.

I should be excited about my presentations today, but my thoughts keep drifting off to a certain melanated goddess. Nina Williams has plagued my mind for the past two months. Well no, she's been on my mind for years. But now that I've kissed her, tasted her, fucked her, I've gone into overdrive.

I've been interested in her since my sister Sasha first brought her around, but I never acted on it. I wasn't in a good place. Honestly, I'm still not. But when my brother, Lincoln, was trying to get to know his now wife, Ciara,— who was working at the bar with Nina—I couldn't resist the opportunity to talk to her more.

She had me hooked from the moment she laughed at my dumbass joke. She has this deep, throaty laugh that turns me on something serious. Her smile is gorgeous. It lights up her entire face and brightens a room. She's got a beauty mark above the right side of her lip that's begging to be kissed. Her dark curls fall down to the middle of her back. Her breasts aren't particularly large, but they fit in my hands perfectly and her hips go on for days. When she swings them back and forth like a pendulum, I'm hypnotized every time. She's pretty tall too. I like that I don't have to bend down very far to kiss her, and when she wears heels I don't have to bend at all. That would bother some guys, but some guys are pussies.

She's really smart as well. We talked about everything from sports to politics to movies to history that night. We didn't agree on everything, but her insight was refreshing. I found myself so intrigued by her that I didn't fall back on jokes nearly as much as I usually do. I'm known as the "class clown" by everyone, and I tend to really ham it up with women. They enjoy my charming sense of humor. She did too, but it was so much more with her.

That scared the living shit out of me.

At first, my intention was just to hook up with her because I don't do serious relationships, but when I talked to her at the bar that night I knew I couldn't just hook up with her and let that be the end. She's definitely a relationship girl. She deserves so much more than a casual hookup, but that's all I can give her. So ever since, I've been trying to avoid her. Pussy shit, I know. But hey, at least I'm not insecure about her height.

Avoiding her doesn't work, of course, because she's best friends with my sister and my sister-in-law. When we do see each other, I'm torn between acting like she's not there and giving in to my deepest fantasies. Sometimes I do a little bit of both, which I'm sure confuses the fuck out of her, but I'm confused as fuck too.

Then her parents died and she became the sole guardian for her younger brother and sister. I went to the funeral, and it was painful watching her. She was clearly on edge but was trying to hold it together for the kids. I wanted to comfort her but I figured the last thing she would want is me and my mixed messages. I decided to do her the favor of staying away from her then; she had enough on her plate. Instead, I relied on Lincoln to check on her for me and let me know what I could do from afar.

All that tension exploded on the night of Lincoln and Ciara's wedding. Seeing Nina in her bridesmaid dress was too much to resist. I'm used to her wearing graphic tees with leggings or tight-ass jeans, which should be basic but she looks sexy as hell in them. But that dress? God damn, I nearly swallowed my tongue. Still, I kept my hands to myself. I looked, a lot, but I didn't touch.

She came to me that night.

When she knocked on my door, I damn near got on my knees and thanked the Lord above. I know I was trying to avoid the casual hookup with her but if she came to me, there was no way in hell I was turning it down.

The sex was phenomenal. There's no better way to describe it. Fucking phenomenal. I have jacked off to the memory of it for the past two months. I sang fucking Katy Perry to try to keep myself from coming early, she was so wet and tight. She teased me mercilessly after the fact and started calling me KP.

The morning after, I wasn't looking for an escape from her. I wanted more. I wanted her to stay and spend the day with me. That was a mind-fuck in itself, but then the perfect night and morning came to a screeching halt when fucking Alexis showed up.

Alexis Bell is one of the biggest mistakes I've ever made. We had what I thought was a casual hookup, but she keeps trying to sink her claws into me. Every time I tell her that we can't hook up again, she dangles that carrot that I can't let go of in front of me and draws me back in. I hate it. I hate her. I hate myself.

Not that morning though. I was more pissed than anything that she not only showed up and drove Nina away—I still have no idea what the fuck she said to her—but she had a fucking key to my house! How the fuck did she get a key? I may be dumb enough to keep letting her suck me back into her demon pussy, but I am not dumb enough to give her a damn key to my place. I demanded she give me the key and any other copies she might have and sent her packing.

The damage was already done though. Nina refused to answer my text messages and calls. I debated going to the bar and trying to force a conversation, but it's probably better this way. If she hates me, she won't come on to me again and I can go back to pretending like I don't want her. Like I'm not dying to have her again. I assume she never told Sasha and Ciara about our hookup because neither one of them bitched me out. I hate that I'm this big dirty secret for her now, but it's what I fucking deserve.

After my morning presentation, I check my phone to find messages from Niecy and Malcolm. We're in a group chat because I'm the coolest uncle ever. Reggie says I'm childish and need a babysitter more than they do, but she's just not fun.

Malcolm: Uncle Zay, we need your help

Niecy: Yeah, it's crucial

I chuckle to myself. What could be crucial to a teenager and a pre-teen? What am I saying, everything is crucial at that age.

Me: Never fear, Uncle Zay is here. What's up?

Malcolm: Well I wanna go to this video game tournament in a couple weeks

Niecy: And I wanna go to a Post Malone concert with my friends on the same night

Me: And??

Malcolm: Mom said no!

Niecy: And we couldn't even get Dad to cave!

Me: LOL guys I'm the cool uncle I know but if you think I can change her mind you're crazy

Niecy: Not exactly what we're asking

Me: Oh hell. Call me.

I step into the stairwell of my building to answer their video chat.

"Are you crazy texting me this shit? Paper trail. Have I taught you nothing?"

"Sorry, Uncle Zay. We'll delete the texts," Malcolm declares. He looks the most chastised between the two. Niecy just looks like a woman on a mission. Her mother's daughter through and through.

"So what exactly are you asking me?"

"My friend's mom already bought the tickets, and her big sister is coming with us! She's twenty-three! She won't let anything happen to us, but Mom still said no."

"And I don't even know what she's got against video games."

I huff. "You guys are not telling me where I come in here."

"Right. So we thought maybe you could ask for us to spend the night with you? And then my friend's sister will pick me up from your house and drop me back off there after the concert. And Malcolm's friend's brother will do the same."

"Ahh, the old bait and switch. It's tried and true. There's just one problem."

"What?" they ask at the same time.

"My sister. Your mother. She ain't dumb. She's gonna know it's the same date and catch you and then beat my ass and yours."

"Well…" Malcolm looks to Niecy like he's seeking permission to continue. Niecy nudges him as if they've come too far to turn around now.

"What? Tell me."

"When we asked her if we could go we sort of told her it was a week earlier than it actually is."

These fucking kids.

"So basically, you knew she'd say no and knew you'd be deviants and do it anyway?"

"Well, it is Mom. We hoped she wouldn't but we kind of saw it coming so we wanted to be prepared with a back-up plan."

"Yeah, so this way she'll think we already missed the concert and tournament, and she won't be suspicious," Niecy adds.

Damn. Kids are getting smarter and smarter these days. I would've never thought of that. I gotta say I'm impressed.

I iron out the details with the kids for another few minutes before agreeing, because let's face it, we all knew I was going to agree. I'm the fun uncle. I have a reputation to uphold. Besides, Lincoln has a firm grip on Nevaeh for favorite uncle. I have to keep my hold on Niecy and Malcolm. I confirmed what chaperones would be with each of them, so I don't see the harm in going.

I may be the fun uncle but I'd never put them in danger, and they are actually going to spend the night with me after their concert and tournament so I'll have eyes on them. The best thing about being the fun uncle is that they tell me everything, so if they ever got in any real trouble, they'd know they could come to me and I'd help. Reggie will thank me one day when we share these stories. In about twenty years. When the statute of limitations is up. Shit, I'm twenty-nine years old and I just started telling my parents about all the dumb shit I used to get into.

Leaving work that night, I pass by a woman wearing a *Poetic Justice* T-shirt, and my thoughts immediately drift back to Nina. Jesus, this is pathetic. I need to get laid and move the fuck on. Unfortunately for me, no woman has so much as turned me on since that night with Nina. My hand and I have become best friends which sucks because I haven't been best friends with that lame ass since high school.

My father calls me and asks me to head over and help him with a project. Thank God, I have a distraction to prevent me from going home and pitifully jacking it to Nina again. For now.

CHAPTER
Five

Nina

WELP, IT'S OFFICIAL. I'M PREGNANT.

Not that I didn't already know that from the five positive at-home tests I ended up taking, but I thought the doctor might hit me with a "those shits you bought were busted, you ain't pregnant."

But nope. I'm eight weeks along.

One night. One magical night changed my entire life. I signed up for special occasion dick. Had I known the special occasion dick in question had permanent resident sperm I would've thought twice.

Okay, I'm lying.

Because as much as the timing of this sucks and as much as I'm having my doubts about being able to be the best mother to this kid, Logan, and Jada, I'm kind of already in love with the little bean.

I just never saw this happening for me. I'm thirty years old and I've had serious relationships but none I ever thought I'd end up with for the long haul to have babies. And I never considered adoption or IVF by myself because I never wanted to do the parenting thing alone. I always wanted to do it with a partner.

And yet here I am. The sole guardian to two kids, pregnant with a baby whose father I don't have a relationship with. A father who could very well decide that's a title he's not interested in taking on.

Wow. I sure know how to kill the fucking mood.

It's not that I think Isaiah will run away from his child. Yes, he's a jokester who doesn't take himself or anything too seriously, but he's not a piece of shit. I don't think. I guess I just have to tell him and find out.

The thought of telling Isaiah makes me nauseous, though. Or that could be the fetus growing in my belly. I choose to say it's the idea of telling Isaiah so I can put it off for a little longer.

Damn, when did I become such a chump? I'm a boss-ass bitch. I'm the woman who started managing a struggling bar and made it into the popular watering hole it is now. I'm the woman who showed up at Isaiah Cole's door and demanded he have his way with me. I can woman the hell up and tell him he planted a baby in there. No problem. I pull out my phone and hit the call button.

I get an answer on the third ring. "You Texans just love you some me today," Brittany teases.

Okay, so, I chickened out. I didn't call Isaiah. I called Brittany. Sue me.

Brittany is Ciara's childhood friend from her hometown. She and I have become really close in the last few months. I clicked with Ciara's other two best friends, Simone and Sarah, too, when Lincoln flew them in to visit her a while ago, but Brittany and I became even closer after she beat me at my own game for the role of Ciara's maid of honor.

Ciara refused to choose which of her friends would be her maid of honor so she demanded we decide amongst ourselves. We couldn't figure out how to do that so I suggested we have a movie trivia game. It was all I could think of at the time, and I knew it was a little unfair since I consider myself somewhat of a movie buff, but everyone agreed to it. But Brittany gave me a run for my money, and she finally beat me on the final question, which was about Harry Potter. Harry Fucking Potter. Those movies are my shit! I'm a proud Gryffindor even though my favorite character is Ravenclaw Luna Lovegood. But it turns out that cute little Hufflepuff Brittany loves the movies a tiny bit more. I knew right then that she too would become my bestie.

The bottom line is, I'm not ready to talk to Isaiah. I need a plan of action, and I need advice from someone who doesn't have their own close bond with him, so his sister and sister-in-law are out right now. That leaves my girl Brittany. So here we are.

"And what were you and Ci running your mouths about today?"

She giggles. She's too fucking cute. "A bunch of nothing. Just filling her in on the latest work drama here. And Dom and I discussed—"

"Wait, what?" I cut her off without thinking.

"What, what?"

"You and Dom? As in Lincoln's friend, Dom? Since when do you guys talk?"

"Oh. Umm…well, we're friends. We got to know each other really well at the wedding and we've just kept in touch."

What an odd friendship. Dom is a great guy, but he's also a broody guy most of the time. If you're not in his inner circle or someone he's helping while on duty as an EMT, the most you'll get out of him is a few grunts. Brittany on the other hand is so sweet she can give you a cavity. I have no idea what they bonded over at the wedding, but the idea of our very own Professor Snape and Luna Lovegood being best friends is something I am rooting for and need to see. "Oh. I didn't know that."

"Yeah, I'm secretly poaching all of you as my friends so you'll move up here with me."

"Or…you could move down here with us."

"Psh. I think not." We'll see, Brittany. We'll see.

"I'll break you down one day. So sorry, you were saying you and Dom discussed what?"

"Oh, just a bunch of dumb stuff. Now it's your turn. What's going on in your world? How are the kids doing?"

"They're good. For the most part. The third one is good too. Healthy."

"What third one? Third what?"

"The third kid."

Silence. "Make this make sense. I'm lost." Well, of course you're lost because I'm talking in circles. I need to pull my shit together and just say it.

Here goes nothing. "The kid I'm carrying. In my belly. Because I'm pregnant."

"You're…wait…I'm sorry, I think I blacked out. Did you say you're pregnant?"

"Yep. I sure am." I try to act as nonchalant as possible, waiting for her true reaction.

It comes three seconds later in the form of the loudest shriek ever. Seriously, I think she busted my goddamn eardrum.

"Eeeek! Yayyy! This is so exciting!"

A laugh tumbles out of my mouth before confusion takes over. "That's it? That's all you've got to say?"

"We'll get to my questions in a second. Don't rush me!"

"Oh sorry, please process your feels."

"Thank you." She hits me with another shriek. Seriously, I'm pretty sure I'm deaf in my right ear now.

"Please process your feels in a way that doesn't cost me my hearing."

She takes a deep breath. "Sorry. Okay, okay. I'm together now. This is really exciting! Simone doesn't plan on giving me any nieces or nephews ever. Sarah and her man are taking their sweet time. Ciara and Lincoln want kids but aren't planning on any just yet, and my siblings don't have kids. So you'll be the first one to feed into my need for baby snuggles! I'm so excited!"

"Well, I'm so glad I could please." Brittany's statement actually makes me feel marginally better. Even if Isaiah turns out to be the complete opposite of what I thought he was, I realize I'm not alone. Sasha, Brittany, and Ciara will all be by my side. They've been with me from the moment I became a parent to Logan and Jada. This will be no different. I'm honestly ashamed that I've somehow forgotten that.

"Now, on to the questions. Who the hell is the father? When are you due? How are you feeling? Have you told anyone else yet?"

"Woah, slow down."

"You asked for questions. You got questions. Let's go!"

She's right. Answering these questions gives me something to focus on. Sticking to the facts so I don't have to deal with the emotions running rampant inside of me. "Okay. Well, I guess I'll start with the biggest question. The father."

"Oh, thank God. I thought you were gonna save that for last and then I'd have to have you repeat everything else you said because I'd be too focused on when you were gonna announce who the father is to listen to anything else."

That gets a chuckle out of me. "It's…Isaiah." She makes what sounds like a choking noise and then continues coughing afterward. I'm pretty sure the bitch is choking to death. "Are you dying? Because I can't really handle another person dying right now so I need you to shape up."

She sputters one more cough before answering. "Sorry. I took a sip of water when you said that and it went down the wrong tube. Holy shit. Isaiah is the father? Like Isaiah Cole. Lincoln and Sasha's brother. Not some random Isaiah you met at the grocery store or something and hit it off with? Isaiah Isaiah?"

Nope, more like the Isaiah I awkwardly met years ago when I went with Sasha to her parents' house for Thanksgiving. "That's the one."

"Okay, so follow up. Why did I not know you slept with Isaiah?!" she yells.

Ugh. I recap the sad-ass story of my roll in the sheets with Isaiah. Again. Maybe I should've told everyone when it happened because telling this story for the second time in the past few days is exhausting, and I know I'll have to tell it again when I fill Sasha in. That'll be a great conversation. *Oh hey, bestie, yeah so I fucked your brother but I never told you about it, and now I'm pregnant but you're gonna be an auntie again so yay.*

Brittany interrupts my thoughts. "I mean, hey. If you had to get knocked up by a hookup, at least he had good dick."

But that good dick is attached to a man I can't escape. "True, I guess. But Britt, what the hell am I gonna do about him? We're not together and we're not gonna be together and that's fine, but now I'm tied to him for the rest of my life. What if he wants nothing to do with the baby? That'll be fucking awkward considering his sister-in-law and sister are my best friends. Or worse, what if he does want to be involved and he gets on my fucking nerves and we agree on absolutely nothing when it comes to parenting?!" I'm getting more irrational as I talk but these are real concerns, dammit.

"I love how him being annoying and not agreeing with you on parenting decisions is worse to you than him being a straight-up deadbeat. But let's be real, do you really think him being a deadbeat is even a possibility?"

"My gut says no, but I don't really know him. We don't know each other that well."

"Okay, so what do you need from me? Do you need me to walk you back from the ledge or do you need real talk advice?" Brittany is different from Ciara, Sasha, and me. We're all smartasses who are always running our mouths, and Brittany can do that too, but she's mostly the sweet, awkward lovebug. But when it comes to getting real and delivering the much needed brutally honest advice, she's a pro like the rest of us. She's exactly what I needed. Honest, unbiased advice.

"Hit me with the real."

"You and Isaiah don't know shit about each other, really. Fine. But you're having a baby together so you better learn. Babies don't ask to be born, and they deserve to be born into an environment that's not dysfunctional and toxic. So you and Isaiah don't have to be together, but you need to be on the same page and soon. You have to tell him and most importantly you need to prepare for whatever reaction you get. You freaked out when you found out, so he's probably gonna do the same. And that's not an excuse to write him off. Give him the time you had to process his feelings and then you can have a real conversation and figure out your game plan."

Well alright then. I have to laugh because even though she just put me in my place, she delivered it with such a smile in her voice. Like a gentle mama bear. I feel like she just slapped me across the face and then immediately gave me flowers after.

"Damn. You're good." I can practically hear her smiling on the other end.

I agree to woman the fuck up and tell Isaiah soon and then fill her in on the rest of my pregnancy updates before we hang up.

Now it's time to text Isaiah and tell him we need to talk. I spend a dumb amount of time figuring out how to start off the conversation with my acquaintance turned star of my sinful dreams turned hookup turned baby daddy, because this man reduces me back to a sniveling teenaged girl. I type out a text and send it before I can change my mind.

Me: Hey KP

Hey? Really? After all that mental warfare, I really just said hey. Good Lord, world just swallow me whole now, please.

But wait, don't take me yet, world, because the man just responded.

Isaiah: Lol never gonna live that down am I?

Okay, this is promising. I haven't returned a text or phone call from him in two months, but he's joking with me now. A good sign. Though not one I take much stock in because his default is always jokes.

Me: Probably not

Isaiah: I could always give you an encore performance. Maybe pick a different artist

Isaiah: I'm very versatile. I could do some Maxwell. Maybe some Drake. Some Bruno. If you're nice I'll hit you with some Jodeci.

And now flirting, his other default. Oh, hell no. Let's get this conversation back on track.

Me: Down boy. I didn't say I was up for a repeat

Especially considering you've got a woman who has a key to your place already.

Isaiah: What if I said that I've got my eyes on you and that you're everything that I see? - hint I just dropped some Drake

Girl, you're just sitting here while he lets his flirt flag fly. Steer this shit around!

Me: Can you come to Neon tonight? Wanna talk to you about something

Isaiah: To talk about our upcoming repeat performance?

Me: You wish. To talk about our last performance actually

Isaiah: Oof now I'm scared

Me: You should be

Me: See you tonight KP

Let him sit on that.

What does one wear under their work button-up shirt to tell a man about his impending fatherhood? Apparently, a *Goosebumps* tee. Because I'm a little bitch. R.L. Stine, please give me the strength to deliver this news tonight. Why did I think telling Isaiah that I'm pregnant with his baby at my bar was a good idea? Because I needed to be surrounded by distractions so I could walk away from him if I needed to, but now the loud noise of the bar is putting me on edge, and I wish I hadn't done this.

Ciara catches my attention then jerks her eyes forward, and I know he's here. I look up to find him staring me down, walking toward me with all the confidence in the world, not looking nervous whatsoever. Jackass.

But damn, is he good-looking. He's got on ripped jeans that sit perfectly on his hips, a tight black T-shirt that expands across his broad chest, and a leather jacket that makes me want to rip it off of him with my teeth. This is gonna be a long night.

"Hey, Nina. Glad you finally admitted you missed me and asked me to meet." I move the back of my hand to his forehead, and his brows rise in confusion. "What are you doing?"

"Checking you for a fever because you are delusional."

He throws his head back in laughter. Laugh all you want. Your life is about to permanently change. "Okay, fine, have it your way. You were the one calling out SOD for the win after our first round."

"Uh yeah, and SOD is exactly that—special occasions. You can't just have SOD on a regular-ass Friday." Though a very sinful, very stupid side of me would gladly make an exception for him.

"Nina, every day is a special occasion with me."

"There you go with the delusions again. You should probably see someone about that."

"I seem to remember our special occasion lasting all night and into the next morning."

"And I seem to remember your little girlfriend crashing that party." His smile falters at that. Fuck, I don't want to be an asshole here, but I don't have time for his flirty banter tonight. Time to rip the Band-Aid off. "Look, I really did call you down here to talk about something. I need to tell you something."

"Yes, I will fuck you again. Gladly." And now I'm just plain irritated. Flashes of that woman walking into his house like she owned the place cloud my vision. How dare he walk in here and think he can flirt me into submission? I'm not some easy lay.

"Jesus, can you be serious for two seconds?"

He throws his hands up in surrender. "Okay, okay, you're right. I'm all ears."

"I'm pregnant." There. I said it.

He blinks.

He blinks again.

Three times.

Four times.

Five times.

I'm beginning to think he's having a seizure.

"Isaiah? Can you say something, please?"

He blinks one more time. "You're pregnant?"

"Yes." He purses his lips, and I'm suddenly on edge. "If you ask me if it's yours I'll shove my shoe so far up your ass you'll taste the gum I stepped on earlier today."

"I…" He opens and shuts his mouth twice and remains perfectly still. I'm channeling my inner Brittany and trying to let him process his feelings, but I need him to say something, anything at all.

I place my hand on top of his. "Hey. You don't owe me anything. You can be as involved or as not involved as you want. I'm not asking you for anything, I just wanted you to know." There's a flash of hurt in his eyes at my statement, but it's gone in a blink. He yanks his hand away as if I've burned him, but he still doesn't speak. "Isaiah, I need you to say something. It can be positive, negative, whatever, but I need you to give me something here."

He shakes his head, and the motion speeds up with his thoughts. "I can't do this." And then before I can even process his words, he's gone.

Well, fuck. I did tell him to say anything, but that's the last thing I wanted to hear.

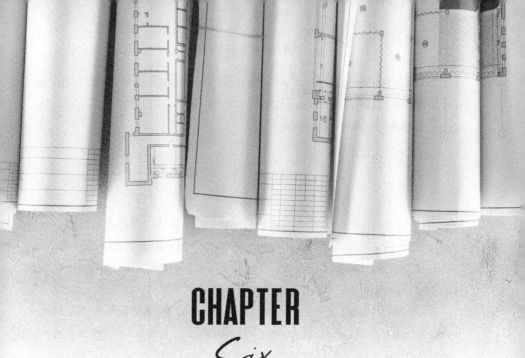

CHAPTER
Six

Isaiah

I'M IN MY CAR BEFORE I CAN EVEN PROCESS WHAT THE FUCK I'M DOING.

She's pregnant.

She's fucking pregnant.

When she texted me, I was surprised, and when she asked me to come see her I was floored but excited.

I thought she wanted to maybe question me about Alexis and squash our issues. I didn't expect her to want to hook up with me again, but I hoped.

What I definitely didn't expect was for her to tell me she's pregnant.

She told me I should be scared, and like the dumbass I am, I thought that was playful banter. But no, I should've been shitting bricks walking into that bar and not walking on cloud nine like I owned the fucking world.

I'm having a baby. She's having my baby.

When she told me, I blacked out. My mind immediately went to Monica and everything I went through with her. In my heart, I know I'm wrong. I know I'm an idiot and that I'm making a mistake. I know in my heart that Nina is not that woman. But my fucking head is driving the car right now.

My head is telling me to get out. That if I go through this again I'll never recover. I'll become someone I don't want to be. God, I don't even want to think about Monica right now.

I pull up in front of our apartment building and grab the takeout from the passenger seat. The minute I step out of the car, my entire body is covered in sweat. Fuck, it's hot out today. This is partly what I miss about Texas. It's hot there, but this shit is unbearable.

The other part I miss is my family. We've never lived so far apart. I would never admit it to the assholes, but I really miss them. I miss being able to just pop in on them anytime I feel like it, swing my niece and nephew around. Sasha had her daughter not too long ago, and I hate that I'm not there, but I've got my own baby to think about. Monica's here, so I'm here. I'll see my family soon enough. They'll be here next weekend for my birthday celebration. I can't wait to see the looks on their faces when Monica and I tell them we're having a baby. It's been killing me not to say anything every time I've been on the phone with them, but it'll be worth it to deliver the news in person. Plus, I'm pretty sure if I told them over the phone they'd all think I was joking. Reggie would definitely think I'm pranking her again.

Monica's been craving meatball subs lately, so that's what I brought home for lunch. She's off work today, so I figure I'll use my lunch break to bring her food, rub her feet, and make her come a few times.

"Fuck!" Monica cries out as I open the door. I immediately worry that maybe she hurt herself, but that wasn't a cry of pain. It sounded like a cry of. . .pleasure.

Is my greedy girl pleasuring herself on her day off? She's been insatiable lately. It's been amazing for me. Another plus for pregnancy. I loosen my tie and make my way back to the bedroom.

What in the fuck? That is not a sex toy getting my girlfriend off. That's a re-al-life man. A man I know. Fucking Harris. I'll kill him.

"What the fuck is this?" I yell at the both of them. Harris doesn't even startle, he just looks down and slowly peels himself off of Monica to tuck himself away.

Monica at least has the sense to look ashamed. She jumps up and grabs a blanket off the bed to cover herself. Imagine that. Covering herself from me. The man who's supposed to see her naked.

"Jesus, Isaiah," she stutters. "What are you doing home?"

What are you doing home? Is she fucking kidding me? That's the first thing out of her mouth? Not "I'm so sorry" or even "It's not what it looks like" though I'm not sure how you can explain away the fact that you were bouncing on my boss's dick two seconds ago.

"Shouldn't you be at the office?" Harris asks. The motherfucker. My boss is in my apartment, fucking my girlfriend, and he's asking me why I'm not in the fucking office? I don't even look at him. If I do, I might really kill him.

My boss.

The boss who Monica knew before we moved here.

A disturbing thought crosses my mind, and I'm trying not to let it take over, but I can feel my anger rising as it settles in.

"How long has this been going on?" I ask, and Monica looks away from me. She opens her mouth and closes it again. "Don't even think about lying to me right now. How fucking long?" She jumps as my voice gets louder, and Harris doesn't move a fucking muscle. This is the fucking guy she picks? He doesn't even defend her. He watches this all unfold like he couldn't care less.

"A while." Her voice is barely a whisper.

"Since before we moved here?"

Her eyes jump to mine then. "No. Not that long. But long enough. I'm sorry, Isaiah. I never meant for this to happen. I just—" She cuts herself off.

"You just what?" I need her to give me something. I need her to give me something to hold on to. I gave up everything for her. I left my job, my family, my city to follow her here. We were supposed to be forever. We were going to build a family together. I need something. I don't know if I can truly forgive her for this, but I also don't think I can live without her. I definitely can't live without our baby.

Please, God, let this be my baby.

Fuck.

"You're too much of a joker, Isaiah. I need someone more...together. Someone who can take care of me."

"I don't take care of you?" The rage inside me is at a fever pitch.

"I don't want to raise two kids! Okay? You're basically an overgrown man-child. All you do is joke around. I can't take it. I'm sorry."

Here I was planning a life with this woman, and she cheated on me because she doesn't take me seriously. Life's a fucking joke. "Is the baby mine?" She looks away, and that look in her eyes tells me all I need to know. But I'm not leaving here until she says it. I want to hear the words. I want her to admit to the ultimate betrayal. "Is the baby you're carrying my child, Monica? Answer me. Now."

The tears start falling down her cheeks, but I can't bring myself to care. Let Harris wipe them from her face.

"No. No, the baby is Harris's. I'm sorry." Harris picks that moment to finally move toward Monica, and the bastard places his hands on her stomach. I don't even realize I've crossed the room at this point, but I do tune in to my fist flying into Harris's face. It's the first time I've taken a breath since I walked in this room.

"Isaiah. Bro, what the fuck?" I look up, and Lincoln is staring at me like I've grown two heads. I look around and realize I've driven myself to Lincoln and Ciara's house. When did I decide to come here? Jesus, all this talk of babies has completely fucked with my head.

I know why I'm here though. My mind was so hazy when I walked out of Neon, but I didn't miss the way Ciara looked at me when I left. Like she was disappointed in me. So she knows exactly what bomb Nina dropped on me. How many others knew before me? Lincoln? Sasha? How many people have been hiding this from me?

"Did you know?"

"There you are. I thought you were having a damn stroke. Did I know what? Why do you look like that?"

"Like what, Linc? Like I just found out I'm having a baby? Because I did. And I'm asking if you knew first."

His eyes bug out of his head. "Pause. What? Just get inside right now."

He ushers me into his condo, and I brush past him to sink down onto his couch.

Linc stands across from me, arms crossed. He's older than I am by two years. He's got a brawnier build than I do. I guess that comes with the territory when you're a firefighter. He's exactly one inch taller than I am, and he never lets me forget it. His beard is full and covers his face while mine is more like a chin-strap. Basically, he usually looks like the older brother that he is. Looking at my brother right now, he looks so…young. He's so unbelievably happy now that he has Ciara that he's always sporting a damn smile, and it makes him look ten years younger. I'm happy for him. No one deserves it more. But I'm not okay with looking like the older brother. If I looked in the mirror right now I'm pretty sure I'd look like I just aged ten years and shaved off five years from my life expectancy.

Linc blinks, waiting for me to say something, but I'm so out of it. I just stare so he continues, "Say that again for me."

Sigh. "I'm having a baby, Linc."

He shakes his head. "By who?" Well, I guess that answers that question. So I guess Ciara is not one of those women who when a friend tells you something and asks you to keep it a secret, she assumes that doesn't include her husband. That immediately makes me like my sister-in-law even more, and I already love that girl to death. I'm glad Nina has a friend like that in her corner.

"Nina." I respond.

Linc steps back from me and wipes his hand down his beard. He doesn't even say anything else to me; he grabs his phone and starts texting.

"What the fuck are you doing?"

He doesn't look up from his phone. He just walks over to the kitchen. "Telling the guys to get over here." Lincoln grabs me a beer from the fridge. See? He understands the gravity of this situation.

Shane is the first to arrive. He complains about being pulled away from a date on a Friday night, but I know him well enough to know that if he was really into his date he would've blown us off. Dom shows up next, and he grumbles about not being in the mood to get into any bullshit tonight so this better be a chill night. Moody motherfucker. Kai's the last to show, but he just walks in, grabs a beer, and plops down on one of the chairs without a word.

I guess it's time to unload on the crew. I tell them everything about my night with Nina, the morning after with Alexis, and the news Nina gave me tonight.

The room is so silent you can hear a pin drop. The silence is driving me up a wall; I want to crawl out of my skin. Is this how Nina felt, waiting for me to respond?

God, I'm such a piece of shit. I just left her standing there. What the fuck is wrong with me?

"Well, okay then," Dom comments, then takes a swig of his beer.

"Okay then? What does that mean?"

"Nothing else to say. You're having a baby, man. It is what it is. Good for you." Dom is the kind of guy who's more broody than anything else. He's quieter than the rest of us. He jokes around, but he's definitely the most serious of this friend group. He drives into you if he thinks you're being a complete dumbass, like Lincoln was with Ciara before they got together, but he keeps his thoughts to himself for the most part on serious shit. So I guess I'm supposed to take comfort in the fact that he must think I'm going to pull my shit together at some point.

I just nod in acknowledgment and wait for everyone else's mouths to catch up to their brains.

"I just can't believe you conceived a baby on my wedding day. Jackass." Lincoln smirks. I punch him in the arm, but I appreciate him trying to lighten the mood.

"So, what happens now?" Shane asks, scratching his head.

"What do you mean?"

The sound of a chair scraping against the floor interrupts Shane before he can respond. Kai, who has been staring daggers at me since I told everyone what happened tonight, is now stomping toward Lincoln's door.

"Where you going?"

"You need to leave," he demands.

"What?"

"You need to get the hell out of here, you fucking asshole."

Everyone's head snaps up at that. What the fuck is happening right now?

"What's your problem?"

"My problem? You're the one with the problem. Nina told you she's pregnant with your baby, and you just walked out on her. And now you're here talking to us when you should be talking to her, like a man."

Shit. He's right about that. I already feel like a dick for walking away from her. I just needed a minute. Hearing her say those words was like an out-of-body experience. I was immediately transported back to the bull-shit with Monica, and I couldn't see what was right in front of me.

"I know, man. I know. I'm gonna talk to her. I just needed to clear my head. I wanted to get advice from my friends."

He clenches his fists. "What's there to get advice about? All she told you was that she's pregnant. You didn't even give her a chance to tell you what she wants to do about that. Is she keeping it? Is she going to have an abortion? Give the baby up for adoption? You have no clue because you walked out like a chickenshit. She came to you and was vulnerable with you and all you said was 'I can't do this.' She probably thinks she's all alone in this now, and that's the kind of stress she doesn't need. So you need to go make this right. Get off your ass and go find her. Now."

I've never seen Kai this fired up. Yeah, he gets passionate when he's working with his clients, but this is pure anger. I've never witnessed rage fly off of him like this. I have no idea why this has touched a nerve for him, but I don't have time to analyze it because he's absolutely right. I'm a piece of shit. I didn't give her a chance to tell me how she felt before I became so absorbed in how I felt.

And the thought of her aborting the baby or giving the baby up for adoption puts an ache in the pit of my stomach.

And that's when I realize the hard truth.

I want this.

I want this baby.

I want this baby with her.

I have to make this right.

I jump up, grab my jacket, and fly by Kai with just a slap on the shoulder.

Walking back into Neon Nights, I don't see Nina, but I do see Ciara, and the look she's giving me has me literally shaking. She's sort of fucking terrifying.

I push my shoulders back and march over to her with all the fake confidence I can muster. "What would it take for you to not yell at me right now and tell me where your girl is?"

She scoffs and rolls her eyes. "You know the only reason I'm not castrating your stupid ass right now is because number one, you're family and number two, we're in public and I don't wanna catch a charge."

"I'm fully aware I fucked up, Ci. I'm trying to make it right," I concede. She'd be well within her rights to drop my ass right now, and I know I'll be groveling to not just one woman but three. Ciara, Sasha, and Nina are like bulldogs when it comes to protecting each other, so I know I'm in for a world of hurt. If Nina doesn't tell Sasha what happened tonight, I have no doubt that Ciara will. I can't wait for that call, but all I care about right now is Nina. I have to get to her.

"And what's making it right mean to you?" She crosses her arms and waits for my response.

"Whatever she needs. Whatever she wants to do, I support her. I just want her to know that." Even though I want her to keep the baby, it's her body and her choice and I'll have to accept whatever decision she makes.

Her eyes soften. "She went home. The kids are at Sasha's so you'll be able to talk to her alone. If she allows it." I smile and start heading for the door. I went to Nina's house for the memorial service after her parents' funeral so I remember where it is.

"Isaiah?" she calls after me.

"Yeah?"

"Don't fuck up again. Because I would hate to have to explain to my husband how I murdered his only brother. Don't forget I write about murder for a living. I know how to do it without leaving a trace. But you're too heavy for me to carry, so he'd have to be the one to bury your body and that would be very traumatic for him."

I snort. "And we wouldn't want that."

"Exactly." There's a slight trace of humor in her voice, but her eyes tell me she's dead serious. See what I mean when I say she's sort of fucking terrifying? Ciara used to work in Human Resources before she went through the traumatizing experience of having a psychopath stalk and try to kill her several times. When she fled from her hometown to here, she decided to pursue her passion of writing thriller novels, and it paid off. She's now a successful published author and is working on her fourth book. She's got a morbid curiosity. Lincoln's always telling me how she gets him to watch all these unsolved murder documentaries and serial killer shows. I have no doubt in my mind she could come up with some very clever ways to dispose of me if she wanted to.

I look her right in the eyes, and I hope she can see the sincerity there. "I'm going to be there for her. No matter what." And I am. The more I think about it, the more ready I am.

She searches my eyes and offers me a curt nod before going to serve a customer at the other end of the bar.

CHAPTER
Seven

Nina

I'VE SHOWERED, CHANGED INTO MY PAJAMAS, AND NOW I'M FOCUSING on channeling my inner patience and understanding.

Fuck. That.

I'm pissed.

I get that it was a shock to him. It was a shock to me too, but he wouldn't even look me in the eye and then he took off and left me standing there like a fool.

I'm irritated. And what I really want is some caffeine or some goddamn alcohol, but the little bean won't let me be great, so here I am. Sober. Non-caffeinated. Hungry. Nauseous. Angry.

I'm stewing in my thoughts while rummaging through my fridge to see what Little Bean would like to eat when there's a knock on my door.

I have no idea who that is, but I feel sorry for them because I'm in a fucking mood and I'm ready to unleash on someone.

Well, well. The petty gods have smiled down on me and delivered the direct source of my frustrations to my doorstep. Isaiah has the good sense to look sheepish at least, but he still looks so mouth-watering good that I want to punch him in his throat even more.

He sticks his hands in his pockets and rocks back on his heels. I cross my arms and lean against my doorjamb.

"What can I do for you?"

He sighs. "Can I please come inside?"

"Yeah, you did that already. That's why we're in this position in the first place."

A surprise laugh falls from his lips. "No, I came inside a condom. Had I known you'd get pregnant anyway, well, I could've amped up the pleasure even more for both of us."

"Enough of that, get in here already. I'm too hungry for this conversation." I don't even wait for him to respond. I just turn and walk back into my kitchen to continue my search. If Little Bean doesn't get something to eat soon, he or she is going to turn against me.

When I turn back around, I can't deny the heat in Isaiah's eyes. He's blatantly checking out my legs and ass. It's then I realize that I have on tiny sleep shorts. Part of me wants to cross the room and pull his lips down to mine. *Lock that shit down.*

"Stop that," I demand.

He throws his hands up in surrender. "Stop what?"

"Looking at me like that." I point my finger in his face and narrow my eyes.

He sticks his tongue to wet his bottom lip, and the motion freezes me in my tracks. "How am I looking at you, Nina?"

"Like you want to devour me." His eyes darken. Holy shit. Is it hot in here?

Wait. No. Fuck this guy. I'm still pissed at him. And even more pissed now that I have to change my panties the minute he leaves.

"I'm serious, KP. Stop looking at me like that." I point to my stomach. "One roll around with you was potent enough, don't you think?"

His eyes fly to my stomach but where I thought I'd see panic and disgust,

I see excitement. I'm not sure what that means. "I know, I know. I'm just playing around. That's not what I'm here for. You must be really pissed at me."

I narrow my eyes again. "No, I'm a ball of fucking sunshine. How'd you guess?"

"Actually, it's because of your shirt."

"Excuse me?"

He points to my shirt, and I look down to see I have my Pixar *Inside Out* T-shirt on. It has the character Anger on it shouting expletives. I didn't even realize I picked this shirt out. My brain is so used to picking shirts to fit my mood, I must've been on autopilot.

I'm shocked and a little impressed that Isaiah has picked up on my dressing habits, but I'm not about to compliment him on it.

"You think I'm wearing this because I'm mad at you?" Nope, not gonna compliment him. I'm going to go in the complete opposite direction and poke at him.

"Either that or you're mad at your kitchen cabinet considering how hard you just slammed it. But I'm willing to bet it's me you're mad at, and I deserve that." He pauses. "Earlier you had on a *Goosebumps* T-shirt so you were probably feeling scared and anxious to tell me about the baby, and instead of realizing that, I acted like a jackass. I'm sorry."

Okay, I'm a little more impressed that he's able to read me so well. That's exactly why I wore my *Goosebumps* T-shirt tonight. I used to read those all the time as a kid and they would scare the shit out of me. I was terrified to tell Isaiah about the baby. Scared of getting the exact reaction I got. The fact that he understands that is unnerving. I need to steer away from his intense gaze. Shit, I'm hungry.

He takes a step toward me. I don't tense this time, so he takes another step before asking, "What exactly are you looking for? You look a little lost over there."

I resume my search through my cabinets and fridge. "I'm hungry but I have no idea what I want to eat. All I know is it has to involve cheese."

"Cheese?"

"Yes. I'm craving cheese."

"Want me to make you something?"

My head pops up from the fridge. He says this like it's the easiest thing in the world. Like he's not here to discuss the fact that he literally ran away from me when I told him I was expecting his child. Like we're friends. And I have to admit, I want to be his friend. We're going to have a baby together. I don't have any hopes that we'll be anything romantic, but I'd like us to be comfortable with each other. "You want to make me food in my house?"

"Yeah, why don't you sit down? I'll come up with something good." He reaches his hand up like he's about to guide me to one of the barstools in my kitchen but thinks better of it and drops his hand.

"You know what, usually I would argue that that's unnecessary, but I don't have the energy for that right now so knock yourself out." I slide onto a barstool and motion toward my fridge.

He chuckles. "Sit down, Phoebe. I'm about to rock your world."

"There will be no rocking of worlds, thank you. And you can't promise that; you don't even know what I have here."

"I don't need to know. I'm just that good. Now sit back, relax, and let me feed you."

"Do you hear yourself when you speak? It's just innuendo after innuendo."

"Hey, I'm not doing it on purpose. You're the one always pointing them out. Admit it, your mind is way dirtier than mine."

Cover your ears, Little Bean. Your dad is acting up right now. Do you have ears yet? I don't think so. I don't know.

I flick my hands in dismissal. "Make my food, asshole."

He laughs and goes back to my fridge to dig around. Watching Isaiah root around my kitchen like he owns the place proves too much to handle, so I make some lame excuse and head out to the living room.

Heavenly smells are coming out of my kitchen, but I refuse to look back there. I'm watching TV and guzzling water. Not paying attention to the gorgeous man back there, making me food because I had a craving. Not paying attention to that at all.

He clears his throat to get my attention. "My lady. I present to you…a gouda and provolone panini with a bacon garnish." He whips a plate from behind his back with a flourish.

I look down at the plate and burst out laughing. "You made me a bacon grilled cheese sandwich? That's brilliant."

Forsaking all manners, I snatch the plate away from him and moan around my first bite. I notice him fidget beside me, but I don't take my eyes off of the delicious sandwich in my hands. The bread is perfectly toasted and buttered. The crunch of the bacon perfectly offsets the gooey cheese.

Wow, I'm really pregnant.

He stands there and watches me inhale the sandwich in record time. I'm not even sure I chewed the last bite. Little Bean seems to have enjoyed it though, so I have no regrets. I try to regain my dignity by using the napkin he gave me to wipe my mouth, but I'm pretty sure the cat's out of the bag at this point. I'm somewhat of a pig when the food is that good. It's high time he learns that. "Thank you. Really." His smile is so wide at my thanks that it makes me smile.

"It's the least I could do. Does this put me back in your good graces?"

"Who said you were ever there?"

And there's that playboy smirk again. This guy never misses an opportunity. "Mmm, the way you laugh at my jokes, the way your nails slide down my back when I'm inside you, the face you make when you come. I could go on." I take another sip of my water, ignoring the way my heart races at his words. Pushing the memory of that night as far away from me as it can get.

"Please don't."

He grabs my plate off the coffee table and takes it to the kitchen. When he comes back he sits across from me and takes my hands in his. "So now that I'm done being an asshole, we should probably talk. About everything."

"Look, I'm not expecting anything from you. I meant what I said—you don't owe me anything. I'm perfectly capable of taking care of myself and this baby, so if you want out, that's fine."

He squeezes my hand. "I don't want out. If you want to keep this baby then I'm happy. And I want to be by your side through everything. I…" He pauses and closes his mouth. It looks like he considers saying something but changes his thoughts at the last minute. "I panicked when you told me. And I reacted poorly. I own that. But I've got my shit together now. I intend to be here with you through each step of this journey, and when this baby gets here, I'll be the best dad I can be. I promise you that."

Now that, Little Bean, is your daddy. I guess he's not so bad, huh?

My stomach rolls and my mouth fills with saliva. No, no, no. Little Bean, don't do this. That sandwich was delicious, but it won't be as good coming back up.

Little Bean has spoken. I excuse myself and run to my bathroom just in time to throw up everything. I was right. That sandwich was not good coming back up.

The next thing I know, Isaiah's strong hand is lifting my hair away from my neck and rubbing my back as I empty the rest of my stomach contents.

"Are you okay? Was the sandwich too much?"

"Nah, it was perfect. This is just the morning sickness. Which they should really consider renaming all day sickness. Morning sickness is very misleading." He chuckles and continues rubbing my back. "You don't have to keep doing that. I know this is probably gross."

"I meant what I said. I'm here for this entire journey. Every step. It would take a lot more than puke to scare me off. You didn't know me in my college years."

"Oh no, you're a sloppy drunk? A puker?"

"Oh yeah. Well, I used to be because in college I thought I was hot shit and I could mix dark and light liquor whenever I wanted."

I can imagine Isaiah in college, walking around with all that unearned swagger. Who am I kidding? I've seen his man-meat; that swagger was definitely earned. He probably was that guy who all the guys wanted to hang out with and all the girls wanted to fuck. And I'm betting he indulged a lot of those girls in their fantasies. I'm tempted to ask about it, but the thought of him with other women makes me want to throw up again, and there's nothing left in my stomach but bile so I'll pass. "Rookie mistake."

"Right? One time I was so drunk, this girl took me upstairs and attempted to give me a lap dance. I threw up all over her breasts."

I laugh and fake gag at the same time. "That's fucking disgusting."

"It wasn't pretty, that's for sure."

"I'm gonna assume that girl never spoke to you again."

"You assume correctly."

It makes me feel a little better imagining him with other women if I also imagine that he threw up on all of them. Ugh, that's so dumb. I can't have a crush on the father of my child. He's not for me. "Good. I suppose you're back in my good graces now." He smiles at me, and suddenly, I don't feel so alone in this. "KP?"

"Yeah?"

"Thank you."

"I got you, Phoebe." He rubs my back and starts humming in my ear.

"Is that...'Teenage Dream'?"

"Well, I know I said I'd try other artists, but KP is kinda my thing now, and 'Hot and Cold' doesn't fit our dynamic anymore. This seemed more appropriate."

"We really need to discuss your knowledge of Katy Perry's discography. You are not passing that on to our child."

He throws his head back in laughter. "Deal."

CHAPTER
Eight

Isaiah

"FUCK!" I CURSE TO MYSELF AS I DROP MY KEYS FOR THE SECOND time. I'm nervous as all hell walking up to Nina's door.

Last night when we were talking, she started freaking out about needing to tell the kids that she's pregnant. She was worried they would take it poorly because they've already gone through so much change in the last few months. This also means a delay in getting them their own rooms, since she will need the third bedroom as a nursery.

I wanted to take all her worries away, and I promised her I'd be here for everything she needed. Before I knew what I was doing, I offered to be with her while she told them. That way if they bombarded her with questions, she wouldn't have to take them on alone.

I don't know why I'm nervous. Kids love me! I've met Logan and Jada before and they're great, but I'm on edge. I guess I want their approval. For what? I don't know. It's not like if they don't like the idea we can do anything to change it, but I want to make this as easy for them as possible.

Knock knock knock.

Nina opens the door, and I'm immediately under her spell again. She has on leggings that hug her hips and demand attention. Her hair is in its naturally curly state. She has no makeup on. I don't mean to sound cliché, but she's glowing. She looks absolutely stunning.

I chuckle when I see she's wearing a Bob Marley "One Love" T-shirt. I know she's hoping this conversation will go well and everyone will come out unscathed. I plan to ask her how many times she's sung "Three Little Birds" to herself this morning.

"Hey. You sure you wanna do this? You can back out right now," she offers.

Yeah, right. I'm in far too deep for that.

"I told you, Nina. I'm in this with you. Don't worry about a thing." She smirks at my last line before stepping aside so I can walk in.

It's a whole different vibe walking into Nina's house when the kids are home. The sexual tension isn't crackling the way it was last night. Well, let me rephrase, the sexual tension isn't the only thing crackling. It's more like consistent background noise today. With the kids here, it feels…homey. Jada is doing all kinds of flips and cartwheels while some weird kid show blasts on the TV. Logan is at the kitchen table with his head in a book, attempting to eat a waffle but missing his mouth a few times. It's like a quiet storm in this house. I like it.

"Hey guys, can you come here a second? I wanna talk to you," Nina announces. Logan looks up from his book, and for the first time he sees me standing there. He takes a double take, like he's trying to figure out if he wants to welcome me or throw his book at me, but he doesn't say anything. He just saves his place in his book and heads over to the living room with us. Jada finishes the flip she was working on before turning the TV down and sitting down on the carpet.

"Hey, I know you," Jada says, sizing me up.

"Oh yeah? How?"

She taps her tiny fingers on her chin. "Mmmm, I've seen you before. You were at CiCi's wedding. You're, umm, Linc's brother."

I snap and smile. "You got me. I thought you were gonna say I look like a movie star."

"You're not in movies, silly." She moves her hands to cover her giggle.

"But I could be, right? Come on, don't I look like I could be the black Superman?" I flex so she can really see my muscles. Gotta get all the angles.

She giggles. "No! You're not big enough to be Superman!"

I slap my hand to my chest and feign offense. "You wound me, kid! Guess I gotta go to the gym more."

"But you don't have lasers in your eyes either. And you can't fly!"

"Pshh, how do you know? Maybe I just keep it a secret like Clark Kent."

She looks me up and down like I might be telling the truth. "Nahh, I don't buy it."

"Tough crowd." I look over at Nina, and she looks away from me quickly, but I caught a glimpse of her face before she turned, and I want her to look at me like that forever.

"Okay, guys. I have some news and I wanted to share it with you."

"Is it good news? I only like good news," Jada says. Same, kid, same.

Nina takes a second to collect her thoughts. "Umm, yeah…yeah, it is." She takes a subtle look at her stomach and smiles. She loves that little nugget growing in there already. She's going to be an amazing mom. Good. That kid is gonna need one worthy parent.

"Yay! Okay, tell us."

"I…we,"—she gestures between the two of us—"we're having a baby."

Logan's mouth falls open while Jada gasps.

"You and…him? Are having a baby?" Logan asks.

"Yes."

"I didn't know you guys were dating."

Nina's eyes widen, and she looks to me but quickly looks back to Logan and masks her features. "We're not. But we're having this baby, and we're going to co-parent."

"Co-parent? What's that mean?" Jada asks, suddenly nervous.

"It just means we're going to be equally responsible for raising this baby even though we're not boyfriend and girlfriend or married." I'm letting Nina take the lead because I don't know what she wants them to know and what she doesn't. I'm pretty sure she just wanted me here as a supporting figure, but I feel useless just sitting here not saying anything. My gut tells me to crack a joke, but I'm ignoring that dumbass right now.

"So there's a baby in there?" Jada points to Nina's still flat stomach.

"Yep. I call it Little Bean since we don't know if it's a boy or girl yet." Little Bean. I like that. Our Little Bean is inside her. I still can't believe this is happening. I thought after everything I'd never have this chance again.

Will our baby look more like me or Nina? I hope they have my eyes and her nose and lips. It would be the perfect combination.

"So is that why you've been sick? I heard you throw up a few times."

"Yeah, but don't worry—it's normal. It's called morning sickness. My body is just adjusting to a little human growing inside of it, so I get sick sometimes, but I'm okay." Watching her explain this to Jada is so sweet. She's so caring with her. So patient. She takes the time to break everything down for her. Is it weird that witnessing her maternal instincts is turning me on?

"Okay." Jada looks relieved at that.

"Is the baby gonna share the room with us?" Nina's smile falls at Jada's question. I know she feels guilty for not being able to give the kids their own rooms. She promised to rectify the weird situation their parents put them in, and having to renege on that is eating away at her.

"No, Mini. The baby will probably have to use the spare bedroom." Jada nods but doesn't say anything else to that.

"Are you gonna move in with us?" Jada turns her question to me, and I'm suddenly regretting my wish to be an active participant in this conversation.

"Umm...no. I don't think so." That's not something Nina and I have discussed. I wouldn't mind living here with Nina and the kids or having them move in with me so that I can be close to them and the baby. We don't live far from each other, but really anything other than together is too far. The idea of living in a separate home from my kid makes my stomach hurt, but I don't want Nina and the kids to be uncomfortable. Nina and I have a lot to figure out with this co-parenting thing.

Jada frowns. "But how will you see the baby if you don't live here?"

"He'll come visit, Mini. That's part of the co-parenting I mentioned."

"Have you guys talked about a plan, though?" Logan asks. He's been letting Jada get all her questions out since we first made the announcement, but I think the shock is wearing off now.

"We've talked, and there's more talking to do but we'll be okay. We have it under control."

Logan turns to me. "So, if you're not going to be living here will you be contributing financially? Because Nina has enough on her plate already taking care of us. She doesn't need to be picking up your slack too."

"Logan!" Nina exclaims.

I hold my hand out to indicate I'm okay. Honestly, I'm proud of this kid right now. He's looking out for his sister, and Nina deserves that. She looks out for everyone around her, and she needs someone to help carry some of the load.

"Hey, I get it. I really do. And yes, I'll be contributing financially, but that's not all I'll be contributing. That baby inside your sister's belly is half me, and I'd never sit back and let Nina do all the work. I'm going to be present all the time and making sure Little Bean knows he or she is loved. Unconditionally. There's not a game, tournament, concert, play, competition, anything that I plan to miss. For as long as I breathe and even long after that, there's not a moment that baby won't know how much I care about and support them. And if you ever feel like I'm not living up to the hype, feel free to call me on shit." Nina elbows me in the side. "Err...stuff."

Logan searches my eyes for a lie, which I know he won't find. When he's satisfied, he turns back to Nina. "Are you happy?"

A faint smile touches Nina's lips. "Yeah, Lo. I really am." A tear springs in her eye and starts to roll down her cheek, and I wipe it away on instinct. She startles at the touch but leans into it. Logan smiles and nods, and Jada jumps up and down.

"Yay! A baby! I can't wait! I'm gonna teach him or her how to play every board game, and when they get older they can do my chores for me."

We all laugh. "That's not at all how that works." She just shrugs.

This meeting is officially adjourned. All of my limbs are still attached and no one is in hysterics, so I'd say it went well. Jada offers to show me how to do some "easy" tumbles. Logan decides to stay in the living room with us while Nina goes in the kitchen to grab a cup of coffee for me and snacks for her and the kids.

Like I said, we have a lot to figure out for our future and our baby's future, but right now I feel like Bob Marley was on to something. Everything is gonna be fine.

 *

The next day, I'm early getting to the office, still riding the high from yesterday's successful conversation. I check my phone, and I somehow have missed an entire conversation in my family group chat.

Sasha: Soooo Izzy…do Mom and Dad know you knocked up my best friend? Because I'm about to see Mom in a little bit so I need to know what's public knowledge

I'm glad Sasha is finally acknowledging me again. I got a mouthful followed by the cold shoulder when she called to inform me that Nina had already filled her in on the pregnancy.

Reggie: Umm…excuse me? WTF?

Ooops. I knew I was forgetting to tell someone. It honestly just slipped my mind to tell her. If Kai hadn't ripped into me I'm sure I would've because Reggie is the person I go to when I need someone to burst my bubble and give me full brutal honesty. There's a reason I never told her about the whole Monica and Alexis situation. I didn't really want brutal honesty about it.

Sasha: Oh you didn't hear? Our baby brother has super sperm. It fought through a condom and Nina's birth control to get it on with her egg

Lincoln: LOL yeah the fucking asshole is gonna be a papa so now Ciara's mom is all up our asses about when we're gonna give her a grandbaby. Thanks for that

WHERE WE FOUND OUR *Heart*

Reggie: Why the hell am I always the last to know shit?! I'm gonna be an auntie again!

Sasha: Oops sorry sis. He probably was in freak out mode. I heard he almost got his ass beat by Ciara because he didn't react well at first

Reggie: *sigh* dumbass

Sasha: Right? It's like we didn't raise him right or something

Lincoln: Here she goes thinking she raised us again

Lincoln: But yeah Ciara was heated when she got home. And Kai almost beat his ass too

Sasha: Kai?! Oh shit he's so laid-back. You fucked up bro

Reggie: *inserts gif of Key & Peele skit with the words 'ya done messed up A-ARon'*

Sasha: LOL

Sasha: And Lincoln I did have a hand in raising you. Respect your elders bitch

Lincoln: *inserts gif of Stanley from The Office rolling his eyes*

Jesus. My siblings are a bunch of idiots. And assholes. Idiot assholes.

Me: Dickheads

Me: I fixed it. Nina and I are good. Sorry I didn't tell you Reggie I was a little busy

Sasha: Sooo does this mean Mom and Dad don't know??

Me: *inserts gif of Kanye shrug*

Me: I mean I didn't tell them

Sasha: *inserts gif of Toy Story dramatic gasp*

Sasha: Izzy wtf! I can't be around Mom and not tell her! She'll kill me when she finds out

Me: So tell her

Sasha: Oh so now I'm in charge of delivering your big news?? Hell no that's too much pressure

Me: I'm just fucking with you I told them last night. I went over after I left Nina's

Mom was surprised, but when I told her it was Nina who was pregnant she perked up. I know she loves Nina, but I thought it would take her longer to get over the shock of Nina going from Sasha's friend to the mother of my child. Dad just smirked and said he was excited for another grandchild. I never told them about the grandchild that never was, so it was a bittersweet conversation for me, but I'm glad they're happy for me.

Reggie: What did they say?!

Me: Congrats?

Reggie: Be fucking serious. What did they say?

Me: They're excited to have another grandbaby. Really that was it. I'm a grown ass man what were they gonna say?

Sasha: Okay tough guy. Stop the cap. I know Mom had to have asked about a million questions about your relationship with Nina.

Me: Oh I gotta run into a meeting sorry guys bye

Sasha: Dickhead

Reggie: Such a damn tease. I will beat this information out of you. Or lawyer it out of you. Whichever is worse

Sasha: No need I'll find out from Mom today I don't need your ass Izzy *tongue out emoji*

Lincoln: Good luck bro. I'm just glad it's not me they're ganging up on

Sasha: The day is still young. Your wife will be here soon so don't tempt me

Lincoln: I was never here *inserts gif of Homer Simpson backing up into bushes*

Sasha: Mhmm

Reggie: Izzy I just wanna say you're gonna be a great dad. That's my one nice comment for the day, take or leave it.

Me: I'll take it

Reggie: Ha! Sucker I knew you were still reading these texts

Me: LOL fucking brat.

I won't lie, my chest expands at Reggie's text. Let's hope she's right. I put my phone in my pocket and get to work.

"Okay, so once we get the final permit for the Gardner building we'll be able to move forward to next steps." I'm in a meeting with my boss, Alan, and two of our partners to discuss the commercial bank building plans I drafted.

There's a knock on the door. Alan's assistant, Carla, pokes her head in. "Excuse me, sir. Sorry to interrupt, but Isaiah, you have a visitor in the lobby."

"Oh, thank you, Carla." Alan tells me to find him later, and I head down to the lobby, and what I find there has my blood boiling.

Alexis Bell is standing in the lobby of my work building. She's wearing skin-tight jeans and a low-cut top. I feel nothing but rage looking at her.

"What are you doing here, Alexis?" She must be looking for her damn mind. I know she's lost it, showing up here at my job. Showing up anywhere I am after I kicked her out of my place last time.

"Hey there, I was in the neighborhood. I wanted to see if you wanted to grab lunch."

I level her with a glare that I hope sets her entire insides on fire. "I don't want to go to lunch, Alexis."

Her lips twist up in a grin. "Okay, no problem. I know you're busy. Maybe we can get together later tonight then." She runs her hand down my arm, and I gently remove her hand and guide her farther away from the front desk.

"No, thank you. I think I made myself clear last time. There won't be any get togethers for us tonight or ever."

"Hmm, that's too bad. I was talking to Monica the other day just catching up, ya know? I thought it would be nice if you and I caught up too. Like old times."

She always does this. She knows how to dangle the Monica carrot in front of me. The two of them have the most toxic friendship I've ever seen. Every time I push her away she offers intel on Monica and I cave, desperate to still have insight into her life. Why? Why do I torture myself like that?

It pains me to admit it, but part of me wants whatever info Alexis has to offer right now, but thinking back to Alexis scaring Nina away that day in my house pisses me off enough to push my desires away. I don't have time to worry about what Monica's doing right now. I've got a baby on the way to think about. A baby that's mine.

"There's nothing for us to talk about. I'm glad you two were able to catch up though." Her smile falters, and I know I've caught her off guard. Good. She should get used to it.

"Have a good day, Alexis." I don't wait for her to respond before walking back to the elevators.

CHAPTER
Nine

Nina

"PLEASE SIR, CAN I HAVE SOME MORE?" I HOLD OUT MY MUG TO Sasha and put on my best British accent, which isn't good at all. The smell of coffee beans and freshly baked bread overwhelms me, but thank God it doesn't make me gag. Little Bean has made me so sensitive to smells I can't take it. We had to remove the buffalo wings from the menu at Neon for the time being because Little Bean is not a fan.

He or she seems to understand my addiction to coffee and Sasha's pastries, so this is my safe haven for now.

Sasha and I built our friendship in this shop. We met four years ago. Sasha had been a stay-at-home mom for the first two years of Nevaeh's life before pursuing her dream of owning her own business. I was trying to take Neon Nights to the next level. We were two businesswomen trying to flourish in this city, and we supported each other. Granted, I don't own Neon Nights. I'm the manager. I'd had my eye on Neon for a while. It was in a prime location, but business was not good. The place was outdated as hell. It was almost empty every single day. I waltzed in there one day and begged to be brought on as a manager, Bar Rescue style. The owner was a man who passed away and left the place to his mom who had no interest in the bar scene and no idea what to do with the place. Her name is Dee, and she lives in Dallas and rarely comes in. She just trusts me to run the place to the best of my ability. It's my dream to one day buy this place from her. When I first took over as manager, I asked her permission for every change I wanted to make, but she encouraged me to be comfortable making executive decisions. The place needed a lot of sprucing up. It had no allure. Before long, I made this place my own, and now it's truly my baby. Well, my first baby, I guess I should say now. I passed by Sasha's shop on my way to Neon one day, and we bonded. We promoted each other's businesses. She'd offer hangover deals in her shop for anyone who went to Neon the night before and posted it on Instagram. I started selling one of her pastries on my menu. She's my rock.

Sasha rolls her eyes and sits down beside Ciara, across from me.

"Girl, I told your pregnant ass no more."

"The doctor said I could have two cups of coffee a day, and I want my second cup, dammit."

Ciara cackles while Sasha waves me off. Can you believe this shit? She is ignoring the pregnant woman's request. That's some bullshit if you ask me.

"You sound like an addict." Ciara tosses that at me as if I would feel any shame about that.

"I am an addict. I'm addicted to caffeine, and I'm okay with that."

"The fetus growing inside your belly isn't, fool," Sasha admonishes.

I sigh. "I can't believe how horrible you're treating me. I'm gonna write you a terrible review on Yelp."

"Ho, I dare you!" Ciara cackles again, and I can't help but join her.

"Well, damn. Fine then. I'll just have my second cup later."

"Yeah, psycho. It's only noon. You might wanna space your two cups out so you don't go through withdrawals and my niece or nephew suffers the consequences." I stick my tongue out at her comment. Whatever. I know when I've lost. I hope Little Bean appreciates this because I sure as hell don't.

"So how is everything going with you and Izzy?" I can't help but laugh when she says that because I know he hates that nickname, but she and Reggie refuse to give it up.

How are things with Isaiah and me? That's a great question. The simple answer is…fine. We talk daily. He's constantly asking me questions about how I'm feeling and if he can do anything for me, but I rarely take him up on it. I don't know how to be around him. We had a weird friendship before all of this so now I'm left wondering exactly where we stand. Are we friends? Are we just getting along for the sake of the baby? He still flirts with me all the time, but he flirts with everyone so I don't know what to make of that. It all just feels complicated, and I'm trying to let him in but keep my distance at the same time. The worst thing that could happen right now is that I catch feelings for him. We need to focus on the baby.

"Things are good. He's requested to come with me to all of my doctor's appointments. And we've decided that on Friday nights when the kids are with you that he'll come over and we'll talk."

"Talk. Is that what we're calling it now?" Ciara raises her eyebrows.

"Oh, fuck off. That was a one-time thing…with very permanent results. No, we just feel like we should probably learn more about each other beyond surface-level bullshit. We need to learn each other's beliefs and values so that when co-parenting really begins we don't kill each other."

"That's true. You wouldn't want to find out that one of you believes in letting the baby cry themselves to sleep while the other picks them up after every sound. You'd confuse the shit out of the baby."

"Exactly. Stuff like that. Or just finding out what beliefs and traditions we each plan to pass down to the baby."

"So these Friday night meet-ups are like getting to know you sessions. I like it. Little ass-backwards but I like it." She puts her index finger and thumb close together for emphasis.

I throw my balled-up napkin at Sasha in response.

"Well, I can't wait to hear how the first one goes."

Yeah, me either. I know one of the things Isaiah will want to talk about is our living situation. I know he wants to be under the same roof as the baby— and that makes sense—but I just can't process that right now. I haven't acknowledged Little Bean's nursery because I feel so guilty that I can't give Logan and Jada the one thing I promised them—separate bedrooms. I was going to make it so special for them and now what? They get put to the side yet again because I gave in to temptation? It feels selfish.

Where the hell would Isaiah even sleep? We're not together. I would not survive sharing my room with him, so what does that leave? My couch? My garage? The baby could sleep in my bedroom and Isaiah could have the spare room, I guess, but all of that feels wrong.

What is the right choice?

"So I heard Ms. Angela is hounding you to hop on the baby train, Ci." I'm grateful to Sasha for turning the subject over to Ciara because I was about to go down a deep rabbit hole over how Friday is going to go.

"Ugh, I blame this asshole." She points at me. "But yes! She's like a damn gnat that will not go away no matter how many times I swat at her. When she first moved down here to be near her nonexistent grandbabies I told her not to get her hopes up for a while." Ciara's mom moved down here not long before the wedding because she couldn't stand being so far away from her daughter and wanted to be close when the grandbabies started appearing.

I think it's sweet. My parents wouldn't have done that. If I'd lived in a different state than them I think I would've seen them maybe twice a year.

"Lincoln and I want kids," Ciara continues, "and we don't plan on waiting too much longer, but after the drama we went through with the psycho and the hell I suffered before that we just want to enjoy each other, ya know? I just wanna jump on my husband's dick whenever and wherever I want without having to worry about waking a baby up for a little longer. Last night, we did it on the kitchen table, the washing machine, and the couch. Do you think I'll be able to do that when there are little hellions running around? Hell, no. And we just booked our trip to St. Lucia for New Year's and I'll be damned if I can't get shitfaced on the beach."

"Before jumping on your husband's dick," Sasha adds.

"You just get me. So yeah, that's where we're at."

"Wait. Can we just go back to the fact you and Lincoln fucked on three different surfaces in one night? I have questions." I lean in, fully invested in the answer. To hell with the fact that his sister is sitting right here.

"Oh girl. I gotta use that firefighter stamina to my advantage while we're young-ish. Plus, I've always wanted to have sex on a washing machine and I just never have. Ten out of ten. Would recommend."

Sasha fakes a gag and gets up to help a customer who just walked in.

"I always figured sex on a washing machine was overhyped. But I'm adding it to my list of places to try. If I ever have sex again, because right now I can barely go two hours without puking. Plus, no one wants to have sex with a pregnant woman. Unless they're one of those weirdos with a pregnancy fetish. No, thank you."

"One, absolutely add it to your list. And I wanna know what else is on this list, by the way. It's worth all the hype. Two, that is not true. Lots of guys without weird fetishes would have sex with a pregnant woman. Including the guy who fathered the baby you're cooking."

"I told you that is not happening. Isaiah and I are in a weird enough place as it is. We don't need to complicate it more by having sex again. Besides, that thing between his legs may actually kill me." But shit, what a way to go.

"Whatever you say, boo." She leans in closer and whispers, "I lowkey wonder if their dad has a big dick too. I mean what are the chances that the two Cole brothers are walking around with grade-A Wagyu beef between their legs? It's gotta run in the family."

"You're disgusting." I laugh.

"Just saying," she sings.

"Just saying what?" Sasha asks as she returns to the table.

Ciara and I look at each other and burst out laughing.

"Nothing at all," I lie.

Sasha looks between us with a scowl. "Nasty bitches." She sits down and we crack up all over again.

75

Later that night, Logan and I play Candy Land with Jada to cheer her up because she had a hard day in gymnastics.

"Ha! I get to take Gumdrop Pass," Jada declares before taking her pawn up the shortcut, inching closer to the Candy Castle than either Logan or me.

"It's not over. If I land on the orange square in my next turn I can take Rainbow Trail and catch up to you." Logan is deep in concentration. He hates board games, but he puts his all into every game we play because he knows it's important to Jada. He's a good big brother like that.

"I bet you you won't," Jada teases.

"I bet you I will."

"I bet you your brownie you won't." Jada points to the brownie Logan has sitting next to him.

I made brownies today because Little Bean was craving them. Yes, I am that pregnant woman that blames her pigging out on her baby. No, I don't feel bad about that. I'm providing Little Bean with the space to live in my body for nine months; they provide me with the excuse to overeat. I think it's a fair trade-off. Besides, Little Bean rejects most food so when I have a craving for something, I immediately go for it with the relief that I'll be able to keep something down.

"You're on." Logan holds out his hand, and Jada shakes it. Apparently, we're deep in the shits now. Who knew Candy Land could be so competitive?

Logan picks up a card, but it's not the orange card that would put him right below the Rainbow Trail. It's a blue card that puts him next to the orange square he needed.

"Yay! You lose, so give me that brownie!" Jada does an adorable victory dance and holds out her hand. Logan reluctantly hands her the brownie, and you would think the world was ending.

"You know there are more brownies, right?"

"Yeah, but they're in the kitchen. That's so far." Fucking kids.

After Jada kicks our asses in Candy Land, we move on to Connect Four. Logan says he'll play the winner of our game, deciding to stop being a lazy-ass teenager and go to the kitchen for a replacement brownie.

"So how's the reading list going this week, Lo?"

"Good. I finished *Fahrenheit 451* last night. I'm gonna start on *The Martian* tonight."

"I loved *Fahrenheit 451*."

"You did, really? Cool. Wait, you mean the book, right? Not the movie because Michael B. Jordan was in it?"

Did I mention he's also a smartass? "Hey, I read as much as you, ya jerk. I just also happen to be lusting after Michael B. Jordan."

He scrunches his nose up. "Eww. I don't wanna talk about that."

I wave him off. "Oh please, you're past the cooties stage."

"Yeah, but that doesn't mean I wanna hear you talking about lust." It did not slip my notice that he said "yeah" to my statement of him being past the cooties stage. Hmm. Could someone have caught Logan's eye? Am I ready to be the parent of a teenager with hormones and a sex drive? Yuck.

"Do we need to have the talk? Because I'm pretty sure your baby niece or nephew's existence tells you I've lusted before."

"I hate you," he teases between laughs. "I don't need the talk again. It was awkward as hell when Dad did it."

I crack up at that. When our mom gave me the talk, Dad walked in on us and as soon as he heard her say the word condom he flew out of the room. I can't imagine him having the talk with Logan. It probably went something like "Sex. Don't do it."

"I bet it was awkward. You know Dad was not good with words. One time, a guy I was kind of dating told me I gave him blue balls, so I asked Dad what blue balls felt like, and he literally shoved a piece of bacon in my mouth and walked away." Logan chokes on absolutely nothing, and I bend over with laughter. "Hey, consider yourself lucky. At least you didn't have Mom pulling up pictures of STDs and YouTube videos of childbirth. Some stuff you can never unsee." And flashes of those videos she showed me are coming back now. Suddenly, I want Little Bean to stay in my belly forever.

"Mom was always so extra. I had a girl over to study once, and she told us she wasn't ready to be a grandmom and to leave the door open. We were eleven."

Logan laughs at the memory, but it's a somber laugh. This is the first time we've talked about happy memories of our parents since they died. It's nice to be able to talk about them without the lingering anger underneath.

I sense Logan shrinking back into himself, so I move the subject back to books. "So, *The Martian*. Is that the one that Matt Damon did the movie version of?"

"Yeah. I heard the book is way better, so I'm going to read it first then watch the movie. Have you seen the movie? I bet you have since you've seen every movie in existence."

"No, smartass, I actually haven't seen this one. So when you're done reading the book we can watch the movie together."

"Cool." He nods then heads to his and Jada's bedroom to no doubt dive into his book.

It's Friday. My heart feels like it's beating out of my chest. My palms are sweating. I feel like there's so much riding on tonight. It's a ridiculous thought. If tonight is awkward or doesn't go well then we try again. This isn't a one or done obviously, but tonight will set the tone for our partnership going forward. Can we really do this together?

I just brushed my teeth after throwing up for the fifth time. I can't decide if Little Bean is wreaking havoc on my stomach or if I'm nervous about Isaiah showing up for our first get to know you session.

Jesus, we're having a baby together, and we're having a get to know you session. Sasha's right, this is ass-backwards. I have to come up with a better name for our meet-ups.

Knock knock knock. Showtime.

I open the door, and surprisingly the first thing I notice isn't how delicious Isaiah's forearms look when he has his sleeves rolled up or how his broad shoulders are swallowing his collar. No, it's how his eyes keep darting to the ground and how he keeps scratching his arms.

He's nervous.

Now that is adorable. It makes me feel a million times better that I'm not the only one freaking out.

I wave him inside, and he greets me with a kiss on the forehead. Dammit, Isaiah. Do not make me swoon right now.

"Hope you like tacos because that's what we've got tonight."

"I'm a human being. Of course I like tacos." Okay, good. He can stay.

"Can I get you a drink? Water? Soda? Beer?" I might have asked Ciara to find out his favorite beer so I could have it stocked for our Friday night meet-ups. That's just me being a good hostess. Nothing more.

He seems to relax the longer he stands in front of me. "I'd love a beer, but I feel bad drinking since you can't. Do you have stuff to make mocktails? I could make you one."

Nothing sounds worse than a mocktail. That's just a painful reminder of the missing alcohol. "Absolutely not. I'm not a recovering addict. You can have a drink, Isaiah." He laughs, and I grab a beer from the fridge for him. Let the getting to know you session commence.

I honestly don't know why I was so nervous about this. At his core, Isaiah is a good guy, and he's easy to be around. We've been laughing and joking all night. I've learned that he puts his toilet paper over, not under, so he's not a complete heathen. His favorite color is red. He's pro-choice. He went to the University of Texas to study architectural engineering. He's more Agnostic than Christian so he doesn't care to give our child godparents or have Little Bean baptized, which is fine by me. His mom will fight us if we don't give our child a Nigerian middle name.

He just finished telling me the story of "Niecygate" where Reggie and their mom almost came to blows over Niecy's middle name and in the end his mom won.

"Honestly, I'm not surprised. I mean Reggie is tough but your mom..." I whistle. "I would not fuck with her."

"Yeah, she's like a mafia boss. Loved by many, feared by all."

"I wanna be a badass mom like her."

"You will be."

"You think so?"

"Yeah. I see it already in how you are with Logan and Jada. You listen to them, and you don't treat them like kids should be seen and not heard. But you also don't take any shit, and they respect you enough to not try you. LB is one lucky kid to have you as a mom."

Can somebody say swoon?

"Thanks. For the record, I think LB is lucky to have you too."

"Jury's still out on that one, but I hope so."

We're washing and drying the dishes together when Isaiah excuses himself to the bathroom. His phone lights up with a text, and I swear I don't mean to look but the light is calling to me and I can't help myself. I sneak a peek at his phone and see a text from someone named Alexis. "Wyd? Come over?" it says.

Alexis. I wonder if she's the girl who showed up at his house the morning after our sexcapades. We never talked about who she was to him. It's none of my business, and if he's not going to bring her up I refuse to ask. I do wonder if he's told her about the baby though.

Why did I look at his damn phone? Because I'm a masochist apparently.

"There was an Uno card next to the sink in the bathroom. When is Jada not playing games?" he asks as he rejoins me in the kitchen.

Oh shit. I try to mask my face but I know he can see the confusion and hurt in my eyes.

"What's wrong?" he asks.

"Hmm? Oh, nothing. I was gonna have some ice cream. Do you want some?"

He wrinkles his brow. "Sure. I guess. If you have the correct flavor."

"The correct flavor? Excuse you, there are hundreds of ice cream flavors. You can't limit yourself to just one."

"Yeah, and a lot of ice cream is good but there's only one that's the best ever."

"And what would that be?"

"Butter pecan."

I blink twice. "Get out."

"Oh, hell no. I won't tolerate any butter pecan slander."

"I mean, Jesus, what are you, an eighty-five-year-old black grandma? Who the hell eats butter pecan?"

"Normal people eat butter pecan."

"Okay, fine, it's a perfectly fine flavor. But the best flavor ever? Get the fuck outta here. I think I'll wait until Little Bean has a baby of their own before I declare it the best."

His eyes narrow to slits. "It is not for grandparents."

"I beg to differ, gramps. It's okay. I'll have butter pecan for you next time you come over, I guess. You want me to get you a cane and some hearing aids too?"

He laughs and shakes his head. "Brat. Fine, what subpar flavor do you have to offer tonight?"

"Well, I'm not an ice cream nazi, so I have options. I have chocolate chip cookie dough, Ben & Jerry's Half Baked, and Neapolitan. Take your pick."

"Which one's your favorite?"

"Guess."

"Mmmm…you're definitely a Half Baked girl." He looks deep into my eyes, and there's a heat there that I refuse to acknowledge.

"I don't know if that's meant to be a compliment or not, but I'm gonna say it is because you're right. Will Half Baked please your taste buds, sir? I know it's not your precious butter pecan." Half Baked is decadent and delicious. Chocolate and vanilla ice cream with cookie dough and fudge brownies in it—what's not to like? But looking at this sinfully gorgeous man standing in front of me, I know the flavors in this ice cream would never even compare to the taste of him.

"There's a lot of things that will please my taste buds right now. Half Baked would be low on that list, but I'll take it. If the queen is willing to share."

Shit. I need a funny comeback, but I'm so busy thinking about his taste buds tasting me that I can't focus. Fuck it, just get the damn ice cream. I walk away without another word, but I hear his snicker under his breath.

When I come back with the ice cream, he's looking at his phone with a frown.

"Did you look at my phone? Is that why you got weird earlier?"

Busted.

"Umm, phone? What phone?"

Jesus.

He takes a deep breath. "I think maybe I owe you an explanation."

"Nope. You really don't. Your love life is your business."

He frowns at that but pushes on. "Sit down, Nina. This is not what you're thinking."

I have a feeling I don't want to hear any of this, but this is supposed to be about getting to know each other, right? At some point, I need to know what his home situation is so I know who he's going to have around Little Bean.

He sits on my couch and motions for me to join him. I feel like I'm walking the plank. "Alexis is the woman who came over the morning after you spent the night. We're not dating. We've never dated, but we have slept together. I don't know how she got a key to my place. Actually, I do. She probably grabbed the spare key from under my plant and made a copy before I noticed."

"Wait, you actually kept a spare key under a plant at your house? Have you never seen a scary movie before? Who does that?" I want to take him under my wing since apparently he doesn't understand that spare keys in easy to find places lead to murders.

He chuckles. "Well, I don't anymore, but I used to. I, umm...when I lived with my ex-girlfriend we used to keep a spare key under our mat because she was constantly forgetting her keys, and I guess it just stuck with me." Oh. "So, anyway. I took the key back from her and told her not to do that again. She's been trying to get me to hook up with her and make things official for a while, and I always say no. Hooking up with her was a mistake."

"Why do you say that?"

"I guess I have to give you the full story for it to make sense. Did you know I lived in Arizona for a little bit?"

"No, I didn't."

"Yeah, I was dating this girl, Monica, a few years ago, and she wanted to move to Arizona for a job opportunity doing interior design. I was crazy about her so I went with her. She knew a guy at an architecture firm there so she got me an interview, which led to me getting the job. I gave up my apartment and left with her. It was great. I was completely in love with her."

So he had an apartment before moving to Arizona? And now that he's back and single he has a single-family home. Considering he's back in Texas now, I have a feeling I am not going to like where this is going.

"She got pregnant." Oh shit. As far as I know Isaiah doesn't have any kids, so I'm already feeling heartbroken for both him and Monica at this point. "I was really happy. I mean I was only twenty-three at the time, so I was scared shitless but really excited too, ya know?"

"Of course."

"So everything was going great. We started planning the nursery and everything. My family was going to come visit for my birthday weekend and we were gonna announce the pregnancy to them then."

My heart is breaking for him. The slight shake in his voice prompts my, "You don't have to keep going if you don't want to."

"No, I want to. I'm getting to the point, I promise."

"Don't rush. I'm here."

He smiles, but it quickly fades. "The week before my family was gonna fly in, I came home early from work to surprise her. I knew she was off that day, so I wanted to bring her food and rub her feet for her. But, uh, she wasn't alone. She was with my boss—the guy she knew who gave me the job. Apparently he was spending his lunch break with her every day. And a lot of time before that."

Oh.

Hell.

Fucking.

No.

Now I know exactly where this story is going, and I just want to beat Monica's ass.

"Holy shit."

"My thoughts exactly. She didn't even try to lie about it. I mean there was no point in trying, considering they were midfuck when I walked in, but still. She said that the baby was actually his and she was leaving me for him. She said at the end of the day I was too much of a joker, and she could never take me seriously, so he was the better choice."

And now I get why Isaiah is the way he is. Why he defaults to humor and flirtation ninety percent of the time. It's easier to just lean into the character people claim you are. You can't get hurt if the version of you people see is just a caricature.

"What was his name?"

"What?"

"Your boss. What's his name?"

"Harris."

"Harris. What the fuck kind of name is Harris for a first name?"

He lets out a genuine laugh this time. "That's exactly what I said. His parents probably scheduled sex."

"And his dad probably left his socks on," I add. His eyes twinkle with laughter, and I want to get lost in them.

"So, needless to say, I called my family and told them not to come visit. But I didn't tell them why."

"They don't know?" I wondered why Sasha wouldn't have told me about his heartbreak with Monica once I told her I was pregnant. He's been carrying this alone all this time? I'm seeing Isaiah in a whole new light. I want to get to know the real him. The one that doesn't hide behind jokes and flirtation.

"Nope. The only person who knows is Lincoln. He showed up anyway, and I was a hot fucking mess and confessed everything to him. He helped me get my stuff out of the house with Monica and figure out a plan to get back to Texas. We never told anyone. I didn't want anyone to know about my biggest failure."

I reach out and take his hand in mine. "You are not a failure, Isaiah.

She's a failure. Because she messed up a really good thing. It's her loss. Let her enjoy vanilla-ass sex with Harris and raise their kid that they probably named Smith or some bullshit."

A dark look passes through his eyes, but it's gone in seconds. "Yeah, I know you're right. It was just hard to let go of." And I suspect he still hasn't. Not completely. I mean how could he? He thought he was going to be a father and that was ripped away from him in the most embarrassing way. "It doesn't excuse how I reacted when you told me you were pregnant. I was wrong that night. But as soon as you told me, my mind just went back to all that shit with Monica. Not that I thought for a minute it wasn't mine when you told me, but I just panicked." I squeeze his hand, letting him know he doesn't need to keep going. I've already forgiven him for that, and he doesn't need to explain anymore. "So you're probably wondering where Alexis comes in, right?"

"Just a little."

"When I moved back here I was a mess. I was just going through the motions—existing but not living. I felt like my heart shriveled up and died. And then I saw Alexis in a bar. She and Monica were friends. And I say that loosely. What's that word, frenemies? That's what they were. They hung out a lot but they were always competing with each other, and it wasn't friendly competition. They were both petty. Anyway, she found me at a bar, drunk as hell, and came on to me, and I guess I just wanted a chance to hurt Monica like she hurt me. So I hooked up with her. And then we hooked up a couple more times. She started getting clingy, and I was coming out of my haze, so I knew I needed to get my shit together and put her and Monica in the past. But every time I would try she would dangle information about Monica in front of me. How she and Harris were doing. How the pregnancy was coming along. When he proposed to her. Where they were living. What the gender was. When she gave birth. Monica and Harris had both blocked me on social media, so Alexis was my only connection to them, and I was desperate for anything I could get my hands on. It was stupid, I know, but she had a hold on me for a while there. She'd give me info that would piss me off, I'd get drunk to deal with it, and then sleep with her again. It was a toxic fucking circle."

"Jesus. That's emotional warfare."

"Big time."

"So, she just keeps coming by with information on Monica hoping she can get you to drown your sorrows with alcohol and then get you to sleep with her?"

"Pretty much. She stopped by my office last week trying to do it again, but I turned her down again. Monica doesn't control me like she used to and neither does Alexis."

"That's…good." I take a tiny bit of comfort in the fact that he wants to move past both Alexis and Monica, but I can't deny that it worries me that Alexis seems to know exactly how to manipulate him. Warning bells are going off in my head. The guard around my heart goes up a little higher.

"So you have nothing to worry about when it comes to Alexis. Or Monica. I'm over both of them."

"Well, I mean, we're not dating, KP, so I wasn't worried anyway. I guess I just wanted to know who you'd have around Little Bean." His jaw ticks.

"Right. Well, it damn sure won't be her. There's only one woman not related to me that I plan to have around, and she's not ready to admit there's something going on between us, so I think we're good."

He stares deep into my eyes, challenging me. Abort, abort. I shove a spoonful of ice cream into my mouth, and he follows the motion, wetting his bottom lip with his tongue as he watches. Fuck me.

He takes mercy on me and gets up to take his dish to the sink. I feel a lot closer to Isaiah after he shared his story with me. I also feel like I'm in a lot of trouble.

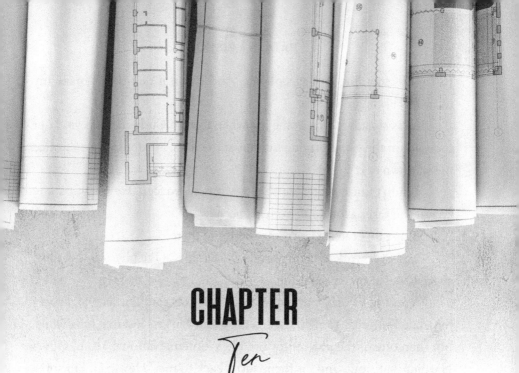

CHAPTER
Ten

Isaiah

I'M ON MY WAY TO MEET KAI FOR A DRINK, AND I'M IN THE BEST mood ever. The client I worked with today tried his best to drag my mood down, but every time I flashed back to the look in Nina's eyes when I implied I wanted to be with her, the smile was back on my face.

I can't deny how badly I want her anymore. I knew she'd have me wrapped around her finger if I spent enough time with her and really got to know her. And here we are. I've never had anyone push my buttons the way she does. It's sexy as hell.

I'm not going to push her. I know she's in a weird headspace right now, but I am going to continue to be here for her, the baby, and the kids to prove to her that I want this. I want to give us a real shot.

I feel like a huge weight has been lifted off my shoulders since telling her what went down with Monica. My own family doesn't even know that story—only Lincoln—and yet I felt comfortable telling her. She just listened to me. There was no judgment in her eyes, no pity, no contempt.

Just understanding and acceptance. And damn if that didn't make my heart feel like it grew a size.

Kai is already sitting at the bar when I get to Corbett's, his eyes laser focused on the game playing on one of the TVs. He doesn't even notice me sit down next to him.

"I didn't know you were so into women's soccer." He startles at my arrival and takes a long pull from his beer.

"Oh yeah. I catch a few games here and there."

"You ever work with any soccer players?" Kai is a physical therapist, specializing in sports medicine.

"A few, yeah." The bartender comes my way, and I order a local porter while Kai's eyes go right back to the game. He gets lost in it for a while, but then one of the players for the US Women's National Team, Olivia Harding, subs out, and his focus turns back to me. "Hey man, I'm sorry for going off on you the other day. I never apologized for it." Honestly, so much has happened since then I forgot all about it.

"No apology necessary. I needed my ass kicked. I should be thanking you for forcing me to rethink things."

He nods slowly. "So everything good with you and Nina now?"

"Yeah, we're in a good place. We started getting together every week just to talk, get to know each other. I hung out with her and the kids on Saturday and Sunday too. It was nice. They're cool kids."

He grins. "You tryna be stepdaddy too? Or step...brother? I guess."

I want to be whatever Nina will allow. Jada reminds me so much of Nevaeh. She's full of light and hope. I just want to wrap her in a bubble and protect her from every monster lurking in the dark. Logan is such a good kid. There's a heaviness clearly weighing on his shoulders. A lost look in his eyes. I know a little something about holding on to your worries with no release in sight. I want to help him get through it. "Nina's pretty much in denial that we're more than friends. So I don't know, but yeah, I plan to be there for the kids. I'm not gonna be there for Nina and the baby and not them."

"Oh, so you think you are more than friends?"

"I wanna be. She's the first woman I've felt like this about in a long time."

Kai arches his eyebrows. "And you sure it's because you actually feel that way, or is it because she's having your baby?"

"I mean, I won't lie and say her having my baby doesn't draw me in more but it's beyond just that. I've been attracted to her since the moment I met her, and I don't think I was ready to address that before, but I am now. I just need to make her see that." Nina and I met three years ago. She and Sasha had grown really close so I'd heard about her plenty of times, but it wasn't until she joined us at our Thanksgiving dinner that year that I met the mysterious bar manager. She was wearing a T-shirt that read "leg day" with a drumstick underneath it, jeans that molded perfectly to her hips, and heeled boots that made her legs look even longer. I was mesmerized by her immediately. She showed up to dinner with top-shelf bourbon for my dad, merlot for my mom, a smile that knocked me on my ass, and an undeniable wit that was unforgettable.

"Good for you, man." His attention goes back to the women's soccer game.

He turns back to me and his eyes are dark, full of regret.

"I almost had a kid once."

I don't know what I thought he was going to say, but that definitely wasn't it.

"No shit?"

"No shit." He draws in a long breath.

"When was this?"

"We were young. Only nineteen at the time. We'd been together since we were thirteen. I wanted to spend the rest of my life with her." This is the first time I'm hearing about this and that he was ever in a relationship that lasted at least six years. Since I've known Kai he's always been perpetually single. He's dated, but he's never been interested in anything serious.

"What happened?"

He pauses, and I can tell he's fighting a memory. "She wasn't ready. If

I'm honest with myself I wasn't either, but I kept telling myself I was at the time. But she had dreams and she had to make the choice that was best for herself. And I supported her."

"Shit. So when did you break up?"

"Right after. She had an opportunity to chase her dream, and I had to let her go so she could do that."

"Shit, man. I'm sorry." I put my hand on his shoulder. I know sorry isn't enough but I don't know what else to say. This is obviously still weighing heavy on him years later.

"Yeah, thanks." He takes another pull from his beer. "Anyway, that's kind of why I went off on you before. It wasn't really about you."

"I get it. I really do." I tell him about my situation with Monica. It feels only right after he shared his story with me.

"I remember that. We all thought you were a little different when you came back from Arizona, but Linc wasn't saying anything and neither were you, so we dropped it."

Lincoln was really there for me when everything went down. He helped me move back to Texas, letting me stay with him until I bought my house. I came back on a mission to prove my worth in some way. I bought a house that would be fit for a family. Even if I'd never have one, I wanted to prove I could provide for one. I started my job at A. Paterson under Alan's mentorship. But in my dating life I was barely holding it together. I lost myself in Alexis and countless other women. "Crazy, right?"

"It's crazy how one experience can shape your entire life and put you on a whole new course."

"Do you think you'll ever have kids?" I ask Kai.

"I don't know. I think the only person I ever saw a future with got away. So I don't know if any of that is in the cards for me at this point. But I do know if she ever came back to me, I'd never let her go again."

Kai is such a laid-back guy. Nothing ever gets to him. He even dresses like he's on a beach vacation ninety percent of the time. But the guy I see in front of me is a man full of regret. I don't want that for myself.

I don't want to watch LB grow up and wish I had taken the chance with their mom.

I lift my glass to Kai. "Here's to second chances." We touch mugs, and I start thinking through my next move.

I'm at my parents' house helping Dad build a new shed for Mom. He doesn't really need my help with this, but building things together has always been how we bonded. I know my dad always wanted me to take over his construction business, but I wanted to find my own way. I needed to build my reputation off of my own name and talent, not my dad's.

I look at his wrist where his Invicta watch sits. I promised myself that I'd buy a watch just like it when I prove myself in this industry. I've come a long way in my career, but I still don't think I've earned that watch.

"So how's Nina doing?"

"She's good. I'm gonna go with her to her doctor's appointment this week."

"And her brother and sister?"

"They're good. I think they're still kinda a little lost, but honestly, Nina is great. She loves those kids with her whole heart, and I think that's more than they were used to, so they'll be okay." I pause. "So you got any advice for your youngest child bringing a child of his own into the world? Besides 'don't fuck it up'?"

"Oh you're gonna fuck it up." He shrugs. I wait for him to turn around and add a "but" to that sentence, but he doesn't.

"Well damn, Dad. Thanks for the vote of confidence."

"It's just a part of the gig, son. Parenting isn't a science. You just keep throwing shit at the wall until you find what sticks."

"So my kid is spaghetti?"

He barks out a full-belly laugh. "Yep. You can take advice from all the parents you want, read all the blogs and articles, but that doesn't mean what they do is gonna be right for you. What's important is that you and Nina are on the same page, and whatever you do, you do it together."

We're getting there. We're starting to trust each other more. I want to know everything there is to know about her. "Huh, okay. Yeah, I get that."

"When we had Reggie we had no idea what we were doing. She cried all day and all night, no matter what. We thought we broke her. The only time she didn't cry was when we'd take her for long drives. She wouldn't take to breastfeeding, and we had to switch her to formula. So we accepted that as our normal. But then we had Sasha and she took to breastfeeding like a champ, and she only cried when she was hungry or had a messy diaper."

"Reggie, a crybaby. I knew that tough girl shit was an act. She's a whole punk. Everything is making sense to me now," I tease. I have all the confidence in the world that Nina is going to kill it as a mom. Me as a dad? I don't know. I just don't know if I'm what any child needs, but I'm determined to be the best. For LB. For Nina. For Logan. For Jada.

"You weren't much better. You refused to let us put you down or you'd scream bloody murder. But at that point we were four kids deep and used to baby screams, so we'd let you cry it out in your crib."

"Now see, that ain't right."

"You'll see if you have more than one." The idea of having more than one baby with Nina doesn't freak me out at all. I could picture that.

I pull out my phone and send a quick text to Nina.

Me: Good news. I've learned that babies are basically just spaghetti

She answers immediately.

Nina: I have no idea what that means but if you say that's good news I say great

Me: Glad I have your trust

Nina: I didn't say all that. So are you gonna explain this spaghetti comment or do I just let my imagination run wild?

Me: I'm curious what your imagination comes up with first

Nina: My gut reaction says that every baby is a different type of noodle and can be combined with a bunch of different sauces but everyone has their own preference?

Me: Da fuck? What does that even mean?

Nina: LOL hey you came to me on some babies are spaghetti bullshit. I can barely see straight

That sets me on edge.

Me: Wait what's wrong?

Nina: I'm just not feeling great today. LB is acting up

Me: What can I do?

Nina: Oh nothing I'm good I promise

Promise my ass. She always does this. I ask her what I can do to ease her load, and she always says nothing. Pregnancy sucks. And I know I have no right to say that when I don't have to experience it, but I hate being useless. I hate being on the outside, not able to contribute anything of value. Nina and I aren't together. I'm not there to fluff her pillows at night or rub her feet. She wouldn't call me if she had a craving in the middle of the night. I go to her doctor's appointments with her, and we've been getting closer every day, but she doesn't need me. I'm disposable. I hate that.

Does she view me the same way Monica did? Like I'm just a joke that wouldn't be able to provide for her? Fuck. This is hard.

"Hey Dad, I gotta take off. Is that okay?"

"Tell Nina I said hi." I give him a sly smile.

"You don't follow directions well." Nina sighs when she opens the door.

"Oh, was there a direction in your evasive text? I must've missed it.

I brought food for you and the kids. And I brought ginger ale for you. You're gonna eat a little and then take your ginger ale with you to bed. I'm gonna be here in case Logan or Jada need anything."

"Isaiah—"

I cut her off. "Nope. Don't wanna hear it. You're doing most of the work right now. You're carrying LB and there's nothing I can do to help carry that load, but I can carry everything else. Let me carry it. Whether you like it or not, you and I are a team, so let me do my part. Please."

Her eyes light up, and her lips tilt up in a grin. I can practically feel a piece of her wall fall down. She steps aside so that I can walk in. "Fine. But after my nap I expect you to explain this 'babies are spaghetti' shit."

I smile. "Done."

A week later, Halloween is finally here.

Usually, Halloween would consist of Lincoln and me joining Sasha, Reggie, their husbands, and their kids for trick-or-treating and then going with Lincoln to meet up with the guys for a drink after dragging Dominic kicking and screaming from his lair. The night would usually end with me going home with some random woman, or worse, Alexis.

This year, Niecy has decided she's too old to trick-or-treat with her parents, aunt, and uncles, so she'll be going with her friends. Malcolm has decided he and his friends need to tag along. I'm pretty sure he has a crush on one of Niecy's friends. He was adamant that he and his friends go along to "protect" Niecy and her friends, but he didn't seem to care about her safety until she mentioned her friend Yasmine was coming. When I was ten I had crushes on plenty of Reggie and Sasha's friends. It never worked out for me. I hope you have better luck, bud.

Lincoln and Ciara are going to join Sasha, Carter, and Nevaeh for trick-or-treating today. Meanwhile, I'll be joining the Williams family. When Jada asked me to come with them, I jumped at the chance. Ciara informed us that we'll all be going to Neon Nights tonight whether we want to or not. I was planning to go as Black Panther, but as soon as Jada told me about Nina's *Beetlejuice* theme, I changed my plan. She's so excited to be Lydia this year. I think what she's most excited about is being a part of something. Matching with her brother and sister.

She told me that Logan took her trick-or-treating every year, but he rarely wore a costume. I don't think Logan has ever really been a kid. I worry about him, but he is a great kid and I plan to take a lot of the burden off his shoulders now that I'm here. I've been spending more time with him, and I can see him opening up a little more. I can see him shrinking from the grown man he's forced himself to be back to the teenager he's meant to be. He's even expressed some interest in architecture, so we've been bonding over that. The kids are embracing me as part of the family. Now I just have to get Nina to let me all the way in.

I'm hoping showing up on her doorstep dressed in this cringy button-up and khaki pants will bring me a step closer to that goal.

"Holy shit." Nina looks me up and down as she opens the door. I hold out the creepy mask for emphasis.

"Are you really dressed as Alan from *Beetlejuice* right now?"

"Of course I am. I was originally gonna be that blue chick whose legs were separate from the rest of her, but I couldn't find my tights so here I am." She chuckles and rests her hand against my arm. Her touch burns a hole through my shirt. I don't even take a breath, because I don't want her to move.

"I'm not sure how you're making that basic-ass costume look good, but you are."

"I had to be on your level." I look her up and down. She's wearing the floral dress Barbara wears in the movie, but her version perfectly hugs to her body accentuating her hips that I'm dying to grab. She's wearing black Converse instead of ballet flats, and that makes me smile.

"Jada's really excited you're joining us. Thank you for doing this."

"I'm happy to do it, Nina." That came out more intense than I planned, but I don't backtrack. I mean it.

I'm realizing that I'd do anything for all of them.

"ZayZay!" Jada runs past Nina to get to me. She's decided ZayZay is a better name for me because Isaiah is too difficult. It's got a nice ring to it. It kind of sounds like zaddy which is what I hope Nina will be calling me soon. I nearly gag at my own joke. Let's pretend that never happened.

Jada jumps into my arms, and I squeeze her tight.

"Hey, Flash. This costume is perfection." She looks exactly like a miniature Lydia. It turned out even better than I thought. She's a goth queen, and it's hilarious.

"Thank you! Nina wouldn't let me get too heavy with the makeup but that's okay! Ready?"

"Oh yeah. Let's do it."

"Do what?" Nina asks.

"Oh, words won't do it justice. You gotta see for yourself. Let's go."

"Flash?" she follows up.

"Oh yeah, it's my nickname for her because she's fast as fuck. I'm actually not sure she's human."

"Facts. If she ever decides to drop gymnastics, track and field might be her jam." I grab her hand and she intertwines our fingers, leading me to the living room.

"Logan! ZayZay's here!" Jada calls upstairs and signals for me to hook my phone up to the speakers.

Logan makes his way downstairs in his Beetlejuice costume, and I bend over with laughter.

"Dude, you look epic." He's got the perfect pinstripe suit on, complete with green wig and makeup.

"Thanks, man. I see you're part of the family tonight, huh?"

"You good with that?"

He offers me a fist bump, and Nina smiles at the image. I can't lie, it feels damn good.

"Okay, Nina, sit down! And join in when you want."

"I don't know what's going on."

"Sit down, babe. You're in for a treat."

She cocks an eyebrow at me but sits down on the couch. Suddenly,

"Jump in the Line" starts playing through the speakers, and Nina bursts into a fit of laughter. Jada takes center stage and closes her eyes, preparing for her big moment. She breaks into character and does the entire dance from start to finish. Logan breaks into a very stupid, very Beetlejuice-worthy dance.

I hold my hand out to Nina, and she takes it without hesitation and we dance around the whole living room.

Best Halloween ever.

CHAPTER
Eleven

Nina

"**O**H FUCK, ISAIAH. RIGHT THERE," I CRY OUT. HIS HIPS SLAM INTO ME from behind. *The sound of our bodies slapping together fills the room. We're up against his bathroom sink. I look at him in the mirror, and his eyes are full of pure carnal desire.*

"You're so fucking sexy," he growls, gripping my hips tighter. I throw my ass back against him with so much force, the groan that comes from him is unnatural.

"Harder," I demand. He smirks, grabbing my hands and placing them higher on the edge of the sink. He grips my hips once again and slams into me so hard I lift off the floor. Fuck, yes.

"Do you like that, Nina?"

"Yes," I answer breathlessly. He leans forward and bites my ear. A shiver runs from the base of my neck down to the tip of my toes.

I don't think I can take much more of this and yet I never want this to end. I need more. I need this every day.

He snakes his hand around my waist and down to my core. I bite my lip in

anticipation. I want to hold off on my orgasm for a little longer, but I'm power-
less when he presses his thumb against my clit.

"Come, Nina. Now." *Oh fuck. That voice. It's like fucking velvet.*

I scream with my release.

My eyes fly open with my release. Ugh, lusty bitch.

We are officially in the second trimester. The good news is I'm no longer suffering from morning sickness. The bad news is I have a whole new
problem. I'm horny as fuck.

This is the third sex dream I've had this week about Isaiah. It's getting
out of hand. I can't take any more. In the dream the night before last there
were three of him. Three! That's far too much dick. I'm actually sore just
thinking about that dream. I'm like a cat in heat. I'm dying for a release and
the release I give myself is not enough.

I've googled it, and apparently being horny during pregnancy is normal.
No. I don't accept that. I can't go another six months like this. I will explode.

Hmm. Exploding doesn't sound bad, actually. Exploding on Isaiah's dick.

No. Jesus, take the wheel. *Lock that shit up.* This is just your hormones
talking. You do not want to have sex with Isaiah. He's just confusing you
with how sweet he's been with you and the kids lately. God, he's spent so
much time with us these last few weeks. Jada loves him, and I think Logan
respects the hell out of him. It's too much.

On a more family friendly note, Little Bean is the size of a peach. I'm
not sure why doctors compare the size of your baby to fruits. Apparently,
next week the baby will be the size of a lemon. I've seen lemons that are the
same size as a peach, so I'm not sure what I'm supposed to get from that,
but I'll take it.

"Okay, everything looks good, Mommy. How are you feeling?" Dr. Hunter
asks me. Isaiah is with me at my appointment, like he's been at every appointment. Being supportive and sweet and perfect. Prick.

"I'm feeling good. No more morning sickness. Now I'm even hungrier."

"Yeah, that's normal. Once the morning sickness starts to fade, your appetite will definitely pick up. I'd suggest carrying healthy snacks around with you."

"She's way ahead of you, doc. I don't know how healthy you'd consider packaged doughnuts and Cheez-Its though."

I glare at him. "Rat." He flashes that smile that I just want to kiss and smack at the same time at me. I mean where does he get off being so good-looking? I'm over his shit.

"What the baby wants the baby gets, right? But you do want to try to have some healthy snacks in there as well. We don't want to have to worry about high blood pressure."

"Okay, you got it."

"So do you have any questions for me?"

"Is sex safe at this stage of pregnancy?" The words are out of my fucking mouth before I can even stop and think. Isaiah immediately starts choking and coughing. And despite the fact that I just made a complete ass out of myself, I consider following that up with "and is it safe if the man in question has a giant penis?"

Dr. Hunter offers me a reassuring smile. "Absolutely. Sex is perfectly safe. You're having a healthy pregnancy with no complications. The baby is protected by the amniotic fluid as well as the uterus itself so sexual activity won't affect the baby in any way. But keep in mind that pregnancy can change your comfort level during sex and your sex drive in general." You don't fucking say.

"Right. Yep. Okay then. That answers that." The ground doesn't seem to be doing me the favor of swallowing me whole, so I push forward and ask a few more questions. Questions I didn't really have. But I didn't want my only question to be about sex so I look like a goddamn sex fiend in front of Isaiah. He does not need to know I'm fantasizing about his ass.

Isaiah and I drove separately to the appointment because he came from work and he has to go back. I was hoping we'd say our goodbyes at the door and go our separate ways but of course not. He walks me to my car and wants to chat.

Even though it's November, it's a cool day for Texas. The wind is crisp. I prefer when Isaiah's arms and broad back are on full display, but he looks damn good covered up too. He has on ripped jeans per usual, matched with a hoodie and a flannel shirt over it. I want to strip him of his layers and lick my way up his chest.

Oh shit. I think he asked me a question. I have no idea what he said.

"Sorry, what did you say?"

He cocks his eyebrow at me, and I roll my eyes. "I said at the midpoint ultrasound in a few weeks do you want to find out the gender or be surprised?"

"Oh. I wanna know. I can't handle a surprise; I need to be able to plan." I don't have a preference in what we have. Boy. Girl. It doesn't matter to me. But waiting to find out until the baby is born gives me too much anxiety. I've got enough balls in the air. I'm not gonna volunteer another.

"Do you have ideas for the nursery yet?" He reaches up to grab the back of his neck, and the T-shirt he's wearing under his hoodie lifts, revealing a brief glimpse of those washboard abs. My brain short-circuits. I'm so embarrassed by the level of my horndoggedness right now. Not embarrassed enough to stop the dirty thoughts running through my mind but still embarrassed.

"Umm, yeah. Yes. I…umm…yes."

"You okay?"

"Yes. Anyway, I have a few ideas for the nursery. Yeah. I haven't fully decided yet."

His eyebrows wrinkle as he slowly nods. "Well, we can plan together if you want. Since we don't live together, I plan to have a nursery at my house too, so we can have them coordinate." And now I'm imagining him rocking the baby to sleep, and I'm about to melt into a puddle right here. "We could do a movie theme. I know movies are your thing. We could take the best children's movies and have one of the walls painted with characters from them." And now he's being thoughtful about the nursery. I have to get out of here.

"Yep, all that sounds great. I'm gonna get going. Thanks for coming, bye!" I hop in my car and start it. I chance a glance in his direction before I pull off, and his eyes are dancing with amusement.

Fuck me.

"Oh my God, I'm dead." Ciara has been laughing hysterically for five straight minutes since I told her about today's doctor appointment. I don't find the humor in the situation. I've looked. It ain't funny.

"I'm glad you think this is funny."

"It's fucking hilarious. You just drove off midsentence. I'm dead."

"Yeah, you said and yet you're still breathing and talking." She laughs even harder at that.

"I don't even understand why you're making this harder on yourself. Just give in. Isaiah has given you more than enough clues that he's down if you are. So get down."

"And I told you I'm not doing that. It's a complication I don't need in my life."

"Good dick?"

"Dating. It's too risky. We're building a friendship, and I'm happy with that but what if we date and we don't work out? Are we gonna be able to co-parent without issues?" What if he doesn't actually want me? What if he just thinks he does because I'm having his baby? My heart can't take that kind of rejection.

"That's a cop-out and you know it."

"It's a valid concern!"

"Yeah, it is, normally. But this is different. If you and Isaiah date and you don't work out, it might be awkward, yes, but it would have no effect on your co-parenting relationship."

"How can you guarantee that?"

"Because neither of you would ever bail on your kid, and we would never let you. You're best friends with his sister and his brother's wife. There's literally no escaping each other anymore. We're basically one big happy family whether you guys are together or not. You'll both be at every family event. The whole family will be at all of your kids' events no matter what. It's not possible for you guys to fall apart at this point. We're all too up in each other's business for that. It's your own fault, really. I mean, what is this, *Friends*? You guys couldn't go outside the friend group for a hookup?"

She's right. Isaiah and I are going to be forever connected and not just because of Little Bean. But that makes it even worse. He's wormed his way into my heart so fast it's terrifying. I still have a relatively strong safeguard around my heart right now, but I feel it breaking down with every touch, every conversation, every look. If I let him all the way in, he could destroy me. And then I'd be forced to keep him close for the rest of my life as punishment. I'd have a front row seat to him moving on with someone new. Getting married. Having more kids with her. I'd be in his life from a not far enough away distance. Present but no longer privy to those special smiles he only gives me or the parts of his past no one else knows about.

"Look, I said what I said. Isaiah and I are not going to happen."

She rolls her eyes. "Mhmmm, okay. Well I hope you and your vibrator have a healthy relationship over these next few months. Sounds like you're gonna need it."

"Carlos and I are just fine, thank you." I'm lying. Carlos doesn't do shit for me now that I've had Isaiah, but she doesn't need to know that.

"You named your vibrator Carlos?"

"Yes."

"Why?"

"Like Carlos Santana. Because he knows exactly how to play my strings." Her eyebrows shoot up to her hairline, and she nods in respect. This is why I keep her around.

The kids and I are eating dinner. Jada is excitedly filling me in on gymnastics practice. I love watching the light in her eyes when she talks about it. She started gymnastics when she was four years old and loved it from the start. Whenever I'd pick her and Logan up she'd tell me all about the new moves she was learning, though she mispronounced half of them.

Jada's love of gymnastics was the source of one of the biggest fights I ever had with my parents. One of the last too.

Logan called me one day, telling me that Jada was sobbing, and he couldn't help her this time. Logan always made it a point to downplay how bad things were with our parents so as not to worry me. Jada just didn't comprehend that she was being neglected in the first place. I knew they were constantly going on vacations and leaving them alone because I was the one taking care of them while they were gone. But I had no idea they were neglecting them while they were home too. He couldn't hide this, though, because Jada was inconsolable. Our parents told Jada that she would probably have to quit gymnastics as they couldn't fit it into their schedule.

Fit it into their schedule. What even is that?

Not because they couldn't afford it. Not because they had no means of transportation to get her to practice and tournaments. But because they simply couldn't make the time. Traveling the world and being free was more important. I lost it.

I drove right over to my parents' and demanded answers. They tried to justify their poor parenting by explaining that Jada's gymnastics schedule was too demanding for a girl her age. Bullshit. She enjoyed every minute of it, and it wasn't too much by any means. They just didn't want to do it.

Voices were raised. Feelings were hurt. I vowed in that moment to do better by Jada and Logan. I took over the payments for Jada's gymnastics and took her to every single practice when she didn't catch a ride with her friend's mom. Logan's robotics club is less involved since he just has to stay after at school to attend, but I took over paying for any sort of dues he may have owed for it so our parents couldn't hold it over him. I also made sure that Jada and I attended his tournaments.

Our parents were gone two months later.

I carry so much guilt with me. I should've stepped in sooner. I should've realized how bad it had gotten. I failed them.

I won't do that again. Never.

Logan is now practicing math problems with Jada while my phone is burning a hole in my pocket. I've been trying to resist checking it, but my willpower is draining by the minute. I cave a minute later.

Isaiah: Hey do you have enough water? I can bring you some if you need it

Umm what?

Me: ??

Isaiah: You just seemed a little thirsty earlier so I wanted to make sure you were properly hydrated.

Isaiah: Ya know, for the baby

Oh, this little shit.

Me: My thirst has been quenched, thank you.

Isaiah: Oh yeah? With your fingers or a toy?

Me: With Carlos

Isaiah: Who in the fuck is Carlos?

Not so cocky now, huh? I leave him on read and go back to my dinner. Sometimes being petty is better than sex.

Sometimes.

After dinner, I'm washing my face in the bathroom when I decide to check my texts. My phone has blown up.

Isaiah: ??

Isaiah: Hello??

Isaiah: This is extremely petty of you

Isaiah: I asked Linc and he doesn't know of any Carlos

Isaiah: He said Ciara just laughed when he asked her

Isaiah: *inserts gif of little boy tapping his fingers waiting*

I don't even think I'm in charge of my texts anymore. I'm thinking solely with the queen downstairs right now.

Me: He's here right now. Wanna meet him?

Isaiah: Nina, I'm warning you. If you send me a picture of another guy's dick I'm blocking you

I grab my vibrator out of my top drawer and snap a picture.

Me: Meet Carlos

Me: *inserts picture of Carlos*

Isaiah: *three crying laughing emoji* Jesus! You got me

Isaiah: Do I even wanna know why you call it that?

Me: That's for me to know and you to never find out

Isaiah: So is Carlos treating you right?

Me: He gets the job done

Isaiah: I'd be willing to help him do a better job. This is one time I'm down for a threesome with a guy

Me: LOL you're annoying

Isaiah: Hey I'm just picking up what you were putting down at the doctor's earlier.

Isaiah: I'm just trying to be a supportive partner

Me: Mhm I'm feeling very supported right now

Isaiah: Good

Isaiah: Wait, because of me? Or are you and Carlos having an intimate moment right now?

Me: LOL good night KP

Isaiah: Good night Nina

Good Lord, I need a cold shower. And Carlos is in for a long night because holy shit. I can't calm down after that.

I step into the kids' room to say good night to them. Jada is snug under the covers waiting for me and Logan is of course reading. I start on Jada's side of the room.

When I get to Logan's side of the room, I take a double take at the book he's reading.

"*The Architecture of Happiness*? What's that about?"

"Oh, it's a book about architecture. It's really cool. It talks about different styles of architecture and also the psychology behind architecture and how our identities connect to the environments we're in."

"Oh. That's really cool. Where'd you get that one?"

"Isaiah gave it to me."

"He did?"

"Yeah, you know I'm into engineering. And we've been hanging out a lot, and I was asking him about his work and he told me about the engineering behind it, and it got me interested. So he gave me this and a couple other books." The slightly higher pitch in his tone tells me how excited he is to have this bond with Isaiah, even if his eyes say it's no big deal. I can see my little brother poking his head out of the sand. Bringing the inquisitive boy full of innocence back to me. That alone makes me want to run to Isaiah and wrap my arms around him to thank him.

"Huh. Well, cool. That was nice of him."

"He's pretty cool."

"He sure is." I say good night and step into the hallway.

The dam has broken. I pull out my phone to text Ciara before I can change my mind.

Me: What are you doing?

Ciara: Nothing why what's up?

Me: Any chance you could come over here? The kids are going to bed I just need someone to be here with them for a little bit

Ciara: Ha! Sasha owes me ten bucks. On my way!

I'm not even going to address the fact that my two best friends are apparently betting on my sex life. Bet away, ladies. Mama needs some SOD.

Twenty minutes later I'm knocking on Isaiah's door. He looks surprised to see me, but his comment suggests he's not.

"Carlos couldn't get the job done tonight?"

"Shut up." I grab him and pull him in for a searing kiss. He immediately pulls me inside and puts his hands under my ass. My body knows exactly what to do. I wrap my legs around his waist and he backs me up against the door, never breaking our kiss.

When he finally pulls away, he runs his thumb across my lips. His are wet and swollen from our kisses. I'm sure mine look the same.

"I could get used to this."

"Get used to what?"

"You dropping by unannounced to have your way with me."

"Maybe I'll start calling you BK instead of KP."

"BK?"

"Burger King."

"I honestly don't know which is worse." He kisses me again, his tongue sliding inside the moment my lips part.

"I can't wait anymore. I need you."

"I got what you need." He carries me over to the couch and falls gently on top of me. He lifts my shirt with urgency, and I lift my arms to help him get it over my head.

His eyes widen when he realizes I didn't even bother wearing a bra over here. He wastes no time capturing my nipple in his mouth and sucking hard. The stimulation is out of this world; I could come just like this.

He releases my nipple with a pop and moves on to the other one. I reach down and stroke him through his sweatpants which makes him growl and bite down on my nipple.

"Oh fuck," I cry out. He rips his shirt over his head and kisses down my body with so much heat, but when he gets to my belly he presses gentle kisses against it that make me want to cry. He hooks his fingers in the band of my panties and pulls them down with my pants, leaving me completely exposed.

"You're gorgeous," he observes, but when I look up he's not looking at my body. He's looking me in the eyes. I bring my hand to his cheek, reveling in the sincerity of his words and the emotion in his eyes for just a moment before need takes back over. I wrap my fingers in his waistband and pull him down on top of me. No more gentle touching. I want him to devour me. He kisses me passionately, and as his tongue enters my lips, his fingers enter my center. I moan right into his mouth. He curls his fingers inside me until they're reaching the exact spot I need him most. I'm shamelessly riding his hand.

"That's it, Nina. Take what you need." Waves of pleasure wash over me. I'm so wound up; I don't want this moment to end but I have no control over it. He gives me no control. He adds a third finger, spreading me wide. He flicks the bundle of nerves, sending me over the edge. My orgasm hits me hard, and I cry out my release. He keeps his fingers inside while I ride out my orgasm, then he slowly pulls them out and I miss him immediately.

That is until he puts his fingers in his mouth and proceeds to suck them dry. Round two, here we come. I pull him in for another kiss, tasting myself on his tongue. He groans in my mouth and pulls his pants and briefs down, releasing that glorious SOD into the wild.

He lines himself up at my entrance but pauses.

I lean up on my elbows. "What's wrong?"

His gaze is on my entrance. Mine is on the precum glistening on the tip of his cock. His voice is strangled with need when he speaks. "I'm sorry—I shouldn't assume. Do you want me to get a condom?"

I let out a half scoff, half laugh before it dissolves into complete laughter. "I'm sorry, are we worried I'm going to get even more pregnant?"

He laughs. "I just wanna make sure you trust me. I'm clean."

I grab his face and look directly into his eyes. "Isaiah, I trust you. Now, fuck me." He bites his bottom lip and thrusts into my core until he's fully seated.

"Shit, you feel even better than I remember. Are you good?"

ery touch, every bite, every moan, every whimper. I've given myself over
to him completely.

He picks up his pace so I match him thrust for thrust. I pull him down
for another kiss where I suck his bottom lip into my mouth and bite down
so hard I think I might draw blood. I feel so full, it's not long before another
orgasm hits.

He lets out a guttural growl and flips me over gently on my stomach. I
arch my back, and he re-enters me from behind. Our moans and the sound
of his balls slapping against my ass fill the room. Images from my dream the
other night cloud my vision. If only we were in his bathroom. I want to watch
the carnal desire in his eyes while he spreads me. I look over my shoulder
to find his eyes rolling in the back of his head.

"Harder," I demand. His eyes fly open then immediately become
hooded with lust again. He smirks just before I feel the palm of his hand
against my ass. Oh fuck. He smacks it again, the sting blurring the line between pain and pleasure.

He bends over to whisper in my ear. "You want it harder, Nina?"

"Yes," I moan.

He tightens his grip on my hips. "I'm not gonna stop until you come
again."

"I...I can't." I don't think I have any more to give. He's wrung me dry.

"You will." He bends me forward over the armrest of the couch and lifts
my leg higher up, causing him to go deeper than I ever thought possible. He
wraps my curly hair around his fist and pulls, the pressure forcing my eyes
shut and a desperate whimper to escape my lips.

"Deep enough, baby?" he asks.

"Oh my God, yes."

110

He's ruined me. I'll never look at another man the same. He owns my pleasure. This wasn't supposed to happen. I needed a release that I knew he could give me, but I wasn't expecting this. This ache.

I can feel my orgasm building, but I don't want to let it go. I may never recover.

"Give it to me, Nina," he orders almost as if reading my mind. I explode with stars in my eyes.

He follows me over the edge, crying out my name with his release. He presses sweet kisses against my back before scooping me into his arms.

"What are you doing?"

"Taking you to my bed. We're just getting started, baby. But first you're gonna rest." He kisses me sweetly and carries me to his bedroom. You'd never know that the man that just ravaged me and brought me to orgasm three times in a row is the same man who's gently placing me in bed, wiping me down with a warm washcloth, and stroking my arm sweetly while I drift off to sleep.

What was that about me being in trouble? Oh yeah, I'm past that now. I'm completely fucked. Pun intended.

CHAPTER
Twelve

Isaiah

I'M EXHAUSTED, BUT IN THE BEST WAY POSSIBLE. NINA AND I SPENT hours exploring each other. She didn't want to stay too late because Ciara was at her house looking after the kids and she didn't want them to know she was gone. I couldn't get to sleep after she left. I was too busy replaying our conversation.

"So I feel like a dumbass asking this but I have to know."

"Uh oh, I don't know if I like where this is going."

"Did you come to me tonight because the hormones are making you horny and I was the most convenient? Or did you come to me because you wanted me?"

She smirks. "A little column A, a little column B."

I stop stroking her arm and my jaw clenches slightly, but I know she notices it.

She releases a deep sigh. "I wanted you, Isaiah. I've been trying to deny the fact that I want you for a long time. You confuse me. You scare me. And we're diving into parenthood together and I'm worried that you only want me because I'm the mother of your child, not because you actually want me. And that gives me pause. But regardless of all my fears and insecurities, I still want you. And I don't know exactly what to do with that yet, so you have to be patient with me, okay?"

"I can do that. And Nina?"

"Yeah?"

"I want you because you're you."

"Prove it."

I'll prove it alright. I want to give her all the patience she asked for and I will. I'll take it as slow as she needs, but in my mind, she's mine. There's no way we can share what we shared last night and she not be mine and me hers.

Last night was incredible. I already knew sex with Nina was amazing but last night was next level. Sliding inside her with no barriers between us was like a religious experience. It took all of my focus to not spill my release too soon. She felt incredible inside and out. I've noticed the small changes in her body from the pregnancy, the fuller breasts, the softer curves, but seeing them up close and personal was earth-shattering. When I saw how her belly had a small bump to it, I lost it. She's carrying my baby in there. It's the most beautiful thing I've ever seen. She's right about my feelings for her being intensified because of her being pregnant but that's only because it's shown me what an incredible person she is. She's the strongest woman I know. She's raising her brother and sister, and I know she thinks she's doing them more harm than good, but she's the best thing to ever happen to them. They admire the hell out of her. She's a smartass and she keeps you on your toes, but she's also got this huge nurturing heart. She's handling this pregnancy like a champ. You'd never know she's panicking on the inside. It's impossible not to fall for her.

My phone rings and my good mood threatens to dissipate when I see it's not Nina calling me but Alexis. What could she possibly want? I consider ignoring the call, but I know Alexis and she'll just keep calling. It's better to answer and try to get her to see that I'm serious when I say we've been done for a long time.

"Hello?"

"Hey there. Are you at work?"

"Do you need something, Alexis?"

"I'm at the coffee shop around the corner from your office. Can you come meet me?"

I sigh. "Alexis..."

"Please? I just need to talk to you." Maybe it's better to have this conversation in person. She can see the look in my eye when I let her down, and we'll be in public so what's the worst that could happen?

"I'll be there in five minutes."

"Thank you!"

Five minutes later, I walk in the coffee shop and there she is. It's eight a.m. but she's dressed like she's going to a party or a nightclub when she leaves here. She's got on a skin-tight black skirt with a deep V-neck pink bodysuit tucked into it. Several of the men in the shop, including some I work with, are staring at her with their jaws on the ground, but I feel nothing. I just want to get this over with.

"Hey, thanks for coming."

"What's up, Alexis?"

"I got you a coffee. Black with two sugars, right?" No. I drink my coffee with cream and no sugar.

"I just feel like we haven't had time to catch up in a while and I miss you. I wanted to check in." Miss me? She doesn't miss me. We never spent any time together. She'd come over and we'd fuck after she plied me with liquor and information about my ex. I honestly don't think we've ever spent any amount of time together sober. And our last hookup was months before I slept with Nina.

"Alexis, look—"

She cuts me off. "You know I was talking to Monica a week ago and she and Harris aren't—" This time I cut her off. Is she kidding me? What does she think is going to happen? I'm gonna call out of work and drag her home with me? Enough is enough. My blood is boiling.

"I'm gonna stop you right there. I don't care what Monica and Harris

114

are or are not doing. I don't wanna hear about their lives. I hope they're happy and I genuinely wish them the best, but I don't care. You can't keep throwing me information about her to get me to talk to you."

"Okay, okay. You're right. Sorry. It's just a habit to bring them up, and I figured you'd want updates. But you're right, we don't need to talk about them. We can just focus on us."

"Us?"

"Yeah, we can just focus on our future." Her voice is shaky. Panicky.

"Alexis, there's no future for us. We're not together."

"Well, we're not now, but we could be."

"No. We can't. Look, I'm sorry if I led you on. We had fun when we hooked up, but I don't want to keep doing that."

"Okay, we can do more than hook up. We can…"

"I'm not interested in any kind of relationship with you." She looks like I've slapped her, and I feel like a complete dick, but if I'm not blunt with her she won't get it. I want there to be no mistaking where we stand when I walk out of this shop.

"I'm sorry. I really am. But you deserve someone who's going to appreciate you and want to give you his everything, and that's just not me. I want to cut all ties."

"That's bullshit."

"Excuse me?"

"That's bullshit. There's a pull between us. I know it and you know it."

"Alexis…"

"No, you're fighting it. Why? Give me a reason." I mean, there are a million but I'll settle for one.

"I'm seeing someone." She gives me an incredulous look like it's impossible to fathom that I'd be with anyone besides her.

"Who? That girl who was at your house when I stopped by?"

You mean when you stopped by uninvited and unannounced and used a key I didn't give you permission to have to walk in like you owned the place?

I laugh to myself when I realize that Nina has showed up to my house uninvited and unannounced twice now. That's different though. I may not have explicitly invited her but I've always wanted her there. Underneath all that manipulation and cattiness, I'm sure Alexis is a good woman. She's just not the woman for me.

"Yeah, her. I'm seeing her and we're happy." At least I'm happy with her. She's confused by me but that's none of Alexis's business.

"Oh, please…"

"And she's pregnant."

Her eyes widen. "What?"

"She's pregnant. We're having a baby together. And she and the baby are all I want to focus on. I want to leave Monica and everything connected to Monica"—I give her a pointed look—"in the past."

She's silent, and hurt flashes across her face for a moment before she narrows her eyes. "Hmmm, I see. Well, good for you both then."

"Thank you." She looks me up and down slowly then gets up and walks out without another word.

I really hope she got the message, but something tells me this might be the calm before the storm.

Nina and I have developed a routine with the kids. I come over every other day after school and work and hang out with them. Jada shows me her gymnastics moves and uses me as her personal jungle gym. Logan and I discuss whatever book he's currently reading, or I answer questions he has about architecture. After dinner, we all play at least one game together. Candy Land is usually involved. And then I go home at some point between sending the kids to bed and them waking up in the morning because Nina's not ready for the kids to see me spending the night. That's the part about our routine that I hate.

Nina and I continue with our Friday night hangouts which I call date nights, but she elbows me in the chest every time I say that. Baby steps.

Nina cringes every time Logan or Jada go to their room or argue over space. She refuses to discuss ideas for the nursery. I know she hates the fact that she can't give Logan and Jada separate rooms like she planned. It's eating her up that she promised them that one thing and can't deliver. She's even talked about not doing a nursery at all and just having the baby share the master bedroom with her. I don't want that for her. Everyone needs their own space.

The kids deserve their own rooms and so does LB. And Nina deserves peace of mind. I vow to give that to all of them.

"ZayZay, when are you gonna move in with us?" Jada has asked this question a couple of times—never in front of Nina—and I've evaded every time, but I wish I had a better answer.

I'd love to move in with them. I promised myself I'd never give up my home, my career, and my life for a woman ever again, but I'd give up everything for Nina and the kids in a heartbeat. But that would definitely be skipping a lot of baby steps. Nina is in no way ready for that.

"I told you, Flash, I'm just not sure if that's gonna happen. Your sister and I are still figuring things out. It's complicated."

She frowns. "It's just that…she's happy when you're here. I don't want her to be sad anymore." My mouth falls open at that, and I'm at a loss for words. She runs outside to continue her practice like she didn't just shake me to my core.

Logan pats me on the back. "She's right. Nina's a lot happier when you're around."

I have no idea what to say to that. It makes me happy but makes me sad for Nina and for the kids.

"It's not like she's mopey or anything. She's always laughing and joking with us even when I can tell she doesn't really feel like laughing or joking, but when you're around she lets loose. She doesn't worry so much. She's so worried that she's not doing right by us. She's trying to fix what our parents broke, but there's no fixing that."

Damn, this kid is wise beyond his years. He's just like Nina. Carrying the weight of the world on his shoulders with a smile on his face. "I'm sorry."

"It's not your fault. It's not hers either. I don't know if our parents loved us. I really don't. We were afterthoughts. They wanted to travel the world.

They wanted to ride off into the sunset together, and we were the obstacle in the way of their happiness. That's hard to live with.

"But with Nina it's not like that. She loves us completely. She'd do anything for us and there's not a day where we doubt that. We'll never be able to thank her enough for what she's done for us. I just wish she'd see that and not be so hard on herself." He looks at me then like he just remembered I was there. "With you here, it's like she remembers that she's not just a guardian and protector. She has someone to protect her for once. Don't ever stop being that for her." This is the first time he's brought up his feelings toward his parents to me. He's mentioned his therapy sessions a couple of times and that he's been sorting out how he feels about them being gone, but he's never gone into details with me. It's obvious that their parents didn't do right by them, but it breaks my heart that he doesn't even believe they loved him at all.

"I promise I won't."

And I mean that promise with every fiber of my being.

It's Sunday night, and I'm sitting at home when I should be between my girl's legs. I didn't even get to taste her before I left because Logan was up at the kitchen table working on a project so Nina felt it was best I head out.

I disagree.

Wholeheartedly.

My fingers itch to touch her. She's like a drug, and I need her like I need my next breath. I get a text alert, and I'm thankful it's her.

Nina: How's your night going?

Tease.

Me: My balls are a little blue but I guess it could be worse

Nina: LOL poor baby

Nina: Can I help in some way?

Ah, good to know I'm not the only one feeling needy tonight.

Me: Are you missing me right now?

Nina: Maybe just a little

Me: Maybe we can help each other then

Nina: What'd you have in mind?

I have a lot of things in mind, Nina. My dick is impossibly hard thinking about all of them.

Me: Are you alone?

Nina: I'm in my room

Nina: Jada's asleep and Logan's still at the kitchen table

Perfect. I take my length out of my pants and into my hands, slowly stroking myself while I think about my next move.

Me: Good. Lie on your bed

Nina: So bossy

Me: I'd spank you if I were there right now. Get on that bed

A photo comes in of Nina sitting up against her pillows. Her tank top is pushed down to right above her nipples, and her full lips are caught between her perfect teeth.

Nina: Now what?

Fuck. This isn't enough. I need more of her. I push the button on my phone to video chat her.

"Did you like the picture I sent you?" she whispers.

"I think you can see how much I liked it." I pan the phone down so she can see what she does to me. She licks her lips at the sight. Fuck, this woman.

"You started without me."

"Let's get you caught up, baby. Take off your shirt. Slowly."

She props her phone up on a phone stand, making a show of slowly exposing the small swell of her stomach and the hardened peaks of her nipples bit by bit. I can make out the small dimple on the side of her hip but nothing past that.

"Now what?"

"Move the phone lower. I need to see all of you."

She grabs the phone and lies down completely, holding the phone up so I can see every curve of her magnificent body. She's a goddess.

"I need to see all of you too." She waves her finger at the phone. She's so cute. I know she's trying not to be too loud since Logan's still awake but I have other plans for her.

I sit back in my bed, panning the phone down for her to see.

"Now take that hand and snake it down your body. Pretend it's me."

"Oh fuck, Isaiah." Her phone goes back into its stand before her hands glide down her slender neck to her supple breasts, cupping them. Her back arches slightly as her fingertips swirl around her nipples, pinching and pulling.

"That's it, baby. It's my body you're playing with. I'm the one teasing you this way. Put your finger in your mouth and suck until I say stop."

A small moan escapes her lips as she brings her right thumb up to her mouth and sucks it with all her might, her other hand still massaging the soft swell. Her breathing becomes labored while my dick becomes damn near painful with need. I grip my cock hard and stroke from base to tip, my eyes never leaving hers.

"Stop," I command. She releases her thumb with a pop. "Good girl. Now swirl that thumb around that nipple again." She hisses as her thumb makes contact with the pebbled area. "Does that feel good?"

She nods, biting that sinful lip again.

"I can't hear you, Nina."

"Mmm, yes."

"Good. Imagine that's my tongue circling you. Tasting you. Driving you crazy."

Her moan is slightly louder this time. "Isaiah, please."

"Please what, baby?"

"I need..." she cuts herself off.

"What do you need? Tell me."

"I need to come. Please."

You and me both.

"Do as I say and I'll let you come, okay?"

"Oh fuck," she whimpers.

"I didn't hear an okay."

"Okay. I'm ready. Make me come, KP."

Part of me is tempted to hop in my car and demand we finish this in person, but at this point I'm so hard I can barely move. The grip on my cock gets even tighter.

"Trail your hand down to where you need me. Pull those panties to the side so I can see that pretty pussy."

Her head flies back against her pillow, but she wastes no time guiding her hand down to her sweet spot. She slides her pink lace panties down her legs revealing the shine of her wetness calling to me. Fuck, I want to taste her.

"See what you do to me, KP?"

"I'm about to do way more than that. Part your lips for me and circle your clit. Don't stop." She uses two fingers to part herself and then she circles that bundle of nerves slowly at first then faster until she's practically panting.

She's close. I can see it in her hooded eyes. Her whimpers are becoming louder, her chest rising and falling rapidly.

"You know what you need, Nina?"

"What?" She can barely get the word out.

"Carlos."

Her eyes fly open at that, and she pins me with a stare so full of desire I almost blow my load right then and there. She takes a hand and swings it over to her nightstand, rummaging around until she finds our third for the night.

Carlos is a discreet toy. Not nearly as big as me, but I know she's going to need the extra stimulation to get her there when I can't be there. She places the toy at her entrance, waiting for my permission to give her relief.

"Do it, baby." The buzz fills the line, and I see the tremble in her hands as she fights for her release. "Harder, Nina. That's me driving into you. Filling you. You need to feel me completely. Fuck yourself like I would."

I'm mesmerized watching her wetness spill onto the sheet beneath her. My balls start to ache and I know my own release isn't far. I stare at the haven between her legs, imagining lining myself up and thrusting home. Nina's moans and cries spur me on.

"Oh shit, I'm coming." Nina cries out as she does. I watch her pussy pulsate as she pulls the toy out, covered in her juices. The thought of her clenching around me brings on my release, and I let the ribbons coat my stomach. I look up, and Nina looks completely sated. "Jesus. I wasn't expecting that."

"I told you I can always make you come. Even with just my words."

"Honestly, I have no comeback for that. You got me." She chuckles and shivers at the same time.

Damn right I do.

CHAPTER
Thirteen

Nina

ALWAYS THOUGHT I WANTED TO OWN A RESTAURANT ONE DAY. WHEN I was a kid, I would bake stuff in my Easy-Bake oven and make my parents taste test them. Sometimes they'd indulge me, sometimes they wouldn't. When I was in elementary school, I'd have friends over and play restaurant, which meant I would "seat" them in different places in my living room and take their orders. The menu would be limited to sandwiches, Hot Pockets, or some other easy dish, but I'd serve it to them and then ask how their dining experience was. In high school, I got a part-time job at a restaurant close to the house and studied my manager's every move. How he greeted the customers, how he treated his employees, how he created the schedule, all of it.

When it was time for college, I went to the University of Houston to study hospitality management. I wanted to get a part-time job at a restaurant for more experience, but my roommate convinced me to come work with her at a local bar. I started as a bar-back because you're not supposed to serve alcohol if you're under twenty-one, but I stepped up one night when both of the bartenders got severe food poisoning and went home. That was all it took. I stayed on as bar-back until I was of age, but I was paid the difference under the table. I fell in love with the bar scene. It's a completely different vibe than a restaurant. People go out to eat in a restaurant to celebrate, to bond, to be amongst family and friends. People go to bars for the same reasons, but there's a layer of freedom at a bar. People come there to lose themselves. To release the facade they put out into the world every other hour of the day. I love it. As a bartender, I've played the part of a therapist, a mediator, and a matchmaker. I've been everything from a mother hen to an enforcer. I knew then that I wanted this. I wanted to cultivate this environment for people to lose themselves in.

When I was in college I never came home for Thanksgiving. Even though it was only two hours away, my parents basically told me it'd be a wasted trip because they'd eat early and then watch TV for the rest of the day. So I'd stay at school and work.

Imagine my surprise and disgust when Logan informed me that they'd eat dinner early and then they'd ship him and Jada to a friend's house while they'd run out for Black Friday shopping or take off for a weekend trip.

What the fuck was wrong with them? What happened to the mom who would make her famous sweet potato pie every year for Thanksgiving and the dad who would play flag football with me? What happened to the parents who would come to my volleyball games and cheer me on? The parents who would help me with my homework? The parents who would give me driving lessons? They weren't perfect. I kept a calendar in our kitchen that listed all of my events, and if I'm honest, I think that's why they remembered to attend. I never saw it as them being neglectful, just forgetful. They didn't spend a lot of time with me if it didn't have to do with school or my after-school activities. I think they didn't know how to bond with me outside of that stuff. But I still knew that despite all their flaws, they loved me.

I was shocked when they told me Mom was pregnant my junior year of high school. I would've thought that their only child going to college and moving out would be a big weight off their shoulders, but Mom seemed so happy that the house wouldn't be empty after I left. I loved my brother the moment they brought him home from the hospital. He was unbelievably chunky, and I was obsessed with pinching his little arm rolls. Mom and Dad fawned over him all the time and it was nice to see. Mom started having weekly brunches with her other mom friends, and while she couldn't wait to share with them the latest cute thing baby Logan did, they couldn't wait to share their latest travel adventures with her. Their kids were grown and moving on which gave them the freedom to spread their own wings and fly wherever they wanted, whenever they wanted. Suddenly, her homely mom life wasn't so glamorous.

They started traveling a lot more. It started with the four of us taking weekend trips together. It was nice. It was normal. The summer before I left for college we went to Napa for a week. I spent the majority of the trip babysitting Logan so that they could go to different wine tastings. I got it. We were in wine country and I couldn't participate and I had fun with Logan, but I didn't understand why that was the location they chose to take a minor and an infant.

They traveled even more after I left for school, and I just assumed they took Logan along. It wasn't until years later that I learned they were dumping him with a babysitter and taking off. They lied to me about it. Like they knew I'd be disappointed in them.

I was the one who found my mom sobbing in the bathroom after she'd discovered she was pregnant with Jada. I stopped by to visit while Logan was at school and Dad was at the grocery store. When I walked in she was hugging the toilet, sobbing uncontrollably, and it was then I saw the positive pregnancy test on the sink counter. She just kept screaming about how unfair it was. That at this rate she and Dad would never get to enjoy their retirement. I stopped myself from reminding her that they actively tried to have Logan. I knew Jada wasn't planned, but she was a gift. A gift they didn't deserve. They didn't deserve either one of them.

I place my hand on top of my stomach. I was terrified when I found out about Little Bean, and to be honest, I still am. But I know I would do absolutely anything to protect him or her. I would do anything just to see Little Bean happy, and I haven't even seen their face. I don't even know if the baby is a boy or a girl yet and I'm already head over heels in love. I will never understand my parents. I don't understand how they could decide to be parents and then completely half-ass the job.

The smoke alarm going off tears me away from my thoughts. "Fuck!" I was so lost in my thoughts I forgot I had a damn pie in the oven.

This year, the kids and I will be spending Thanksgiving with the Cole family. I've spent Thanksgiving with them before, but that was as Sasha's friend. Now the waters are muddy as hell. Isaiah and I are…what exactly? Having a baby together? Yes. Having the best sex of my entire life? Hell, yes. Dating? I guess? This feels so childish wondering if we're together or not, but I'm genuinely confused. We haven't had that conversation, and I think we need to lay everything out in the open.

"Are you okay, Nina?" I bend down so I'm on Jada's level.

"Yeah, Mini. I got distracted and I burned the pie."

"Oh. Were we gonna take a pie to Nevaeh's grandparents' house?"

"Yeah. I guess I can try to make another one." Logan comes into the kitchen and grabs a soda.

"Is that Mom's sweet potato pie?"

"It was supposed to be, but now it's more like a flambé. That's burnt, right?"

He shudders. "I have no idea what that is."

"It sounds like something that'd be burnt, so let's go with it."

"You know Mom stopped making those pies years ago."

The shock takes over my entire face. "She did?"

"Yeah, she started just buying those Patty Labelle pies and calling it a day."

Jesus, Mom. The kids weren't even worth your famous homemade sweet potato pie once a year?

I look at the pie and back at the kids and my heart breaks for them. They are so amazing. I wish Mom and Dad had given these wonderful kids they produced the time of day. But they have me, and I will never leave them alone again.

"You know what, screw the pie. I think it's time we created our own traditions."

"Really?" Jada's eyes are as wide as saucers.

"Absolutely. What should we make to take to the Cole house today?"

"How about cookies? We could decorate cookies to take over." Logan shrugs at his own comment and I smile, so proud to see the real Logan shining through.

"Ooh, and we could make them into turkey shapes!" Jada jumps up and down with excitement.

"Hell, yeah, let's do it!" We get to work on our new tradition, and it feels like we're going to be okay.

The cookies took longer than expected, so we're the last to arrive at Isaiah's parents' house. As soon as we get there, Nevaeh drags Jada off to play while Niecy and Malcolm beckon Logan over to them. I notice Logan seems a little fidgety around Niecy. That's adorable as hell. I'm gonna have to tease him about that later.

"Oh my God, you look so cute!" Sasha exclaims. She walks up and gives me a huge hug. Ciara is right behind her.

I look down at my outfit. I have on a "Pour Some Gravy on Me" T-shirt with a pair of nice jeans and ankle booties. It's cute but it's not cute enough for all the fuss Sasha's making.

"Umm, I have on a T-shirt and jeans. Why are you freaking out?"

"Because you have a slight baby bump! I'm so excited."

Ciara steps closer to me. "Aww, you do. The little bean is finally making an appearance. I've been waiting for that thing to pop."

"Yeah, well, so far I haven't changed my wardrobe at all. I'm not ready to make the switch over to maternity clothes."

"You're gonna love those stretchy pants, trust me," Sasha adds.

I feel a hand on the small of my back, and I melt into it. I know it's him without even looking. No one has the effect on my body that he does.

I turn to face him, and the heat in his eyes almost knocks me over. We're standing so close our lips are only inches apart. His breath grazes my ear when he speaks. "Hey, beautiful."

"Hey, KP."

"Happy Thanksgiving. I heard from a certain lightning-fast birdie that you brought turkeys with you, so now I have to know if you've staged some sort of Thanksgiving hunt for us. I gotta say I'm not big on hunting wild game but it's a nice gesture."

I laugh and smack his shoulder. "Oh well, there goes my big plan for the evening. The turkeys will be happy though. Especially Randall. He'll peck you if you get too close, but he's a sweetheart deep down."

"Oh, well, I've gotta meet him then."

"Yeah, I'll introduce you. Just sing him some Katy Perry as you approach. It'll calm him down."

His shoulders shake with laughter. It's then that I realize that Sasha and Ciara are still standing in front of us, watching our entire interaction.

"Oh yeah, we're still standing here. That was the most intense eye fucking I've ever witnessed. Excuse me, I'm gonna go find Carter and see if we can get a quickie in before dinner." She shuffles off, and Ciara laughs before winking at us and heading to the backyard.

"You look beautiful." He lowers his lips onto mine, and I hesitate for a moment before giving in and wrapping my arms around his neck.

He moans into my mouth and pulls away. "Hmm...I'm willing to bet Sasha is gonna pull Carter into the downstairs bathroom so that's not an option, but we could sneak upstairs for a quickie of our own." He wiggles his eyebrows at me. Dumbass.

"I'm not gonna fuck you in your parents' house, idiot."

He chuckles while tracing my bottom lip with his finger. "I had to try. Come on, let me get you a drink. I know you don't want a mocktail but maybe some tea or lemonade?"

"Tea would be great."

"Coming right up. You don't need alcohol anyway; you can just get drunk off of me instead."

"I'm gonna punch you in your dick one day."

He shivers, and I laugh at the gut reaction. "Don't do that, baby. If you do, how will I do my duty of pleasuring you?"

"I'll be fine. I could always go back to Carlos."

He rolls his eyes. "Mmm. That is true, but Carlos doesn't do that thing with his tongue you like so much."

And now I need new panties. Dinner hasn't even started. *Save me.*

I glare at him and leave him standing there while I go to the backyard to join the rest of the party. Ciara's mom, Angela, stops me to congratulate me about the baby. She mentions that she's jealous of Isaiah's parents, David and Trinity, because she's ready to be a grandma herself.

"Yeah, it would be great if Ciara and Lincoln started trying soon. I'd love for the baby to have a little cousin closer to their age to play with." Behind Angela's back Ciara shoots daggers at me and flips me off. I try to hide my amusement but to no avail.

Shane walks over and gives me a big bear hug. He usually spends Thanksgiving with the Cole family because he's not close with his own family. That's the kind of people the Coles are. They accept everyone.

"Hey there, you're looking good, Nina. Got that pregnancy glow going on," he compliments me.

"Thanks, Shane. Fun fact, it's not a glow. It's just sweat. I'm always hot now, but if you want to call it a glow, who am I to stop you?"

He chuckles. "Your secret is safe with me."

Dinner is great. The conversation is flowing. The food is delicious. I could get used to this. And then Trinity turns to me and I know the baby flood of questions is coming.

"So Nina, how are you feeling these days?" Trinity asks me.

"Oh, I feel great. Minus the leg cramps and the increase in body temperature. I swear I'm taking cold showers twice a day just to keep from overheating."

"I'm sure there are other reasons you need so many cold showers." Sasha snickers. Reggie, Ciara, and Shane join her while I give her my best death glare.

"Oh yeah, I had leg cramps too. I'd like to say it'll get better, but it probably won't. Truth is you're just gonna feel more and more like your body isn't yours from this point forward."

"Oh, that sounds exciting. I should start charging rent." David laughs at that.

"Have you started thinking about names?"

Isaiah answers "yes" at the same time I answer "no."

I turn to him. "You have?"

"Yeah. I've just been tossing ideas around in my head. We can brainstorm together though." He squeezes my knee under the table, and the anxiety that threatened to overtake me a moment ago subsides.

"Do you know what you wanna do for the baby shower?"

"I haven't thought that far out yet." I'm still trying to figure out what I'm going to do about the nursery.

"We can plan it for you," Ciara declares.

"Sure, that'd be nice."

"Is it gonna be women only or will you be there, Isaiah?" Reggie asks.

He answers, "I'll be there" at the same time I answer, "women only." Fuck, we look like a dysfunctional mess right now.

"Really? I didn't think you'd have any interest in that."

"I'm down to play some baby games and eat cake. I wanna experience everything with you." He gives me an unsure smile until I squeeze his hand under the table, and his face splits into a wider grin.

"Of course. It'll be fun to see you and all your hulking friends play 'what's in the diaper.'"

"I think I'm gonna be sick that day," Lincoln interjects. He sticks his tongue out at Isaiah, and Isaiah scratches his chin with his middle finger.

The questions keep coming, and Isaiah and I answer everything else as a unit. Trinity moves the conversation to Neon Nights which I have a much better handle on answering.

"How are things with the bar, Nina?"

"Things are great. We're busy all the time which is good. I have a lot of ideas for a special Christmas drink menu this year so I'm gonna try that out."

"That's great. I remember how that bar was before you became the manager. You definitely made that place the success it is today."

My chest fills with pride at her words. That bar may not be mine, but it's my baby. I'm constantly implementing new ideas.

"She's amazing at what she does. She should own that bar outright. It's basically hers anyway," Isaiah adds. For some reason, his comment irks me. My dream is to buy the bar from Dee one day. He knows that's a goal for me. With my parents' life insurance money, I could probably afford to do that now, since I've already set money aside for Logan and Jada's college funds. But Isaiah also knows that I'm not ready to buy the bar yet. I don't want to take on the financial risk of owning it until I plan for whatever else Logan and Jada and the baby may need. I try not to let his comment irritate me. I know he's just proud of me and wants me to go after what I want, but it's not something I want to discuss with the whole damn family.

"When you have the baby, will someone else take over as manager?" David asks.

"Actually, Ciara and one of my other bartenders, Lindsay, are gonna co-manage. I trust them both completely. They could run the place in their sleep."

Ciara offers a shy smile in response. "Thanks for trusting us with it. We'll try not to let it burn down while you're gone."

"Linc, maybe you should quit your job temporarily and stay with them. With a hose at the ready," Sasha jokes.

"Oh yeah, no problem, I can get that cleared."

"So when the baby comes, will you continue to live separately or will one of you move?" Trinity ponders out loud. I'm thrown off by the question, but I know evasion won't work on her like it does on Jada.

"You know, it might be nice if you guys moved somewhere completely new. Somewhere that belongs to both of you," David suggests.

Jada jumps down from her chair and stomps her foot. "No!" All eyes snap to her. Tears well in her eyes and slice me in half. "I'm not moving!" She takes off into the house, and I take off after her.

She really is fast as hell. By the time I get inside, she's already in the downstairs bathroom sobbing.

I turn the doorknob but it's locked, so I knock.

"Jada? Jada, can I come in, please?" She opens the door just a crack, and I walk in and shut the door behind me.

"What's going on, Mini? What was that back there?" I'm down on my knees so I can look in her eyes, and they look so lost.

"I don't wanna move. I want to stay in our house."

"Okay. I hear you. No one is saying we're moving. It was just an idea. It doesn't mean anything."

She sniffs, and I wipe the rogue tear that fell down her cheek.

"Okay. When I asked ZayZay about moving in, he said he didn't know. He didn't say anything about us moving. I don't think I want that."

"Wait, you talked to Isaiah about this?"

"Yeah. I ask him all the time if he's going to move in with us. I want the baby to see him all the time instead of just some of the time. You're so happy when he's with us."

There's a lot to unpack with that comment. Does she think that I'm not happy just being with her and Logan? That's not my intention at all, and that makes me feel like I'm as big of a failure as our parents. And why did Isaiah not tell me that Jada asks him all the time about moving in? He should've given me a heads up so I could talk to Jada or at least be better prepared for this conversation.

"I promise you we're not moving out of our house right now. But I do want to be honest with you that it's possible we could move one day. There may come a time where we need more space or we have to move for some other reason, but I promise you that we will not move before I've talked to both you and Logan first. Okay?"

That seems to appease her because her mouth tips up in a small grin at that. "Okay!"

"Okay. And I don't want you to think that Isaiah is the only reason I'm happy." Although I'm not happy with him at all right now. "Nothing makes me happier than you and Logan."

"Really?"

"Yeah. You guys are the best brother and sister I could ask for. I'm so lucky to have you. If it weren't for you I would've fallen apart when we lost Mom and Dad."

"Really? You?"

"Oh yeah. I would've been so lost. But you guys made it all better. I knew that I had you guys, and I wasn't alone."

"I love you, Nina."

"I love you too, Mini."

Once we dry Jada's tears and she's calm, we decide now is the best time to present our cookies to everyone. I recruit Logan to help us pass them out, and everyone carries on like nothing happened.

Isaiah tries to catch my eyes, no doubt to make sure I'm okay, but I don't want his comfort right now. I avert my eyes and get through the rest of the dinner without acknowledging him.

CHAPTER
Fourteen

Isaiah

YOU KNOW WHEN YOU KNOW YOU'VE FUCKED UP, BUT YOU HAVE NO idea how you fucked up and therefore have no idea how to fix your fuckup?

That's where I am right now.

Nina has been cold toward me since she had her heart-to-heart with Jada at dinner. I checked on the little munchkin, and she seems fine with me. I still got a huge hug and our special handshake with my cookie. But Nina is not having my shit.

I rode with Ciara and Lincoln to my parents' tonight so that I'd be able to ride home with Nina and the kids. The ride home is agonizingly quiet. Jada is passed out from eating too many cookies and Logan is smart enough to stay away from Nina's wrath. I'm on my own.

I keep racking my brain to see what I said that was wrong tonight. I can't think of a damn thing. The mood between us was so cold that Lincoln and Shane even started texting me under the table before we left.

Shane: Dude what the fuck did you do?

Lincoln: Yeah your girl is pissed right now

Me: I have no idea! Did I say something dumb?

Lincoln: Of course you did

Me: What did I say?

Lincoln: I don't know I must've missed it but I'm sure it happened

Me: *middle finger emoji*

Lincoln: You wanna just ride back with me and Ci tonight?

Me: No I promised the kids I'd ride back with them

Shane: Protect your balls, man

Shane: And your head

Shane: Maybe just play dead and she'll leave you alone

Lincoln: And whatever she says just say sorry

Me: I'm scared

Lincoln: You should be

Shane: You should be

We pull up to the house and Logan picks Jada up with ease. He offers to get her ready for bed, and Nina thanks him while I silently plead for him not to leave me. He does not hear my cries.

When the door closes behind Logan, Nina whirls on me.

"What the fuck?"

"Umm...my thoughts exactly?"

"Why the hell wouldn't you tell me that Jada has been asking you to move in with us?"

Oh. Oh! Okay, yes. I fucked up.

"I'm sorry."

"Yeah, you are. Go on."

Well, damn. "I'm sorry I didn't tell you. She asked me a few times if I was going to move in with you guys. But I knew you weren't ready to have that conversation with me again, so I didn't want you to think I was trying to pressure you. I told Jada that you and I had a lot to figure out but we had plenty of time so not to worry about it right now. I was hoping that would get her off the scent for a while. I was just trying to help. I'm really sorry." Okay, that's three I'm sorrys so Lincoln would be happy. But Nina is not. I can practically see the steam coming out of her ears.

She turns around to make sure the kids aren't near the door. "Listen, when it comes to those kids, it is not your job to protect me. They are my kids. It's my job to protect them, and I can't do that when secrets are being kept from me."

She's absolutely right. I can't say that it doesn't hurt but she's right. She's their guardian, not me. As much as I care about them and consider them my family too, they aren't my responsibility.

But damn, I want us to be a unit on all things. And it pisses me off that she doesn't see that.

"I'm trying to undo years of damage my parents did to them. I love my parents, but they were assholes and Logan and Jada got the worst of it. I'm fighting an uphill battle here. What I don't need is you not telling me when Jada is coming to you saying she thinks I'm only happy when you're around. That's bullshit."

And another slice to my heart.

"I don't mean to say I'm not happy when you're around because I am. But they need to be my number one. Logan, Jada, and this baby. They've never been anyone's number one before, and I'll be damned if they think they aren't important to me."

"I understand that. I do. I wasn't trying to step on your toes. I was just trying to help."

She sighs. "I know, I know. This is hard. We're both in uncharted territory here and we're trying to figure out which way is up."

"Can I ask you something?"

"Yeah."

"Will you go on a date with me?"

Her eyes widen, and her mouth falls slightly open. Damn, she's cute. I'm still absolutely terrified that she's going to knee me in the balls, but she's so fucking cute.

"What?"

"Can I take you on a date? A real date."

"How is this at all relevant to what we're talking about?"

"You said we're in uncharted territory, and we're trying to figure out which way is up. I think part of the reason we're so stuck is because we haven't established what kind of partnership you and I have. During the day we're either with the kids playing Mom and Dad or at the doctor's talking about LB, and at night we're in each other's bed. I haven't done my job of making it clear to you that I don't want our relationship to be kept strictly to the bedroom. I don't want a friends with benefits situation. I want to be yours, one hundred percent. Mind, body, and soul. And make no mistake, I know that you and the kids are a package deal. I want it all. I want you to trust me to help with them too, not just LB. But I need to earn that. So I need to show you how much I want that. And that involves dates. Not play dates and not Friday night dinners at home. Real dates. Will you please do me the honor of letting me take you out?"

She blinks several times and points her finger in my face. "You think you're so slick right now. Don't think that you can just spew some romantic shit, and I'm going to fall on my knees and suck your dick."

"Jesus." And now my dick is confused as to whether it should stand at attention or cower in fear. Who am I kidding? I'm definitely at half-mast right now.

"The kids and I are ready for bed, so you can go home."

Sigh. I wasn't planning on needing to call an Uber this early, but I know I fucked up.

"Tell the kids I said good night. Good night, Nina."

"Good night. And Isaiah?"

"Yeah?"

"Tomorrow night I'll be dressed for a quote, unquote date which may or may not include heels, depending on how I feel about you at the time. So it better be good."

I can't hold back the smile that splits my entire face. "It'll be more than good."

I'm nervous walking up to Nina's door. It's ridiculous how anxious I am. I've been to this house a million times. Our entire relationship has been ass-backwards. We've had sex, gotten pregnant, then started having regular sex and now we're going on our first official date. But this date is important. It's the first step to showing Nina that I'm serious about her. That I don't just want to co-parent with her, I want to be her life partner. It has to go well.

Nina opens the door before I even knock, and all the air goes out of my lungs. She's got on a T-shirt because that will never change, and I love that about her. The shirt has a picture of Sade on it so I'm not sure what mood she's trying to convey, but I like it. She's wearing a black-and-white plaid ruffle skirt that stops midcalf but has a slit on the right side that goes almost all the way up to her hip. My fingers itch to trace the dimple there. To top it all off, she's got on black strappy heels. Her hair is in its naturally curly state, falling down her back. Her makeup is subtle but gorgeous. She's a vision.

I hold out the bouquet that I almost forgot I was holding. I have no idea what the different flowers are, but it's a vibrant mix of whites, yellows, and purples. I told the florist what I imagined—a bunch of wildflowers— and she made it happen.

Nina hesitates for just a moment before taking the bouquet from me, holding it up to her nose.

"These are gorgeous. Thank you."

"They're not as gorgeous as you, but it's my pleasure."

"What made you pick these? I wasn't expecting flowers at all, but I definitely wouldn't expect something so unique."

"You wound me. They remind me of you. You're a wildflower."

Her eyes jump to mine. "Really? And why is that?"

I step into her space, placing my hands lightly on her waist. "That's for me to know and you to find out, Wildflower." She wrinkles her nose but makes no move to step out of my grip. "Heels, huh? So is it safe to assume you feel pretty strongly about me tonight?"

She squints her eyes at me before stalking inside to put the flowers away. My eyes can't get enough of her ass in that skirt. I'm ten seconds away from stepping inside and forgetting all about dinner, but we need this date. She glides back over to me, each click of her heels going straight to my dick. "Jury's still out." She walks past me and heads toward my car. I try to hide my smile, but when she narrows her eyes at me I know I've failed. Worth it.

We pull up to Lo Scoglio, an Italian restaurant she's been wanting to try.

"Oh wow, I'm so excited you chose this restaurant. I'm not normally into Italian food but I've been craving it lately." I place my hand on the small of her back and kiss the top of her head. It seems to catch her off guard at first but she quickly melts into me.

The food is amazing. Nina ordered the chicken cacciatore while I ordered the eggplant parmesan because it was the other dish she was considering. I asked her if she wanted a bite of mine, and somehow half of my dish ended up on her plate.

We haven't stopped talking all night long. There are no awkward pauses between us.

"Okay, so what's one thing you want to implement at Neon?" I ask as we finish our entrées.

"I have a bunch of ideas. You know I'm a movie junkie, so one of my ideas is to have a monthly movie night. I would play movies on the TVs instead of sports and have drinking games that everyone can play. Like if I'm playing a *Harry Potter* movie I could say "take a shot every time Snape smacks Harry or Ron" and I could have specials on the drinks that are part of the game. I could even have different themes every month, like one month could be a ladies' special and I'll play a rom-com, or October could be scary movie month. Stuff like that. I figure it could bring in the same kind of crowd that a karaoke night or trivia night would, but it's unique."

"I like that. I like that a lot." I really do. It's brilliant. It's a great way to have a fun event at the bar and drive sales.

"Thank you."

"Do you think you'll pursue trying to buy the bar at some point?"

"Ugh, I mean…I would love to do that. That's the goal."

"So what's stopping you?" She mentioned before that she has the money to do it but she hasn't done it.

"I just don't like the uncertainty of it all. The bar is doing great right now, but what if I buy it and it goes under? You know, like how celebrity couples date for twenty years and then they get married and boom, five months later they're divorced."

She looks at me as if that's supposed to make any sense to me at all. "So you think because you've been managing the bar for so long that if you buy it it'll jinx all your success?"

"Yeah. It's just a lot of financial risk to take on. And I have three kids to think about now."

"And you have me to help with all of that now. Plus, you said you already set aside their college funds from your parents' life insurance money, so you at least have that in place."

"Yeah, but there's so much else that could go wrong. What if one of the kids needs a major surgery one day and my insurance won't cover it? I would feel extremely selfish that I sunk my money into this bar—that I for the most part already had—when the kids needed me."

I reach across the table and grab her hand. She gives me a shy smile and squeezes it. "Nina. You have to have a life of your own outside of the kids. You are the best parent these kids could ask for, and they know that. But you are a woman with hopes and dreams of your own."

"I know."

"Do you? Do you want the kids to go out and chase their dreams? To take chances and live life to the fullest?"

"Of course I do."

"They learn how to do that at home. You going after what you want is going to be the blueprint for them to do the same. They'll follow your lead."

"Okay, you have a point there. It's something to think about. And what about you?"

"What about me?"

"What are your dreams? You're this successful architect at an esteemed firm, but your dad has a highly respected construction business that I know from Sasha he'd love to hand over to you. Do you think you'll take over for your dad eventually? Or stay where you are?"

It's a question I've asked myself time and time again, and I still don't have a straight answer. "Honestly, I don't know. After everything happened with Monica and I moved back home, I think I was on a mission to prove myself. I let my personal life fall to the wayside and became the joke that Monica said I was. But in my career I was determined to make something of myself, and I didn't think I could do that working under my father. I wanted to build my reputation on the strength of my talents alone—not that my dad ever offered me any handouts. He wanted the company to go to me, but he expected me to work for it. But I never wanted anyone to be able to doubt that. I met Alan Paterson and he took me under his wing. I've always had a natural talent for the engineering side of architecture but Alan helped me broaden my skills. He's my mentor. So now I'm torn. I'd love to take over my dad's company and continue his vision and put my own mark on it. But I've grown so much where I am now, and I think I owe it to myself to see where I can go with that."

"That makes sense. You don't have to make any decisions right now. But if you ever want to talk out your feelings—maybe make a pros and cons list—I'm here. And you, Isaiah Cole, are a lot of things. But a joke is not one of them." That makes my heart race.

The rest of dinner flies by. We argue over whether she should have a cup of coffee for dessert. I think she shouldn't. She thinks I should shut my mouth because the doctor said it was okay and she'll kill me if I stop her.

She wins.

Her jaw drops when we get to the next destination.

"The Community Cinema? I love this place!" The Community Cinema & Amphitheater is a giant outdoor theater, basically like a drive-in. Anyone else might think that dinner and a movie is a boring first date, but Nina isn't anyone else. She is obsessed with movies, and I wanted to incorporate that into our date.

"I figured this would be more fun than a regular movie theater."

"Definitely more fun. I wish I would've worn my sneakers now though."

"Oh, I got you." I reach into the backpack I packed for tonight and pull out a pair of slides I bought for her. I noticed she had similar ones at her house.

"Holy shit, you brought me comfy shoes?"

"Of course. Can't have you struggling. I brought blankets too." She looks at me with hooded eyes and it takes everything in me not to push her back in the car to slide inside her.

"You're trying to get laid tonight, I see."

"Oh you have no idea, Wildflower." Her eyes twinkle with laughter. She places her hand on my shoulder for balance so she can change into her slides. When she's done I expect her to release me, but she wraps her arms around my neck and plants a kiss on my cheek instead.

"Thank you."

I place my hand on the back of her neck and pull her in for a kiss. She immediately deepens the kiss and bites my bottom lip. The back of the car is looking better and better, but tonight is not about sex. It's about showing my girl a good time. Showing her she's appreciated.

I smack her ass, and she jumps in surprise then giggles. It's the sweetest giggle I've ever heard. I'm half hard already. Jesus, get the hell away from the car. I grab her hand and lead her to find a place to sit.

She's excited because they're playing *Antebellum* tonight and she never had a chance to see that. We talk about the best movies to come out of the last couple of years. She plans to rectify the fact that I didn't watch *Waves*. We both agree that 2019 had some of the best movies we'd seen in a long time come out from *Us* to *Once Upon a Time in Hollywood* to *Knives Out* to *Avengers: Endgame*. She still cries every time Pepper tells Tony he can rest now.

"What's your favorite movie of all time?" I ask.

"Easy. *10 Things I Hate About You.*"

I shake my head in disbelief. "That is not at all what I thought you were gonna say."

"What were you expecting?"

"I don't know. I was expecting a classic."

"That is a classic."

"No, like a cult classic, I guess. Like *Pulp Fiction* or *Breakfast Club*. Or if you wanna stick with the rom-com theme, *When Harry Met Sally.*"

"Ah. No, *10 Things I Hate About You*, one hundred percent."

"What do you like about it?"

"I hated reading Shakespeare growing up. I thought it was boring and pretentious. So when I saw movies like *10 Things I Hate About You, She's The Man, Romeo Must Die*, and *West Side Story*, they made these concepts that seemed so absurd to me make sense. It gave me a much better appreciation for Shakespeare and helped me look to see what was under the surface of everything. And then the movie itself is just great. You've got the darker, more cynical love story between Kat and Patrick but then you've got the sweet, innocent love story between Cameron and Bianca. It's a perfect balance. And the grand gestures! If a guy ever serenaded me in front of my entire school I would've given him the goods immediately." I choke on my water and she pats my back in laughter. "Plus it's got Heath Ledger. That's enough said right there."

"Fair." The movie starts playing, and she leans in to my side. I pull the blanket over us and hold her for the entire movie, my hands only finding their way under her skirt a couple of times.

When we get back to her place, she looks happy but hesitant. She looks like she's trying to figure out the best way to tell me something, and my shoulders are tense with anticipation.

"Tonight was amazing. Thank you again."

"You don't have to thank me, Wildflower. I want to do lots of things like this with you."

"I do too." I can hear the "but" in that sentence. "But." And there it is. "About the living situation." Ahh, here we go. "I don't want to move out of our house, because Jada's not ready for that. But I'm also not ready for you to move in with us. I think we should wait until the baby comes and reassess where we are then."

In other words she wants to wait to see if the two of us will still be together when the baby comes before making a decision. It stings, but I get it. For now.

"Whatever you need. I'm okay with that."

"Okay."

"So are you willing to admit that we're dating now?"

"You move fast. You think one date is enough for us to be dating?"

"We've been dating for a while; you've just been in denial."

She pretends to think it over. "I guess you could say we're dating."

"Now we're getting somewhere. And how do you feel about sex on the first date?" She coughs out a laugh.

"Have you ever seen *Girls Trip*?"

"With Tiffany Haddish? Yeah, I have. Why?"

"I just bought some grapefruits at the store today, and I'm pretty hungry." She looks me up and down before getting out of my car and walking up to her door.

I sit there confused for a minute until I remember the grapefruit scene from the movie and I'm out of my seat quicker than I can blink.

CHAPTER
Fifteen

Nina

"Everything looks healthy. Have you decided if you want to find out the sex?" Isaiah and I are at our midpoint ultrasound appointment, which means we're now able to find out Little Bean's gender.

Isaiah looks at me and I nod my head enthusiastically.

"Hit us with it, Doc," Isaiah responds.

"Congratulations! It's a girl."

A girl. Holy shit. Little Bean is a girl.

"Oh my God." Isaiah puts both hands on my face and stares into my eyes. A tear forms in the corner of his eye and it spurs me on to full-on sob. He catches my tears with his thumbs and kisses me on the forehead.

"Are you happy?" I ask.

"A mini version of you is coming. I couldn't be happier."

I smile. Images of Isaiah swinging a little girl who looks just like him and acts just like me cloud my vision. God, he's going to be such an amazing father. I don't even think he knows how great he's going to be. He doesn't see the effect he's already had on Logan and Jada. Logan has been absorbing information on architecture like a sponge. The wheels in his brain never stop turning, but now he has a clear vision of where he wants to take his genius. Isaiah has been guiding him but never tries to force his opinions on him or steer him in one direction over another. And Jada. My sweet girl. She's always been a ball of energy, but her confidence has gone through the roof now that she has Isaiah cheering her on.

"Are you happy?" he turns the question around on me.

"Happier than I ever thought possible." He drops a chaste kiss on my lips. Dr. Hunter runs through a few more items with us, but all I can think about is the fact that Isaiah and I created a little girl.

How did I get so lucky?

I'm on cloud nine after yesterday's appointment. I'm feeling like a bad bitch, so I'm going to ride that wave before I change my mind and make the call I've been putting off for too long.

"Hello?"

"Hi, Dee, it's Nina."

"Hey there, sweetie, how are you?"

"I'm good. How are things going over there?" Dallas isn't far from Austin, but I get the feeling that Austin brings a lot of bad memories for Dee after her son, Victor, passed, so she stays away. Her daughter and granddaughter keep her going.

"They're just fine. Kaylee won her school's spelling bee so we're going out to celebrate tonight."

"Oh, that's nice."

"So what's going on? Everything okay at Neon?"

"Yeah, everything's great. I just wanted to run something by you. What would you think about possibly selling the bar to me?"

She's silent for a moment, and my stomach sinks until she speaks again. "You know, Neon Nights was my son's dream. I didn't see his vision, but I tried to keep it alive for him." Stomach cancer took Victor way too early. I never got to meet him. He passed two years before I came onboard. That's another reason I've been hesitating to come to Dee about this. The bar was important to Victor. It thrived under his leadership, and when Dee took over she wanted to honor his memory, but her depression over his loss and lack of understanding of bar ownership caused the bar to freefall into disaster. She doesn't want the bar, but I always felt like she didn't want to lose it either. "He'd be very proud of what you've done with the place."

"Thank you, Dee."

"I have to run now, but let's set up a time to talk details. I think you're the best person to take over that place."

Holy shit. "You mean that?"

"Yep. It's time. Thanks for calling, honey."

Holy fucking shit. It's happening. It's really happening. If it weren't for Isaiah, I don't know if I would've ever worked up the courage to make that call.

He's definitely getting laid later.

"Holy Christmas. I feel like all of these decorations should look tacky, but it looks amazing!" Brittany exclaims as she walks into Neon. Her job shuts its doors from Christmas Eve to New Year's, so she decided to take the week before off as well, and now she's here for an extended vacation.

"I know, right? I told Nina that this place has inspired my next book. I'm thinking there's a serial killer who only kills during the month of December and only strikes with Christmas-themed decorations like a strand of garland or a sharpened candy cane lawn decoration." Ciara is a bestselling thriller author. She was in the process of writing her debut novel when she moved here. After the news broke of everything that happened with her tormentor, her book sales skyrocketed. Her second novel was an even bigger hit than the first one. Now she's on book four.

The bar looks like Christmas threw up but like Brittany mentioned, it all works together. Colored lights line the entire ceiling. I've covered the bottom of the bar in wrapping paper. Stacks of wrapped presents hang from the ceiling. It's Santa Claus's wet dream.

"I like that idea. And the killer can leave Christmas cards at each crime scene," Brittany adds. They descend into maniacally planning this hypothetical story. I give them shit for using my bar for their murder ideas but—I can't lie—I would absolutely read that book.

"Alright bitches, it's time to go shopping!" Sasha walks in like she owns the place. The kids and I stayed the night with her last night because Nevaeh had been begging for a sleepover. Today, Logan and Jada are spending the day with Reggie and her kids while Sasha, Ciara, Brittany, and I go shopping for maternity clothes. I'm only four months along and barely showing, but Sasha insisted that I need to just get it over with because once I do pop, I won't want to do the shopping.

"Woohoo! Let's go, preggo." Ciara drags me from behind the bar. We leave Lindsay in charge and head out.

"Have the leg cramps gotten any better?" Sasha asks while holding up the ugliest maternity dress I've ever seen.

"Put that shit back. And yes, somewhat. Isaiah has been rubbing them every night, so that's helped me get to sleep."

"I bet he's been rubbing something every night to put you to sleep, but I don't know if it's your legs," Ciara teases. Brittany and Sasha laugh, and I flip her off. She's right though. I have no idea how sex is going to change once I'm as big as a house, so we've been getting it in as much as possible.

"How are things going with you two anyway?"

"Annoyingly good."

"Annoyingly?" Brittany questions.

"Yeah, we're so cute I want to vomit sometimes."

"That could be less to do with the fact that you're in a good relationship and more to do with the fact that you have an adorable parasite growing in your belly." Ciara sinks to her knees in front of me and places her hands on my stomach. "I'm just kidding, Little Bean. You're an angel, and I can't wait to meet you and be your favorite auntie."

"Hey bitch, don't try to come for my crown." Sasha throws down the gauntlet.

"Right, sorry. Second favorite auntie." She leans down and whispers, "We'll let her think that."

"You're so stupid. Get off me." I shrug her off with a laugh. "No, but really. Things are good. Everyone dismisses him as the joker or the flirt—and yeah, he jokes around a lot and he is definitely flirtatious—but that's not all he has to offer. He makes me feel like I can do anything. I just feel safe with him. He gets me. I couldn't have asked for a better man to have a child with."

Sasha's lip trembles slightly, and she sniffles before turning toward a rack of clothes. "I'm so glad you have each other."

I am trying not to cry in the middle of the maternity clothes section, so it's time for a subject change. "Hey, what are Simone and Sarah doing for Christmas this year?"

"Simone is gonna spend it with her family like usual, but she's got a new boy toy and they're going to New York for New Year's," Ciara explains.

"And Sarah and Jordan are going to Colorado this year to visit his uncle," Brittany offers.

"And what's your family doing this year, Britt?"

"My parents are staying in Florida. Courtney is off saving the world somewhere, I don't know where, and Greg is going to be in Puerto Rico. I have no idea what he's doing there but those are his plans." Brittany isn't close with her older brother and sister. She's a little closer to her parents, but they don't make the trip up to Baltimore often and she rarely visits them in Florida. From what I understand, Brittany has spent most Christmases with Ciara and her mom, so I wasn't surprised when she said she was spending her entire Christmas vacation here since Ciara and her mom have both moved to Texas.

"Well, Mom says you're still in charge of the eggnog this year, so remind me we need to get you to a liquor store this weekend." Brittany salutes Ciara in agreement.

You hear that, Little Bean? I'm giving up perfectly good eggnog for you this year. I hope you appreciate it.

Almost as if she can hear my thoughts, Brittany turns to me. "Sorry, boo, but since you can't have raw eggs and alcohol, you're out. I can make something virgin for you though."

I scrunch my nose. "Ugh. I love you, but no thanks. I expect my own batch next year."

"Your wish is my command."

I end up buying three pairs of maternity jeans and two maternity dresses. That's really all I'm willing to buy. I'm going to keep wearing my graphic tees without a care in the world. If my belly hangs out of them, then the world will get a view of my giant belly and like it.

I pick up Logan and Jada on my way home, but when we get there Isaiah is waiting for us outside the door, looking nervous as hell. He runs to the car and opens the door for me. He and Jada do their special handshake and Logan gives him a fist bump.

"Are you okay?"

"I'm great."

"Okay, so why are you waiting outside like a creep?" I question.

"I wanted to give you guys your Christmas present early."

"Early presents? I love early presents!" Jada shouts.

"You love all presents," Logan teases.

"Well, who doesn't love presents?" Jada asks. She does have a point. Isaiah holds his hand out for me. I narrow my eyes before taking it and following him to the door. What is he up to?

I expect something to jump out at me when we walk in the house, but everything seems normal.

"Follow me." He leads us upstairs and stops in front of Logan and Jada's bedroom.

"Okay, so I know you wanted the kids to have their own rooms, but with the baby coming it was hard to figure out the logistics for that. I think I figured out how to fix the problem."

He opens the door, and all three of us gasp in surprise. He has transformed the kids' bedroom into Jada's personal paradise. It's Candy Land themed. One wall is painted blue, one is painted purple, one is painted yellow, and the other is painted green. There are Candy Land characters and locations painted on the walls. Her bed is covered with pink-and-white striped sheets. The yellow wall has "Jada's Game Corner" painted on it, and there's a handmade shelving unit below it that holds a bunch of Jada's board games and puzzles. The room is loud, it's vibrant, it's one hundred percent Jada. She runs into the room and starts literally hugging every piece of furniture. It's safe to say she's in love.

"This is amazing!"

"Thank you, ZayZay, it's perfect!"

"And the tour is just getting started. Next stop, Logan's room. Follow me." I expect him to walk over to the spare bedroom but instead he goes back downstairs, out of the mud room, and into the connected garage.

"Ta-da!" He flicks on the light, and I'm completely speechless.

I never thought about transforming the garage into Logan's room before because of the heat. He's thought of everything though. The garage doors have been replaced with real doors to make it a true bedroom, and there is air coming in. The garage has become this cool library/teenaged version of a bachelor pad. The walls are painted gray and green. The entire back wall has been converted into a giant bookcase where Logan's library nearly fills each shelf. He now has a huge platform storage bed to keep his clothes and other things in along with a large armoire since there's no closet out here. A TV hangs on the wall opposite his bed, and underneath it is a really cool desk that has his laptop set up along with a reading lamp. There's another reading lamp over his bed that I know will get plenty of use. It's absolutely amazing.

"Wow. This is awesome. I don't know what to say. Thank you, Isaiah. Really," Logan gushes. The two of them share a bro hug, and my control snaps. I burst into tears, and Jada grabs my hand to comfort me.

"Why don't you guys explore your rooms for a bit. I wanna show Nina one last thing." Jada does not need to be told twice, and she takes off upstairs while Logan starts looking closely at the books on his shelf.

I don't think I can take another surprise. My heart is close to exploding from pure joy, but I let Isaiah lead me back upstairs. He stops us in front of the spare bedroom.

"So. Now that the kids have separate rooms, I thought you might get excited about planning the nursery. I didn't want to do any of that without you, but I did make one thing."

He opens the door, and in the middle of the room sits a gorgeous handmade crib. It's a cherry-wood color and absolutely stunning. I let out a gasp as my fingers trace the edges of it.

I turn, and Isaiah is looking at me like I'm the only girl in the world. I hold out my hand. He grabs it and lets me pull him into me. I wrap my hands around his waist, and he rests his chin on top of my head.

"I can't believe you did all this. How did you do all this?"

"I've been secretly getting measurements of all the rooms for a while. I had all the furniture ordered or created a few weeks ago, so that was easy. All I had to do was get the painting done."

"You did it alone?"

"Absolutely not. I called the goon squad. We were here all day yesterday and today while you were with the girls. Dom's sister is a really talented artist, and she did all the artwork in Jada's room."

I suddenly understand why Sasha was so insistent on going shopping today and why Nevaeh was desperate for a sleepover last night.

"So everyone knew?"

He chuckles. "Yeah. The girls will probably be blowing your phone up later to see how you like it."

I lift my head to look him in the eyes. "You're amazing. You didn't have to do all this but you did, and I am so grateful to you."

"I just want you guys to be happy."

God, this man. I was so scared to give us a real chance, but he just keeps proving over and over again that I'll never be able to let him go. I'm falling hopelessly in love with him.

"Kiss me." He obliges immediately. I slip my hands under his shirt to trace each of his abs. He groans into the kiss and deepens it. I bite down on his bottom lip, and his hands fall to my ass.

"Don't start something you can't finish, Wildflower," he rasps.

"Who says I can't finish?"

"Fuck." He grabs my hand and hauls me down the hall to my bedroom, locking the door behind us.

I'm on him the second the lock clicks, grabbing his waistband and un-buttoning his jeans. He quickly steps out of his jeans, and I'm greeted by the glorious dick that I love as much as I love the man attached to it. I lick my lips in anticipation before sinking to my knees.

"You don't have to do that. You shouldn't be on your knees," he says, but little Isaiah seems to be just fine with me on my knees.

"Shhh. This is my thank you. Enjoy it." I lick the tip of his dick, causing him to twitch and shudder. I take as much of him in my mouth as I can and use my hands to massage the rest of him.

"Shit, that feels good." His eyes close for a moment and then fly open as if he doesn't want to miss a moment. He looks at me with so much heat it has me snaking one of my hands down to my clit. I moan around his shaft and his hands fly to my hair, but he doesn't add pressure.

I love that I'm doing this to him. Making him lose control. I feel naughty knowing that the kids are in the house. We've had sex with them home be-fore but usually they're sleeping. He loves to make a game out of seeing if I can stay quiet enough. I always lose. I'm counting on them being so en-chanted by their new rooms, they won't come looking for a while, so I have time for a game of my own.

My tongue glides across his entire length and swirls around his tip be-fore I suck him completely and pump his balls with my hands. He groans loudly, and his fists fly behind him into the door. I smirk at him, releasing him with a pop.

"Shh. Don't wanna alert the kids, right?"

"Oh fuck. Don't tease me, Nina."

"Or what?" His eyes darken. I can feel my arousal pooling between my thighs. "Let me make you come, KP. And keep quiet."

He blows out a harsh breath and closes his eyes briefly. I continue massaging his balls as I slide his cock back into my mouth. Tears spring to my eyes as I hollow out my cheeks, and he hits the back of my throat. He tries to ease himself out, but I don't want him to be gentle with me. I grab his hands and place them in my hair, silently telling him to guide me.

It doesn't take long before his grip tightens and his hips thrust up forcing me to take more. He's fucking my mouth. It's intoxicating. It looks like he's controlling me, but I have all the power. I've never felt sexier. One of my hands flies up to his waist. My fingers trace his happy trail, and his stomach buckles under my touch. I can't help the moan that falls from my mouth.

"You like seeing what you do to me, Wildflower?"

I nod around him. He pulls my hair just enough that it stings. Fuck, he drives me crazy.

"Touch yourself, baby," he commands. I drop my hand down to my slick entrance and tease myself. The sensation is almost too much.

He pumps into my mouth while I stroke my clit, my orgasm building quickly.

"Oh fuck, I'm gonna come," Isaiah warns. I hum my approval and keep up my pace until he comes, and I swallow his release. I rise to my feet and kiss him on the lips, letting him taste himself.

"I need to taste you."

"Nope. That was all about you. I told you it was my thank you."

"Okay, so now let me thank you for your thank you."

I giggle. "I'm gonna save that for later tonight. Don't worry, I'm far from done with you." I smack him on the ass and leave the room in search of the kids.

"Merry Christmas, beautiful," Isaiah whispers in my ear Christmas morning. He spent the night last night. The kids were having so much fun with him that by the time they went to bed it made no sense for him to drive home when he was spending Christmas morning with us anyway. This is the first time he's spent the night when the kids are home, or at least still been here when they wake up. I haven't wanted them to get the wrong idea about our relationship, so I didn't allow it, but what am I waiting for? We are together. In every sense of the word. I trust him with the kids' lives and hearts. We're ready for this.

"Merry Christmas, handsome." I roll over and give him a quick kiss on the mouth. He tries to deepen the kiss but I push him away.

"Eww don't do that, I have morning breath."

"I've tasted every inch of you. I think I can handle some hot dragon breath."

"I didn't say it was hot dragon breath, ass." I slap him on the arm and he grabs mine to place a teasing bite on my forearm. His other hand starts wandering down to my bare legs when the door bursts open and Jada runs in. There goes that.

"It's Christmas! It's Christmas!" she announces.

"Woah, is it really? I had no idea! I wonder if Santa brought you any gifts."

She jumps up and down with excitement. "Come on, we gotta go see!" She doesn't wait for a response before running downstairs and yelling for Logan. She obviously didn't care that Isaiah was in my room just then, so I hyped that up for no reason. I'm sure the presents waiting for her under the tree helped with the distraction.

"Apparently I'm on the naughty list because I didn't get my Christmas present," Isaiah pouts, brushing his hand over my thigh again.

"Technically you did. We rang in Christmas with a bang, literally, if you recall."

"Oh I recall. But I wanted to unwrap my gift under the tree before the kids woke up. It'll have to be after they go to sleep now." He winks and heads to the bathroom to brush his teeth. I wonder if Jada would kill me if I took the time to take a cold shower before coming downstairs.

We make our way downstairs where Logan is still rubbing the sleep out of his eyes while Jada is already looking under the tree and grabbing anything with her name on it.

The kids dig in and absolutely love all their gifts. Jada gets board games, a Wii, and new gymnastics gear. Logan gets books, a sketchpad, and a few robotics kits.

Now it's time for the kids to present their gifts to Isaiah. They worked really hard on them, and they really want him to like them. Especially after his epic bedroom reveal.

"Can he open mine first?" Jada asks Logan, and he nods his approval. Jada proudly shoves her box into Isaiah's hands. She attempted to wrap it herself, and we exchange a smile at how it looks.

"Well, first of all," Isaiah starts, "I just wanna say this is the best wrap job I've ever seen. I almost don't want to open it." Jada's face splits into a huge goofy smile, and I fall a little harder for this man.

He carefully unwraps the box and gasps at the inside.

"Do you like it?"

"I love it!"

"Nina helped me order it but I picked the picture."

"It's a fantastic picture." It's a custom two-hundred-piece puzzle. The image is a picture of the four of us that we took on Thanksgiving.

"I thought we could do it together." Isaiah scoops her up into a giant hug and kisses her on the cheek.

"Of course we will. Thank you. I love it so much." Jada beams with pride and gives him one more hug before sitting down.

"Guess it's my turn." Logan reaches under the tree and carefully slides his gift over to Isaiah. Isaiah eyes it curiously and removes the covering.

"Woah!" It's a LEGO architecture set that Logan put together by himself. It's of Dubai's skyline because that's what Isaiah told him was one of his favorites. Logan shrugs like it's no big deal, but we all know it is.

"This is amazing. Thank you." Logan shares a reluctant smile.

"You're welcome."

"Maybe we can start making these together now. I love stuff like this."

And now Logan is smiling from ear to ear. "Yeah, that'd be cool. They have a bunch of these. Like New York, Vegas, Tokyo, and London." The guys talk animatedly about architecture in different places before Jada gets bored and reminds them gifts aren't done.

"Sorry. It's your turn, Nina." Jada hands me a huge basket, and Logan hands me a box. After they tell me there's no particular order I'm tearing into the basket.

"It's a bunch of your favorite movies to add to your collection." The basket is overflowing with DVDs and movie snacks. My eyes immediately fall to *10 Things I Hate About You,* and I wink at Isaiah. I laugh when I see the copy of *Beetlejuice* in there. *Moana* is in there, which is Jada's and my favorite movie to watch together. *The Sandlot* is in there too which the kids and I have watched together no less than thirty times. It's perfect.

"Don't cry, Nina. You still have one more!" I didn't even realize the tears were falling until Jada called me out. Get it together, Nina.

I open the box and am met with a photo album. The very first page says, "To Our Big Sister…". As I flip through the pages there is picture after picture of the three of us throughout the years. Me and Logan at Jada's gymnastics tournament. Me and Logan at one of his robotics tournaments. Us on a game night which could've just been a random Tuesday. Me standing next to Logan while holding baby Jada. Us on their first days of school. Some of these things I forgot about, but the memories come flooding back with every picture. I'm a blubbering mess when I get to the last page which reads, "Thank you for being our Mom." If I thought I was sobbing before, I don't have words for what I'm doing now. I'm blown away.

"You've always been there for us. You've always been more of a mom to us than anything, and we love you for that," Logan offers.

"Yeah. But even though you're our mom, you're still a really cool big sister." Jada squeezes my hands. I pull them in for a group hug and shower them with thank yous and kisses. I look over Logan's shoulder at Isaiah who's watching us with all the love in the world. I motion for him to join us, and my heart is full when he does.

I'm getting a headache from all the crying, and I still have to give Isaiah his gift. Lord help me.

"Okay okay, sit down. We still have one more gift and then we're watching cartoons and eating pancakes because I can't take any more tears."

My nerves are on one hundred as I hand Isaiah his gift. I know he'll like it, but I also don't want him to think I'm overstepping. He opens the box and gasps in shock as he pulls out the watch box. It's the same Invicta watch his dad has.

"I know you wanted to buy this for yourself when you proved yourself, but I know you never would. Isaiah, you have earned your reputation through blood, sweat, and tears. It's yours and no one can take it from you. You deserve to be celebrated and appreciated." He looks at me and starts to speak, but the words get caught in his throat. He nods and moves on to the last gift in the box. A mug that says, "World's Best Dad."

He laughs. "I haven't earned this yet."

I pin him with a hard stare. "Little Bean is the luckiest girl in the world to have you." He pulls me in for a kiss, and everything melts away. He rests his forehead against mine after and whispers his thanks.

"That was yucky." Jada scrunches her nose. Thank God for children and their comedic timing.

Isaiah and I are in the kitchen whipping up pancakes and bacon while the kids watch *A Charlie Brown Christmas*. We move in unison like we've been cooking meals together for years. I can't help but wonder if we'll be doing this years from now. Making breakfast with the kids and Little Bean like one big happy family. I can see it so clearly.

"You know, I didn't give you your gift," Isaiah whispers in my ear.

"I thought that was gonna be tonight under the tree." I wink. He chuckles and swats my ass.

"No, I meant your real gift."

"Yes, you did. Remember the whole HGTV kids' rooms reveal?"

"That was more for the kids."

"I swear if you make me cry again I might slap you. My headache is just now starting to subside."

"I promise it's more lowkey. You'll probably laugh." I give him a skeptical look but nod in acceptance. He tiptoes out to the living room and returns with a giftbag.

He wiggles his eyebrows at me, daring me to open it. My initial reaction when I open it is to bust out laughing.

This man got me graphic tees. But not just any graphic tees—custom-made graphic tees. The first shirt has a picture of Logan in deep thought on it with the word "Mood" under it. The next shirt is another "Mood" tee, but this one has a picture of Jada bouncing off the walls with energy. There's one with a picture of me with all the girls at Ciara's wedding. That one says "Squad" on it. Then there's one with a picture of just me on it that says "Mom, sister, all around badass."

I'm torn between crying and laughing, but in the end laughter wins out as I wrap Isaiah in a hug on what has turned out to be the best Christmas ever.

Later that night, the kids are in their beds. Jada completely wore us out wanting to play with every single new toy for at least an hour. Isaiah is taking a shower because he plans to stay the night again. We're diving right into this thing.

My eyes are firmly planted on the bathroom door. The steam radiating from there is nothing in comparison to the heat I feel in my very bones. Images of Isaiah spending Christmas with the kids and me—like our own makeshift family—part way to darker, more sinful thoughts. It's sexy as hell watching him step into this father-like role.

Suddenly, my palms feel extremely sweaty and sticky. Maybe I should wash them. I mean, Isaiah wouldn't mind if I came into the bathroom to innocently wash my hands, right?

Let's find out.

I slowly open the bathroom door. Isaiah's back is to me. I stand in awe of the water cascading down his broad shoulders all the way to his tight ass. Oh man, pregnancy has made me insatiable. Or maybe it's just him. No one plays my body like he does. He owns my pleasure. It's intoxicating.

He startles. "Oh shit, Nina. You scared the shit out of me." The top half of his body is turned toward me, and I can make out one side of those delectable abs.

"Sorry about that."

"Are you okay?"

"Oh yeah, I'm good. Just came in to wash my hands." His eyes turn to slits. His lips tilt up into the wicked grin that I know leads to the best kind of trouble.

"Wash your hands, huh?"

"Yeah. Hygiene is important."

"It sure is, Wildflower."

I smirk and head over to the sink. He doesn't shut the water off, but I hear him move the shower curtain out of his way, and his large feet step out of the tub, padding their way over to stand directly behind me.

"What are you up to?"

"I realized that I didn't unwrap my present under the tree like I planned, but this is even better." His hands snake around to the robe belt tied around my stomach. He makes quick work of untying it, exposing me to him. I look at his reflection in the mirror, frozen in place by the heat in his gaze.

"Um, excuse me, sir, I just came in here to wash my hands. Not to disturb your shower."

"I like when you play coy, Wildflower. It's cute." I push back just slightly against his groin but enough to elicit a sinful groan from his mouth. That SOD is already at attention, standing between his stomach and my backside.

"Playing coy, am I? Let me make it clear for you then. I want you."

"Where do you want me?"

"Inside me."

His hand traces a path down to my sex and cups me, one finger slipping into my wetness.

"You're already wet for me. I left the shower running to cover your noises. You ready?"

"Yes. Now." I barely get the word out before he enters me. My head falls down between my shoulders, trying to contain the loud moan threatening to leave my lips when I feel the slap of his hand against my ass followed by a soothing rub.

"Look at us, Wildflower." This is better than the dream I had that night. I look at where our bodies connect in the mirror, losing myself to this moment and this man.

Our eyes connect. I try to stay present, but I'm lifted to the future. The future I want so badly with him. Breakfast with the kids in the morning, sweet kisses before leaving for work, tender moments at the dinner table at night, ravaging each other's bodies every day. I see it so clearly. I hope it stays just like this. He grabs my hand and snakes it down to my clit, our hands working together in perfect harmony to push me over the edge.

His name is on my lips when I come, and he follows me a moment later. He bends down and kisses me with such tenderness I feel the promises he's making coating my skin, settling on my heart. He turns me around and pushes my robe completely off my body, before lifting me into his arms.

"What are you doing?"

"Taking you to the shower. Hygiene is important, Wildflower."

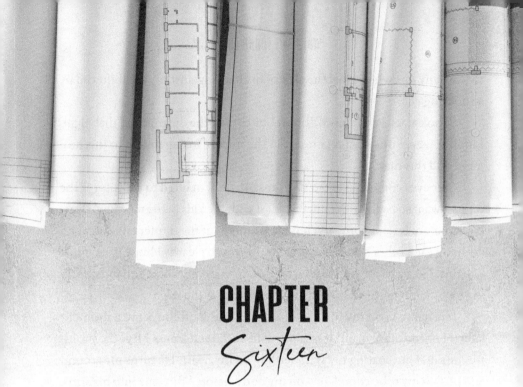

CHAPTER
Sixteen

Isaiah

"**B**ABE, IF YOU DON'T SIT YOUR SEXY ASS DOWN I'M GONNA SPANK you."

Nina sticks her tongue out at me and ignores me, continuing to walk over to the fridge for Lord knows what. She's six months along and has officially popped. Her cravings have also gotten really weird. I cringe as she pulls out the leftover pizza from last night and pours ranch dressing over it.

I've spent damn near every day here since Christmas. We've basically been one big happy family, and I couldn't be happier about that. It feels right. I'm just glad we're past the point of acting like I go home every night. We're still not at the point where I actually live here, as in my mail gets delivered here, but we will. I'm sure of it. Nina usually gets leg cramps at night and her ankles have started swelling, so I like that I can be here to help her.

She takes another bite of her nasty-ass pizza and moans in delight. "Mmm, this is so good." I'm not one hundred percent sure but I'm pretty sure she just came. Pregnancy is one hell of a drug. "Do I look good enough to kiss?" She wiggles her belly at me.

"Wildflower, you always look good enough to kiss." I kiss her on the lips. "And to eat." I wiggle my eyebrows.

She chuckles around another bite. "I can't even watch you do that anymore. All I see is a big-ass belly."

"I'll just have to do it in front of the mirror from now on." She misses her mouth when I say that, and a giant glob of ranch dressing ends up on the corner of her mouth. I don't think I've ever loved her more.

"Well, well, well. If it isn't Papa Cole," Shane teases when I walk into Corbett's. I'm meeting the guys tonight since we haven't seen each other in a while.

"Yeah, yeah. That's right, I'm Papa Cole. And y'all are my sons. Someone buy me a beer."

The guys boo me and punch me on the shoulders as I sit down.

"How's she feeling? Still eating weird shit?" Kai asks.

"Gets weirder every day. But the doctor said her cravings will probably lessen in the third trimester, and we're almost there."

"I still can't believe you're having a baby. I didn't think any of us would have kids ever, but I thought if anybody it'd be Lincoln first since he has Ciara now," Shane says. I look over to Kai and I know he's thinking about the baby he never got to have.

"Yeah, it's crazy."

"I'm proud of you, man. I know you're gonna be an amazing dad. I still hate you for how much Ciara's mom is up my ass and gets worse the bigger Nina gets, but still you're gonna be great." Lincoln pats me on the shoulder and I see the pride in his eyes.

"Knock your wife up, and you won't have to hear it anymore, bro."

"Working on it." He winks.

"We're gonna have to stop calling you the funny friend and start calling you the dad friend," Dom teases.

"Nah, I'm always gonna be funnier than you fucks."

"It's okay. I'll take over that torch for you. It's my time to shine." Shane pops the collar on his jacket. There's silence at the table before everyone bursts into laughter.

"You know what? I'm gonna let you be great. You take that torch on, buddy. I don't need to be the class clown anymore."

"They grow up so fast. So are you thinking about marrying her?" Dom questions.

Every day. But she won't even let me officially move in. I know she's not going to appreciate it if I propose. She'll think I'm doing it out of obligation.

"It's not something we've talked about. I'm definitely in love with her, but there's a lot going on already so I don't think we're there yet."

Kai laughs and Linc joins him. "What's funny?"

"You know that just because you're not married doesn't mean you're not settled, right? You have a baby and you and Nina are together," Lincoln says as if that's supposed to mean something to me.

"Your point?"

"He means, dumbass, that this still counts at two of the five of us being settled."

"Oh, fuck off. It's not about trying to keep the pact intact. Bunch of jackasses." Dom laughs this time, and I throw a sugar packet at him. The story of how Lincoln and I met the rest of the guys is embarrassing, ridiculous, and just plain insane. We promised each other we'd never share the story with anyone until the day every single one of us is married and settled down. It was my idea. Not my smartest idea but I was nineteen at the time. Marriage wasn't even on my radar, and I never wanted that story getting out. Now that I'm older and have found Nina, I wish I had suggested the terms be something more out there—like we can't share the story unless aliens attack and we're all about to die or be abducted. "Besides, I have nothing to worry about. Linc and I are Cole men. And Cole men are irresistible. But who the fuck is gonna put up with you jackasses?" I raise my eyebrows as I bring my beer to my lips. Dom and Shane raise their hands in surrender while Kai looks at me with challenge in his eyes. Interesting.

I'm watching Jada today because Nina took Logan to pick up his suit for his upcoming school dance. I offered to take him for some male bonding time, but she wanted to share her sage sisterly advice with him. I know all about that. Sasha and Reggie gave me plenty of advice about girls growing up. I stupidly ignored it all. Logan's a smart kid though—way smarter than I was at his age—so hopefully he listens.

Right now, Jada is trying to school me at a virtual game of tennis. We've played four games of Uno, five games of Connect Four, put together one puzzle, and now we're on to the Wii. I've been informed that after this game we'll be moving on to gymnastics practice. She keeps me busy.

"Aww, dang-it," Jada whines after missing a backhand.

"That's okay. You'll get it next time."

"I know I'm getting good at this game. I even beat Malcolm once!"

"Oh yeah? You're pretty tough then." She flexes her tiny little muscle at me before getting ready for her next serve.

She gives it her all, but in the end I come out victorious. That's right. I absolutely did not let her win. I don't believe in letting kids win just because they're little. If you don't teach them the art of losing when they're young, they'll be in for a rude awakening when the real world hits them and doesn't give a fuck about their feelings. Jada might want to pursue gymnastics for a living. She's talked about going to the Olympics before. She needs to learn now that sometimes you don't always get your way, but you never stop working for it. She boos as my Mii character does a dance on the screen, but then she hugs me and tells me I did a good job. She's competitive as all hell but she's already a gracious loser. I'm proud of her.

"Ready for practice?" she asks.

"Ready, Freddy."

"I'm not Freddy, I'm Flash, silly." She sticks her tongue out at me. It's our ongoing joke that the only nickname I'm allowed to call her is Flash now. She won't accept anything else.

"My bad, Flash. What are we working on today? Tumbles?"

She nods and runs to her room to change into her practice clothes, but as she does she trips and bumps into the frame on the wall. It falls off the nail, but I manage to catch it before it hits the ground.

"Oh no! I almost broke it!"

"Almost doesn't count, Flash. It's okay, no biggie. Even if the frame had broken we could put the picture in a different one. The important thing is you didn't hurt yourself. How about I hang it up a little higher?" I look over to her, but her eyes are fixated on the frame. It's a picture of us. After we put together the two-hundred-piece puzzle she got me for Christmas, I decided I wanted to frame it and hang it up. When I first suggested it, Jada was confused.

"How will we do the puzzle again if you glue it into a frame?" she asked.

"Well we don't, Flash. It'd be a one and done."

"Oh." Her face falls. "You don't like the puzzle? You don't wanna put it together again with me?"

I sink down to my knees in front of her. "No, that's not it at all. I love this puzzle. But when we finish putting it together, I want to save it forever so everyone can see it."

"But how come we can't just print out the picture and frame that?"

"We could. But I think framing the puzzle would be even cooler. Because it's special."

"It is?"

"Yep. Wanna know why?"

"Why?"

I look over at the picture on the puzzle box. We had Sasha take the picture for us on Thanksgiving. It was right before we sat down for dinner. I have my arm around Nina's waist, and if you look real close you can see her tiny baby bump. Logan has his arm around Nina's shoulder, and Jada is holding on to my leg. We look like a true family. It's my favorite picture in existence. "Because we built it together. Each puzzle piece represents us. It's every laugh we've ever shared. Every game we've ever played. Every book we've ever read. Every cookie we've ever dunked. Every balance beam routine we've ever practiced. Hidden right there in the bones of this puzzle. And it formed this beautiful picture. When *people come over they're gonna see a cute photo. But us? We'll be able to look at this and see our whole story."*

She looks up at me with the biggest grin on her face before face-planting right into my chest and squeezing her little arms around my sides.

"Thank you, ZayZay."

"I got you, Flash."

I look down at Jada, wondering what's going through her mind. I nudge her shoulder. "Hey, you okay?"

"How come Mommy and Daddy didn't take pictures like this with us?"

Fuck. This kid breaks my heart. No disrespect but I want to punch their parents every time I see this very look in Jada's eyes. Logan's too. He's better at hiding it, but it's there.

"I'm sure they wanted to. Sometimes we forget to stop and enjoy the little moments. We're so busy living them, we forget to take the time to memorialize them."

She wrinkles her nose. "What does memor…memor. What does that mean?"

I chuckle and slow down the pronunciation for her. "It means to preserve the memory of something. Basically, every time you take a picture of something, you're freezing that moment in time so you can look back on it later."

"Oh. Okay. I don't think Mommy and Daddy wanted to look back in time."

Another shred to my heart.

"Listen, sometimes people aren't good at showing the people they love how they feel. It doesn't mean they don't feel it though. It doesn't mean there's anything wrong with you."

"So it's not my fault they died? They never wanted to be home. I thought I chased them away. They didn't want me to do gymnastics. They fought with Nina about it. They didn't think I heard them, but I did. Maybe if I had listened to them—"

I move my hands from her shoulders to her hands and grasp them tightly in my own, forcing her to look at me when I cut her off. "No. No.

No. Nothing that happened is your fault. Your mom and dad had their own stuff to work out but that was on them. You did everything right. And don't you ever let anyone tell you not to follow your dreams. I don't care if it was your parents, if it was kids at school, or even me and Nina. No one gets to tell you what you can be except you. Do you want to do gymnastics?"

She gives me a shaky nod. "Yes."

"Then that's what you'll do. And if you ever change your mind, that's okay too. It's your life, Jada. You can do anything. I believe in you. And so does Nina. That's why she fought with your parents about it. But that doesn't mean they didn't believe in you. I think they were just scared."

"Scared of what?"

"Scared of you getting hurt. Mommies and daddies want to protect their kids from all the bad stuff in the world. They probably were scared you'd get injured or something." I'm pulling straws out of my ass. I have no idea why they tried to stop her from doing gymnastics. I'm willing to bet if Nina fought with them about it that they were being the selfish assholes I've learned that they were. But damn if I'm gonna say that to this innocent girl.

Tears start falling from her eyes, ripping me apart. "So you think they loved me?"

"I know they did. How could anyone not love you? You're a pretty amazing kid." She nods, the idea seemingly sinking in, and then she wraps me up in a hug.

"You're the best, ZayZay."

"Nah, that's you, Flash. So what do you think? Should we hang this bad boy up a little higher and get to practicing?"

"Yeah! I'm gonna go change." She runs to her room while I run to the storage closet to get a hammer. I make a mental note to tell Nina about my conversation with Jada. I won't make the mistake of not keeping her in the loop again.

As I'm walking back from the closet, my phone starts blowing up with messages. I smile thinking it's Nina, but it quickly falls when I see Alexis's name on my screen.

Alexis: We need to talk.

Alexis: Isaiah, call me. You can't keep ignoring me.

Alexis: I won't keep your secret forever.

What secret? I have no idea what she's talking about, but I refuse to let her drag me back into her shit again.

I exit out of the messages and toss my phone back in my pocket.

CHAPTER
Seventeen

Nina

Y OU COULDN'T PAY ME TO BE A TEENAGER AGAIN.
School dances, the uncertainty of whether the boy you liked liked you back, the unnecessary drama. Bleh. You can keep all that.

But watching Logan try on his suit for his school dance one last time before I pay for it puts me in my feels. He's growing up so fast. This is insane. There are times when I still see him as that chubby baby whose arms I used to pinch. And there are other times when I see him as a young man who has had to take on too much too soon. He couldn't be bothered with this dance a few months ago, but now that he's finally getting to act like the kid he is again, he's excited. Which makes me excited. I want everything to go perfectly for him.

He turns around to face me. He looks so handsome. He decided to go a non-traditional route with a burgundy suit that makes his brown skin pop. His shoes are light brown leather loafers. His shirt is a cream button-down with a neutral tie, though he mentioned possibly wanting to go without a tie and unbuttoning his shirt a little. Okay, Rico Suave. He thinks he's grown now because he's hit a growth spurt. He's taller than I am which trips me the fuck out. Who told him he could get so tall? Isaiah says as long as he doesn't outgrow him it's fine. Men.

"So what do you think?" he asks with his arms up.

"You look so cute."

"Cute? I don't wanna be cute."

"Oh, excuse me, you're a manly man. You look very suave and handsome."

"That's better." He moves to sit on one of the couches in the dressing area, and I join him.

"So how are you feeling about the dance?"

"Good. It'll be fun."

That's it? That's all I get? "Do you have a date or are you going with friends?" His eyes widen at the mention of a date. Suddenly everything in this room is way more interesting than me. Hmmm. What is that about? "You can talk to me, you know. Is there someone you want to ask? Niecy maybe?" I ask, remembering how fidgety he was around her at Thanksgiving. I completely forgot to tease him about that then. To be honest, I forgot it even happened until this minute. I thought pregnancy brain was an exaggeration. Nope. It's the real deal, and it's a bitch to put up with.

He looks at me like I've lost my damn mind. "Niecy? Why would I ask Niecy?"

"I just thought that you might have a little crush on her."

He balks at that. "Crush on her?" What is he, a damn parrot? "I don't have a crush on Niecy."

I start to tell him that me thinks he doth protest too much, or whatever the phrase is, when he continues. "Niecy and I are just friends. And also it'd be really weird if we did like each other."

"Weird how?"

"She's Isaiah's niece."

I wait for him to elaborate but he doesn't, so I guess it's up to me to ask. "And that matters because?"

"She's practically family. You and Isaiah are together. And having a baby. That baby is gonna be both my niece and her cousin. That's disgusting."

Huh. Never thought of it like that. Isaiah and I aren't married though, so they'd both be related to Little Bean but not to each other, not even by marriage. Crazier things have happened, so who cares? I let him know that, but he proceeds to tell me that I'm crazy and that's gross. I guess the case is closed.

"So then…do you have a crush on anyone? Because you kind of freaked out there when I asked if you had a date."

His eyes drop to the floor. "Oh. There is this one girl in my class. But I can't ask her."

"Why not?"

He sighs. "Because she's her and I'm me."

What the hell does that mean? No, don't be combative. He's expressing his feelings to me. I need to give him the space and freedom to do that. But I swear if anyone at that school made my brother feel unworthy, I'm kicking everybody's ass. Teenagers or not, they can catch these hands. "Please explain." There, that sounded calm, right?

"We're too different. I'm the quiet guy focused on my grades and engineering crap. She's the cheerleader focused on what everyone else thinks of her. But she's so smart. She doesn't let anyone else see that, but I've seen it. I'm her tutor, but she doesn't even need me. I have a feeling she could run circles around me in math."

Holy shit. He's really into this girl. "I'm still not getting why you can't ask her to the dance."

"She has a boyfriend."

"Oh." That changes things.

"Yeah, but her boyfriend sucks. He thinks he's hot shit…umm, I mean stuff…because he's a sophomore and already captain of the varsity football team. Who cares?"

Oh Lord. My brother is trying to become Mr. Steal Yo Girl. "Is she happy with him?"

He hangs his head. "I don't know."

A painful silence passes between us. "Logan…"

He puts his hand up to stop me. "Don't. Okay? Just don't. I know what you're gonna say. I'm not gonna do anything." Ugh. I wish I could fix this for him. I wish I could fix this for this mystery girl, because I have a feeling her life isn't so perfect after all. I thought I had a couple more years before I had to tackle relationship problems, but we're jumping right in to the deep end.

"Listen. All you can do is be a good friend to her. A real friend. I get the feeling that she needs more of those. She has to make decisions for herself. If she chooses you then great. But if not, that's not on you. Maybe the timing isn't right. Maybe it's just not meant to be. But either way, you deserve to be someone's first choice."

"Yeah, you're right. Can I ask you a question and you not get mad?"

The fact that he even prefaced the question that way means I'm about to either get pissed or get my feelings hurt, but I'll be damned if I tell him he can't talk to me about something. "Go for it."

"If you weren't having the baby, would you and Isaiah be together?"

Ouch. Way to tap right into my insecurities. I was hoping he'd ask a question that would piss me off, but nope, he went straight for the gut punch. He seems to notice that I'm struggling to answer, and he pipes in again. "Don't get me wrong. I think Isaiah's a great guy. I wasn't sure at first, but I like him now. I just wanna make sure you're really happy. Because if you don't want to be with him you don't have to be. I can help take care of us. I'll get a job as soon as possible, and I don't have to go to college. I can just keep working."

Oh, hell no.

"No. Let me stop you right there. First of all, even if things don't work out with Isaiah and me, you don't need to worry. I got us no matter what. It's my job to take care of you. And it's my favorite job in the whole world, so I'll be damned if you try to take it from me, okay?" He nods his agreement. "If you don't want to go to college, I'm not gonna force you. You can be just as successful without a degree. But I know you have dreams of going, so if that's what you want then no one wants it for you more than I do. Second of all, to answer your question, I don't know if Isaiah and I would be together if it weren't for Little Bean." I decide to approach this with honesty. "I'd like to say we would be. I care about him a hell of a lot." I'm in love with him. "It may have taken the baby for us to get where we are, but I've never connected with any guy the way I have with him. So am I happy? Yes. I have him. I have you. I have Jada. I have Little Bean. We have a whole extended family who loves each of us to pieces. I could not be happier, Lo. I promise you that." He smiles, seemingly satisfied with my answer. "What about you? Are you okay? How's your heart?"

He chuckles. "That was so cheesy."

"It's a valid question."

"It's fine."

"Be honest. How are you?"

"Honestly?"

"That's what I just said, isn't it?" I nudge him with my shoulder to show I'm teasing.

"I'm good. Jada's always smiling now, which is really good. I'm having fun for the first time in a long time. You're here, which is cool. I've never lived in the same house as you twenty-four seven." Not that he remembers. He was two years old when I went off to college, and I never moved back home. "You're kinda cool, I guess. No complaints." He laughs, and I lightly slap his shoulder. I'll take it though. "I feel good about life. I'm happy." Hearing him say that takes a huge weight off my shoulders. That's all I want for both him and Jada. To be happy. To not fail them. "So are we good now? Can we lay off the heavy stuff for the day? You're giving the therapist a run for her money."

"Yeah, yeah, I guess. Okay, go take that suit off before you stink it up with your teenage boy odors." He takes off one of his loafers and waves it in front of my nose. It actually doesn't smell like anything, but eww, feet. I bow my head to get away from him. He follows me for a minute before I push him and he falls off his seat onto the floor. We laugh for longer than necessary until we catch the eye of another customer giving us the stink eye and then we laugh even harder.

"I'm going to change. Can we go get lunch before we go home?"

"Yeah, we can. I'm surprised you're hungry. You had a huge breakfast."

He had five scrambled eggs, a big-ass bowl of oatmeal, bacon, toast, and strawberries.

"I'm a growing boy." Jesus. Kids really do eat you out of house and home.

"Right." I drag out the word. "Well, get going so we can get you fed then."

I text Isaiah while I wait for Logan to change back into his regular clothes to check in on him and Jada. He says they're having a great time but wants to talk to me about something Jada said when I get home. My stomach is in knots. Logan's right, Jada has been smiling pretty much all the time these days, but I know she confides in Isaiah when something is wrong. I'm a little jealous of that, but I'm trying to rein it in because it's amazing that she feels so comfortable with him. At least she's confiding in someone.

Logan comes out, suit in hand, and I put my phone back in my bag. Isaiah says he has it handled, so I have to trust him. Right?

We opted to head to Logan's favorite barbeque spot. Little Bean decided that we wanted wings while Logan ordered ribs.

There's not much conversation happening right now. Logan is invested in his ribs, so he can barely spare a glance my way. That's fine because I'm having a full-on orgasmic moment with these wings until I spot a familiar face headed toward me.

Her attention is laser focused on me, but I have no idea where I know her from. And then it hits me. She's the woman who marched into Isaiah's place like she owned it. Alexis. Here we fucking go.

"I'll be right back." Logan grunts in response. Boys. I have no idea why Alexis is seeking me out, but I'm not about to let her put on a show in front of him. We're sitting at one of the outdoor tables, so I get up and start making my way inside.

She finally catches up to me as I turn the corner in front of the bathroom. "Hi again."

"Hi."

"Not sure if you remember me." I refrain from rolling my eyes. She knows damn well I remember her.

"Yep."

"Good, so we don't have to waste time with introductions." Ugh, this bitch. "I just wanted to warn you."

I already had zero interest in what she had to say, but somehow I just became even less interested. Warn me? Spare me the bullshit. I don't trust anything that comes out of her mouth. Part of me feels bad for her because she clearly has deeper feelings for Isaiah than he ever had for her, and she's desperate to hold on to him. But then I remember our interaction at his place all those months ago and what Isaiah told me about her plying him with alcohol and telling him stories about the ex he wasn't over, and that part of me shrivels up and dies. "Did you follow me here?" I ask.

She scoffs. "Don't flatter yourself. I was shopping a few doors down. You probably wouldn't be interested in the store." I'm wearing a Fresh Prince shirt—because I always joke that Logan is the Carlton to my Will—and maternity leggings. Alexis looks me up and down like my outfit is beneath her. I'm comfortable so I give zero shits. "Anyway, I saw you when I was leaving, so I figured I'd do you the courtesy of warning you."

"Warn me about what exactly?"

"Isaiah." Shocker. I raise my eyebrow and wait for her to get to the damn point. "He's not who you think he is."

"Ah, this is the part where you tell me he's not a good guy and yet he was good enough for you to keep fucking for years and want a relationship with. Got it. Thanks for the warning. I'm gonna go now."

She lets out a deprecating laugh and steps directly in my way. "I'm serious. You're having a baby with this guy. You should know the guy you're getting mixed up with. If only my friend Monica had listened to my warning, she'd be better off too." And now she has the nerve to bring up Monica to me. This is getting more pathetic by the moment.

"I appreciate the warning." Not. "But I think I'll take my chances."

"Suit yourself."

I step around her and make my way back to the table with Logan.

"You okay? You were gone for a while." There seems to be more bones on Logan's plate than there should be. Did he order more ribs while I was gone? I'm honestly impressed. I look at my empty plate. He didn't order more wings for me? That motherfucker.

"Yeah, I'm good." I catch the server's attention and order more wings to go along with a bunch of stuff for Jada and Isaiah.

We make our way back to the house where Jada bombards us looking for her mac and cheese that she claims to have smelled all the way from the driveway. Logan gives her a piggyback ride to the kitchen while Isaiah greets me with a breathtaking kiss.

"Hell of a greeting," I say. He just smirks in return.

"So how was the fitting? Did you get my boy right?"

"Yes, your boy looks really nice in his suit."

"You didn't tell him he looked cute, did you?"

"I can neither confirm nor deny this information." He gives my ass a smack before wrapping his arm around my shoulders.

"How was the rest of your day out?" I consider telling him about my run-in with Alexis, but what would be the point? If I mention it, I'm feeding into her bullshit just like she wants.

I look up into his gorgeous eyes and smile. "It was good." I lead him into the kitchen and tell him about Logan's annihilation of ribs before jumping into Logan and Jada's conversation and enjoying this family time.

CHAPTER
Eighteen

Isaiah

NINA AND I ARE SHOPPING FOR BABY THINGS TO ADD TO THE NURSERY. We did decide to go with a movie theme. We recruited Dom's sister, Fernanda, again to paint movie characters from children's movies on one of the walls, and the rest we painted plain gray. Our color scheme is gray and yellow. Nina refused to buy into the notion that a girl's room needed to be pink. Fine by me.

We have most of everything we need, but we're looking for a changing table and a few other things today. Nina points out a bassinet that we absolutely don't need but will probably walk out with anyway when I feel eyes on me.

I look up to see none other than Alexis walking toward us. Why the fuck is she in this store and why the fuck is she coming this way? I never answered any of her weird-ass texts, but apparently she's not getting the message.

"Hey there, Isaiah." Her voice is an octave higher than normal, and she doesn't even acknowledge Nina.

"Alexis."

"I was just walking by and I saw you in here, so I thought I'd say hi."

"Well hi. Bye." I go to turn Nina away from her when Alexis shifts, as if noticing Nina for the first time. She looks down at her stomach.

"You look adorable. Your extra weight looks like it stuck mostly to your belly. Good for you." She made sure to emphasize the "mostly." Jesus.

"Yeah, I've kept most of the weight off by staying away from carbs and bullshit. Come to issue me another warning?" Nina replies. My chest puffs out with pride at the snark, and I have a brief moment where I imagine Nina in a sexy wrestling outfit laying the smackdown on Alexis but then my ears catch up. Another warning? What the fuck is going on?

"I was hoping it wouldn't have to come to this, but somebody has to save this poor girl from you, Isaiah," Alexis replies snidely.

"What the hell are you talking about?" My blood is starting to boil.

"I just mean I hope you're a better father to this baby than you were to Monica's." My hands tighten into fists, and Nina gently places her hand on top of mine. I don't know what the hell is going on, but I'm getting more and more pissed.

"Stop talking in circles and say what you want to say."

"Oh, come on, Isaiah. You can give up the act now. We both know that Monica's son is in fact your son. It's a shame you let your pride get in your way. Just because Monica didn't want to be with you anymore didn't mean your son deserved to be abandoned."

No.

No.

She's lying. She's fucking lying. She has to be. Monica flat out told me the baby wasn't mine. Would she have lied to me just to make Harris happy? My gut tells me Alexis is lying, but I wouldn't put it past her to keep a secret like that to herself until she needed a trump card on me.

I know if I say anything to Alexis right now it will be cruel, so I don't say anything at all. I loop my arm around Nina's and lead her out of the store.

The drive home is a blur. I don't remember much—all I can see is red—but I do know that Nina didn't even attempt to talk to me. I can't blame her. I can only imagine the deadly look on my face right now.

I park in her driveway and she unbuckles her seat belt, but I make no move to get out.

"Hey. Are you coming in with me?" She looks hesitant to touch me, but she gives in and rests her arm on my shoulder.

"No, you go ahead."

"Isaiah."

"Go inside, Wildflower. I'll call you later. Okay?" She sighs and with a nod steps out of the car to head inside.

When she gets out, she bends over so that I can see her out the window. "You know, Alexis approached me on the street one day to warn me about you," she says with air quotes. "Warn me that you aren't a good guy. I didn't tell you about it because I knew it was all bullshit. And you do too. Don't let her tell you who you are." With that, she makes her way up the driveway and in the house. The door barely closes behind her before I'm peeling out of her driveway and headed to my own house.

I don't know if Alexis is lying or not, but I need to find out. Because if she's telling the truth then I've missed out on five years of my son's life. And that's something I can neither accept nor forgive.

CHAPTER
Nineteen

Nina

I KNOW SHE'S LYING. I DON'T BELIEVE FOR A SECOND ISAIAH WOULD deny his child. He told me himself that Monica said the baby was the other guy's child. The guy with a last name for a first name. Harris.

So yeah, I have no doubt in my mind that Alexis is lying. What I can't wrap my head around is why Isaiah got away from me as soon as possible and hasn't spoken to me since. I'm tired. I'm hungry. My legs hurt. I'm quite frankly not in the mood for bullshit. I just want him to talk to me. Let me be there for him.

I call him for the third time in the last four hours, and unlike the other two times, it doesn't even ring. It goes straight to voicemail. Did he turn his phone off to get me to stop calling?

I know he probably just needs time to process the bomb Alexis dropped on him, and I know I should probably give him space, but fuck being rational. I'm irritated that his immediate response was to shut me out. We're supposed to be a team. He's been feeding me this bullshit about how we're entering the biggest adventure of our lives and we need to be a unit.

I don't feel much like a fucking unit right now.

Am I being a brat right now? Quite possibly. Do I give any fucks? Zip. Zero. He has a lot of explaining to do.

The next day, I drive myself to my doctor's appointment since I still haven't heard back from Isaiah. I stopped calling him, but I did text him last night to ask if he was okay when what I really wanted to say was answer me right fucking now. No response.

I sit on the table in the exam room. The door opens, and I'm expecting the nurse but it's Isaiah walking in. He looks like shit. My initial reaction is to run to him and comfort him, but I dismiss that as Little Bean taking pity on her father because I'm still pissed, so I stay where I am.

"Hi. I wasn't sure if you were coming."

He makes eye contact with me for the first time since he's walked in, and I'm undone by the misery I see there. "I'm here." That's all he says. *But are you?* I want to ask him but I bite my tongue.

Dr. Hunter comes in at that point, so any potential conversation between Isaiah and me is wiped out.

"Mom, how are you feeling today?"

"You know, I've been better."

Her face morphs into one of concern. "Really? What's going on?"

"Oh no, physically I'm fine. I can barely see my feet and I still get leg cramps, but I'm fine. It's just my moods. I feel like my moods are being jerked around, ya know?" Yep, I'm definitely a brat.

"Ah, okay. Well, that's bound to happen. But you're feeling okay otherwise?"

"Yep, just great."

"And Dad? How are you doing?"

I turn to him then. "Yeah, Dad. How are you doing?"

He scowls at me. "I'm fine, Doc. Thanks for asking." He emphasizes the "Doc" in his sentence to let me know he wasn't addressing me. Fine, fuck you too.

Dr. Hunter chuckles to herself. "You know, just a friendly reminder that tensions and emotions always run high at this stage of pregnancy. Let's just remember you created a precious little human together."

And now we're being scolded by our doctor like children. I am going to smack this man.

"Let's listen to that heartbeat, shall we?" I lift my shirt, and she drips that cold goop on my stomach, spreading it around.

Little Bean's heartbeat fills the room, and every piece of anger I felt leaves my body. We made her. We really made her, and she's so perfect. She's not even fully formed yet, but she's perfect.

Okay, Little Bean. I hear you. But if you don't want me to be mad at your daddy he's going to have to get his shit together.

Isaiah and I walk outside together after the appointment, and I notice he parked right next to me. He walks by my side with his hand on the back of his neck.

When we reach the cars, he turns to me and clears his throat.

"I'm sorry," he says. Good start. "I shouldn't have run off last night, and I shouldn't have been an asshole today. My head is all over the place."

"So talk to me. We're supposed to be a unit, remember?"

He smiles, and it soothes my soul just a little. "I know. I know."

"What's going on in that stubborn head of yours?"

"Alexis is lying. I would never deny my child. Monica told me the baby was Harris's and that she didn't want to be with me anymore."

"I know that."

"But my problem is...what if Monica lied to me?"

"What do you mean?"

"What if her son was mine, and she lied to me about it because she wanted to be with Harris?"

Shit. Fuck. "Have you tried reaching out to her?"

"She blocked my number and blocked me on all social media, but I still had her fucking email address so I've been reaching out, but I've gotten no response. And I refuse to go through Alexis because she's manipulative as fuck."

"So what are you going to do?"

"I don't know, babe. I really don't. This is fucked. But now that this has been brought up, I can't shake it. I have to know."

"Okay, then we'll figure it out. Together." He pulls me in for a hug. I hold him and listen to his heartbeat for so long I almost forget we're standing in a parking lot. I can't imagine the torment he's going through in his mind. If Monica lied to him and her son is actually his child, he's missed out on so much of his son's life. That has to be eating him up.

He helps me get settled into my driver seat and follows me home so he can have dinner with the kids and me.

Jada is so excited to see him when he walks in. He slips a little bit when he does their special handshake, but she doesn't seem to notice.

He and Logan discuss architecture and robotics during dinner, and he helps Jada wash dishes after, but he seems off the entire time.

He opts to go home after dinner instead of spending the night. The chaste kiss he lays on my lips as he leaves is a blow to my heart. I feel like I'm losing him and a chunk of my heart at the same time.

I try not to give in to my selfish thoughts that night as I lie in bed. If Monica's son is his, he should absolutely be involved. I would welcome his son with open arms, but something tells me Monica wouldn't make it easy. She would probably refuse to let her son come visit Isaiah here. She'd make Isaiah go there all the time. And then what? He's a part-time dad to both of his kids? I hate everything about this.

I want to take away Isaiah's pain. I want to make this easy for him. But if Monica did lie to him, I struggle to regret that, because at the end of the day if she had told him the truth he would've stayed in Arizona and then I wouldn't have my Little Bean, and how can I possibly wish her away?

This fucking sucks.

CHAPTER
Twenty

Isaiah

I'M AN ASSHOLE.

A complete fucking asshole.

It's been a month since Alexis turned my life upside down, and I'm no closer to answers. I've been emailing Monica nonstop and she hasn't returned a single one. I'm losing my mind.

I'm not being fair to Nina. She notices I'm distracted all the time, but she's stopped calling me out on it. The kids don't seem to notice, thank God. I don't want to be in this funk anymore, but until I have answers I'm going to keep wondering.

Nina is seven months along. LB will be here before we know it, and I don't want to miss a moment. I think I know what I have to do, and fuck, I don't want to do it.

I pull out my phone to text her.

Me: What are you up to?

She answers immediately.

Nina: Currently basking in my shame

Me: Umm what?

Nina: Let me ask you a question

Nina: How many people does it take to tie a pair of shoes?

Me: Hmm I feel like this may be a trick question

Nina: *inserts girl shrugging emoji* take a guess

Me: 2?

Nina: Nope!

Nina: 3

Me: I'm dying for some context here

Nina: Well my shoes came untied and I'm no longer able to reach said shoes. So I recruited Jada to come help

Nina: And let me tell you six-year-olds do not make the best shoe tie-ers. She needs more shoes with laces. I've now noticed most of her shoes are fucking Velcros

Me: LOL so she couldn't tie your shoes?

Nina: She did. And then they came untied five minutes later. So she tied them again. Same result. So I had to recruit Logan. So far so good. Let's hope teenagers are better at this shoe tying thing.

I'm cracking up at this image but also kicking myself because I should be there doing that for her. Instead, I'm at my house obsessively trying to reach Monica.

Me: Here's hoping. If not, is it too early to sign him up for summer school?

Nina: LOL I mean we might have to see if we can send him back to first grade

Me: Oh even better that'll make school schedules easier if he and Jada go at the same time

Nina: *three crying laughing emoji* good point

Nina: How you doing today?

She asks me this every day. Checking on me when I don't deserve it. I need to hear her voice. I need to see her face.

Me: I'm okay. Need to talk to you though. Are you at Neon?

Nina: I am and if you're gonna come by I think Little Bean might appreciate a maple bacon doughnut from Sasha's

This woman. She's like a beacon of light in all the darkness.

Me: She told you that huh?

Nina: Oh yeah she's been very vocal about it

Me: Well who am I to deny her then?

Nina: I mean only a monster could

Me: See you soon

Nina: *kissy emoji*

I stop by Sasha's and grab a half dozen maple bacon doughnuts, because I'll be damned if I let LB down.

I walk into Neon, and Nina waddles—yes, she actually waddles now and it's the cutest fucking thing I've ever seen—from behind the bar toward me.

"You are a god amongst men," she says as she grabs the box from me. I pull her in for a lingering kiss before releasing her to unleash hell on those poor unsuspecting doughnuts.

"So what's going on?" She tries to sound as casual as possible but I can tell she's on edge anticipating what I might say.

I tear off the Band-Aid. "I think I need to go to Phoenix."

She stops midchew. "When?"

"Soon. Like this week. I want to go so I can be back in case you go into labor early."

"Bite your tongue. I won't be this early."

"Well, the earlier I go the better. If she's not gonna answer my emails and I can't reach her any other way then I need to confront her in person."

"You know where she lives?"

"I found out." I had to do some pretty heavy stalking to get my hands on that info, but I did it.

"Okay. Yeah, you should go."

"Really?" I don't know why but I expected her to have objections here. She's being really understanding, and I'm waiting for the other shoe to drop.

"Yeah, really. You need these answers, KP. You deserve them. And frankly, so do I. Because I need you to fully be here. And you can't do that until you know what your next move should be with her. So go. But hurry back, okay? And if he is yours, fight for him. If he's yours he's a part of this family, and we need him here."

And with that, I fall a little more in love with this woman.

I meet Nina and the kids at the house later that day because I want to tell them myself that I'm leaving. I know they have issues with travel, and I don't want them to think I'm abandoning them.

"So you're leaving?" Jada asks after I tell her about my upcoming trip.

"Yeah, just for a little bit. I have to take care of something, but I'll be back before you know it."

Jada's eyes are full of worry. "Okay. If you say you'll be back I believe you. I have my gymnastics tournament soon. Will you be back in time?"

"I wouldn't miss it for the world."

"You promise?"

"I promise." I hold out my hand for our special handshake, and she joins me enthusiastically. She gives me a hug and wishes me safe travels before running to her room.

"See you when you get back then."

"Yep. You'll have to take my place as Jada's tumbling partner till I get back. Think you can handle it?"

He smirks. "Better than you, old man."

I grab my chest in fake offense. "Ouch. That's low." He gives me a fist bump before heading to his room, no doubt to get lost in a book.

I'm so lucky to have these kids in my life.

When I land in Arizona, I'm already crawling out of my skin. At one point in my life I thought that this would be my home forever. I never wanted to leave Texas but Monica did, and I would've done anything to make her happy. It's crazy how times change.

I waste no time jumping into my rental car and heading to the address I found for her. I have so much energy running through me I can hardly sit still.

When I pull up to the house, I notice a brand new, sleek, silver Mazda CX-5 in the driveway. It's very shiny, very Monica. I take a quick peek inside and see a pair of Tory Burch sunglasses and a tube of lipstick sitting on the dash. Very Monica. There's also a booster seat and a stuffed giraffe in the backseat. These are all good signs. I get ahold of my nerves and march up to the door to knock.

The door opens and I'm face to face with the woman that haunted me for years. She's always reminded me of a slightly shorter Gabrielle Union. I used to get lost in her mocha eyes for hours. Now the spell's been lifted. Now I see her for who she truly is, and I'm okay with that. I'm here on a mission, nothing else. Nina's face flashes in my mind, and I realize how truly gone for her I am. The feelings I had for Monica couldn't even come close to what I feel for Nina and that's scary. I love her and those kids so much. I need to get back to them ASAP.

"Isaiah…what? What are you doing here?" She looks behind her, I guess to see if anyone notices I'm at the door.

"You blocked my number and blocked me on all social media, so I've been emailing you like it's fucking 2005 and you're not answering. We need to talk."

"Umm, I don't know what we could have to talk about that required you to fly out here."

I stare her down. "Monica."

She shudders against my gaze. "What?"

"Is Brandon mine?" I remember when Alexis told me that Monica and Harris named the baby Brandon. It was one of the names I told her I loved when I thought the baby was mine. That led to one of my many drunken hookups with Alexis.

She startles at my question and looks behind her again before stepping outside with me, forcing me back. She shuts the door behind her.

"Why would you even ask me that?"

"Cut the shit, Monica. I talked to Alexis and now I need answers from you." She scowls at the mention of Alexis, but it quickly falls to a look of remorse.

"I can't talk to you right now." I start to argue, but she cuts me off. "Please. I can't. Just...meet me at our spot later. At noon."

I scoff. She refers to the park as our spot. I mean it used to be. We spent long afternoons there. We even had sex against one of the trees late one night. But that was a lifetime ago. What game is she trying to play? I agree to meet her there at noon, and she quickly retreats inside, closing the door in my face.

A while later, I'm sitting on a bench in the park with my head in my hands. A throat clears, and when I look up, there she is. She looks more like the Monica I'm used to. Earlier, she wore sweatpants with a T-shirt and no makeup. Now, she has on barely-there shorts with a tight tank top, and her makeup is carefully applied. I realize now that the whole time I was with her she was always "on." I wonder how exhausting that is for her.

"Hey. Thanks for meeting me here." She sits on the bench, too close to me.

I scoot away so I have room to turn and face her. I want to look in her eyes as I ask this question. "Alexis told me that you said you told me the baby was mine but I didn't want anything to do with you or him because you had Harris. We both know that's a bold-faced lie."

"I never said that."

"But did you tell her that he was mine?"

She looks away then. Fuck. "Damn that Alexis, she can't ever keep her mouth shut. I didn't say he was yours." She hesitates before continuing. "I said that I wasn't sure if he was yours or not."

"What the fuck?"

"I was with you both at the same time, so it was kind of impossible to tell. But I wanted to be with Harris so I just said it was his."

"And you never found out for sure?"

"No." She looks ashamed, but I get the feeling there's more she's not telling me. There's a long pause between us. I don't even know what to say. Thank God she speaks first. "I miss you, Isaiah." Okay, I spoke too soon. I wish she hadn't spoken.

"Monica, don't."

"No, really. I'm just saying I miss you is all. The grass isn't always greener on the other side." Is she kidding me with this? "Don't get me wrong, I love Harris. We're happy. I just wonder sometimes, ya know? What would've happened if I had chosen you?"

What's crazy to me is that she says what if she had chosen me. As if there's no question that I would've stayed with her even after discovering she cheated on me with my boss and the identity of her baby's daddy was left up to question. Is she right? Would I have stayed if she had chosen me? I'd like to say no, but I was a fucking idiot then.

Not that I'm not an idiot now, considering I'm here instead of at home in Nina's arms.

"There's no point in living in what ifs, Monica."

She looks me up and down with her head tilted to the left. "You seem so different." I start to speak, but she cuts me off. "I want you to meet him. Brandon."

All the air rushes out of me. I came here expecting to confront her about what I was told and demand a DNA test. I didn't expect her to actually let me meet him until we had answers. I can't deny that the idea of meeting him makes me anxious and excited at the same time. He could be mine. My son.

"Okay. I'll come over and meet him tomorrow." She wraps her arms around me in a hug, and I give her a quick pat on the back before pulling back.

Something feels wrong here, but I push those thoughts aside and get as far away from Monica as I can.

When I get to my hotel, I see I have a missed call and text from Nina.

Nina: Hey, did you get there okay?

I call her back, and the sound of her voice immediately calms me. I tell her about the weird meeting with Monica and her request for me to meet Brandon.

She's quiet for a moment. "Did you ask her for the DNA test?"

"Not yet but I will. I just want to meet him first. See him with my own eyes. Maybe it'll be painfully obvious that he's not mine and I can rest easy."

"Oh, so you mean if you meet him and he's a cocky asshole who likes Katy Perry, he's clearly yours, but if he's shady and a fan of tube socks, he's obviously Harris's?"

I laugh. "Well, he's five so I don't know if we can call him an asshole."

"Oh, kids can absolutely be assholes. You mean to tell me you've never called a kid an asshole before?"

"Yeah, you're right. Malcolm was a pretty big asshole when he was younger. He's gotten better. Shit, I was definitely an asshole when I was a kid."

"Oh, and you think that's changed?" God, I just want to kiss her right now.

"But I'm your asshole now."

"There's a joke in there somewhere but I'm too tired to reach for it."

We keep talking about the Monica situation until she announces she needs a nap. I promise to check in with her and the kids tomorrow and that seems to soothe her worries. I want to tell her I love her, but I don't want the first time I say that to be over the phone. And then I just wonder why I haven't said it to her yet. I absolutely feel it and I say it in my head all the time, but I haven't said it out loud to her.

What the fuck is wrong with me?

CHAPTER
Twenty-One

Isaiah

T HE NEXT DAY I'M BACK AT THIS DAMN HOUSE TO TRY THIS AGAIN. Monica answers seconds after I knock and looks at me expectantly. I say a quick hi before stepping past her into the house.

I hear little footsteps coming toward me, and I gear myself up to meet my possible son for the first time. He comes skipping around the corner and I'm…underwhelmed. Not by him—he's adorable and I'm immediately captivated by him. But I was expecting to see him and have this overwhelming sense of clarity. I thought I would take one look at him and see my eyes or my dimple and the clouds would part, revealing the truth. But that doesn't happen. He looks just like Monica. I don't see any of me or Harris in this kid. Shit. There goes that miracle.

"Hey, little man, how's it going?" I get down on his level, and he approaches me cautiously.

"Brandon, this is Mommy's friend Isaiah. Can you say hi?"

"Hi." He gives me a shy wave and then goes back to looking at the floor. I notice he's holding a Transformers toy.

"Blitzwing, huh? I'm impressed. Most people don't know who that is."
His eyes light up. "You know who Blitzwing is?"

"Oh yeah. I know the Decepticons are the bad guys, but most of them
are really cool-looking."

"Yeah!" he exclaims. "Blitzwing turns into a jet AND a tank. How cool
is that? All my friends like Bumblebee or Optimus Prime, but that's boring."

I give him a high five for that, and he seems a lot more comfortable with
me now. I look up, and Monica is watching us with a strange look on her face.

"Where's Harris?" I ask.

She clears her throat as if it helps to clear her thoughts. "He's on a business trip." That's weird. I assumed she was acting shady when I showed up
yesterday because she didn't want Harris to see me, but if he's away what
was going on with her? Maybe she was just uncomfortable with me seeing
her in sweats with no makeup on. I don't know. I don't really care to figure
that out. My focus is on the cute kid in front of me.

"So, Brandon. Your Mommy was hoping I could hang out with you
guys today. Is that okay with you?"

He looks at Monica and back at me. "Yeah. Do you want to see the rest
of my toys?"

"You bet I do. I bet you have Starscream, don't you?" He beams at my
comment.

"Yeah!"

"I call dibs." I take off, leaving him behind even though I have no idea
where his toys are, but he quickly catches up and pulls ahead of me. I vaguely
hear Monica calling after us to have fun, but we don't stop.

We spend hours playing everything from Transformers to Connect
Four. Jada would love this. We even play a bunch of games on his Wii. I've
completely lost track of time hanging out with him, and I'm shocked when
Monica calls upstairs to say it's dinnertime. I wasn't planning on sticking
around for dinner, but he begs me to stay so of course I do. At dinner, he
has all the time to tell me about all the stuff he couldn't before because he
was too wrapped up in the games.

I learn that his best friend's name is Mikey. Mikey likes Bumblebee the best so in that I'm cooler than him but otherwise Mikey has me beat, so now I have to find and beat up a five-year-old for popularity.

His favorite thing at school is math. He really likes adding and subtracting but he doesn't know his "times tables and dividy stuff" yet because his teacher told him that's not until third grade.

He doesn't like his gym teacher because he makes the boys and girls pair up for games and girls are yucky.

In short, this kid is awesome. He's incredibly smart, and I'm having so much fun with him. I have no idea if he's mine, but I find myself wishing the results say he is. What would that look like? Would he spend half his time here in Arizona with Monica and Harris and half in Texas with me, Nina, and the kids? I hate that. I'm tempted to say if he is mine then I demand full custody for the next five years to make up for the years I was deprived, but I know that wouldn't go over well. I need to get a grip and figure this shit out once and for all.

Over the next few days, I find myself over at Monica's for hours spending time with Brandon. I'm soaking up all the moments now before the bubble bursts and we're thrust back into reality. Nina and I can't seem to get our schedules lined up. I keep missing her calls, and when I call her back she's already in bed. We're not texting as much either because when I'm with Brandon I'm giving him my undivided attention, learning everything I can about him. I also have a text from my mom asking me to bring Nina over for dinner one day next week so they can spend time together. I make a mental note to ask Nina about that when I get back.

I wake up one morning to a text from Nina.

Nina: Good morning. I'm just reminding you that Jada's gymnastics tournament is coming up. You think you'll be back in time for it?

I look at my calendar and see my reminder that her tournament is in two days. Shit. How did I not realize how much time has passed? I planned to only be in Arizona for two days max, but that was when I thought I'd be dealing solely with Monica and Harris. I thought I'd demand a paternity test and we'd all go to get one together, and I'd be on my way home waiting for the results to come via email. Apparently, that's not how it's done now. How the fuck would I know? I haven't watched *Maury* since I was a kid. Monica ordered a paternity test online, and it took three days for it to arrive. We're only testing my DNA since Harris isn't here for a swab, but my results are the only ones I care about anyway. When Monica sent the test in, she only put her email on the list to get the results. She said she didn't realize she could put additional emails on the form, but I know Monica and that shit was shady, so now I refuse to leave until I see those results with my own eyes the moment she gets them. The only bright side to this is that I'm getting to spend so much time with Brandon. I never thought I'd be allowed to actually meet him and get to know him. It's been amazing.

I look at my calendar and see that Nina's first Lamaze class is tomorrow. Shit. I'm fucking this up.

Me: I'll definitely be back for the tournament. But I'm gonna miss Lamaze. I'm so sorry.

Nina: Ciara will be my baby daddy for the day so you're off the hook. Just get your ass back here for Jada, okay?

Me: I will baby. I miss you guys.

Nina: We miss you too. How's everything going?

Me: He's amazing, Wildflower.

Nina: *sad puppy eyes emoji* Aww

Me: Hopefully the results come in soon. But what if he is mine? How do I tell him that the guy he's been hanging with as a sort of friend is his real dad? He'll probably hate me.

Nina: You can't think about that now. Enjoy the time you have

with him and we'll worry about next steps when we find out the truth.

It's exactly what I've been telling myself for the past week, but now that I know the results have to be coming soon I'm becoming anxious again.

I look down at my phone and panic because I've typed out the words "you're right. I love you." What. The. Fuck? I actually almost told her I love her for the first time in a damn text message. I must be out of my mind. I've been dying to say it, but this isn't the way. When I get home, I'm gonna lay it all out for her and tell her the truth. But until then I need my fingers to not type shit without my permission. I go to delete the message when a call comes in from Monica, who has now unblocked my number.

"Hello."

"Hey, Isaiah. Brandon was wondering if you could take him to the zoo today."

So far all of our hangouts have been at Monica's house with her nearby. She's actually going to let me take him somewhere by myself? I mean it's not like I'm some sort of predator, but I highly doubt Harris would be okay with this if he were here. I know I wouldn't be okay with that fucker anywhere near my son if the roles were reversed. I wonder if she even told him I'm in town.

"Oh. Yeah. I can definitely do that. Sounds fun."

"Great! He'll be so excited. I'll have him ready in the next thirty minutes. Is that enough time? It's better to get there earlier in the day."

"Sure. I'll be there to get him soon."

"Okay, see you soon."

"Monica?"

"Yeah?"

"Did you get those results yet?" I need to get my ass home.

She lets out a frustrated sigh that does absolutely nothing but piss me off. "I told you I would tell you as soon as they come in, Isaiah."

"I know what you said but I'm just making sure you're telling me the truth. Aren't they only supposed to take two days?"

"Yes. Two business days. You forget we sent it in on a weekend. I'll call them, okay?"

"I can call them."

"I said I'd take care of it, Isaiah. Jesus. Look, if you don't want to see Brandon today I can just..."

"I didn't say that." There's no way in hell she's taking this day from me. We don't know what the results are going to be. If this is my last day hanging out with him, I'm gonna make it a great one. "Just call them today. Please. I'll be there soon to pick Brandon up."

"Okay. Bye." I press the red end button before she has a chance. I jammed my finger against the button but it did nothing to curb my anger. Times like this are when I miss fucking flip phones. Slamming that shit closed when you're mad is so satisfying.

I go back to my texts with Nina.

Me: I gotta go baby. Have a good day, okay?

Nina: You too. Remember what I said.

I take a minute to look up flights back home. Jada's tournament is in two days. I should really fly home tomorrow, but I don't want to miss those results hitting Monica's phone. The flights for tomorrow night look shitty. There are no more nonstop options available. It looks like my only options for tomorrow night are a four fifteen p.m. flight that makes one stop in Denver and gets me home close to midnight or a two fifty p.m. flight that makes one stop in Houston and gets me home close to ten p.m. A flight from Houston to Austin means it would probably be on a tiny ass plane. No thank you.

I could fly back the day of Jada's tournament. There's a nonstop flight that leaves at six a.m. and gets me home a little after ten a.m. Jada's tournament starts at noon so I could make it. That doesn't leave a lot of room for error though.

I can't risk it. I book the four fifteen p.m. flight for tomorrow night and head out to get Brandon.

"Giraffes, duh!" I chuckle at Brandon's energy. I asked him what we should see first and that was his response. So giraffes it is.

"So what's so cool about giraffes, buddy?"

He turns to me like I'm the dumbest human he's ever come across. "Have you ever seen a giraffe?"

"I have."

"Then you know why they're cool!" Well, when you put it that way, it makes perfect sense. Duh.

We get to the giraffe exhibit, and it is pretty cool how much space they have here. Brandon is fascinated by one giraffe in particular. He's taller than the rest of his friends, and one of his spots looks like a big heart.

Did you know that you can adopt a giraffe at this zoo? Me either, but you can.

You just pay a fee and you get a certificate with your name on it that says you adopted a giraffe, a photo of your giraffe, a fact sheet about your giraffe, and a stuffed giraffe to take home.

Two hours later when we're leaving the zoo and I'm watching Brandon swing his new stuffed giraffe around with pride, I know it's the best seventy-five dollars I ever spent.

We decided that the real giraffe's name is Blitz, and the stuffed animal giraffe's name is Blitz Jr.

It was on this day that I surpassed Mikey as the coolest guy Brandon knows.

CHAPTER
Twenty-Two

Nina

I NEED A NEW PAIR OF PANTIES.

And not in the sexy "I'm so wet" way. No. In the "I peed a little yet again" way.

Little Bean gives zero shits that she is sitting on my bladder and I have to go every five minutes.

A sneeze? I pee.

A cough? I pee.

A laugh? I pee.

Lying around doing absolutely nothing but existing? I pee.

It's getting ridiculous. I've considered wearing an adult diaper to bed just to minimize the number of times I have to get up and pee in the middle of the night. That's sexy, right?

I'm diaperless out in the wild right now, and it's not going well for my poor bladder and panties. I'm sitting at lunch with Sasha and Ciara. I have no idea if Isaiah has told Sasha what's going on with him, so I refuse to talk about him. I've talked about it with Ciara and Brittany because I needed a sounding board, but I didn't want to cause drama between the siblings. Lincoln already knows what happened between Isaiah and Monica all those years ago, so I didn't feel that telling Ciara was a breach of trust. Besides, the girl is a vault. I asked her not to mention any of my concerns to Lincoln, and I know she won't. Case in point, her not telling him about my pregnancy. Sasha may be my best friend but she's his sister and I don't feel it's my place to tell her about Isaiah's history.

I'm losing my mind over Isaiah.

He was planning to only be gone for a couple of days, but it's been eight days. He says he's going to make it back in time for Jada's gymnastics tournament, but he hasn't even given me any return flight information. He hasn't given me much at all. We've barely talked the entire time he's been gone. We're always missing each other. I did manage to get ahold of him this morning, and he put on a good front but I know he's spiraling. Well, so am I.

I hate that I'm feeling insecure right now, but that's just where we are. Do I think he's licking, fucking, sucking, and doing all the sexy things with Monica? No. But do I feel like he's wondering what his life would've been like if things had gone differently with her back then? Yes. How could he not? If Brandon is his child then he's missed out on five years of his life, and I'm sure he's regretting that and wondering what they could've had. That's the family he's always wanted. I'm the family he never asked for but got anyway.

"Nina, did you hear what I said?" Sasha asks.

Was she talking? Damn. I must've zoned out.

"No, sorry. What was that?" Ciara gives me a look of concern. I don't meet her eyes.

"I said my mom told me to ask you when you and Isaiah are coming over for dinner next week. She said Isaiah hasn't given her an answer."

"We're supposed to come to dinner next week?"

"Isaiah didn't tell you?"

No. He didn't. What am I supposed to make of that? He doesn't want to take me to dinner with his parents? Is he questioning our relationship?

"No, I think he did, I just forgot. Pregnancy brain." Of course my instinct is to protect him. "I don't think we picked a day yet. It's just been crazy. Tell her I'm sorry."

"No biggie."

"Is that…" Ciara's question is cut off by my bartender, Lindsay, plopping down in the seat next to me. Where did she come from?

"Hey boss lady. Hey Ci. Hi there." She greets us before darting her eyes around the restaurant. I'm used to Lindsay being happy, bubbly, and rambling about something, but I've never seen this nervous-ass look on her face before.

"Lindsay, are you okay?" I ask.

"Umm, yeah. Yeah. I'm fine. Can I join you for a second?"

"Of course you can. Why do you look like you stole something?"

"Oh fuck. Fuck." She looks down at her lap. This is so fucking weird but comical.

"I just need to know if I should be reaching for a weapon or my phone to call a lawyer." Ciara picks up her steak knife and Sasha follows her lead and puts her car keys between her knuckles. I'm pretty sure my big belly could take on anything, so I grab my phone poised to call nine-one-one.

Her eyes widen before she breaks out into laughter. "No, no! It's nothing like that. Sorry to be a weirdo. I just saw my ex-boyfriend outside. I didn't even know he was back in town, so I ran in here to avoid him and saw you guys, so I thought I could sit and chat until he was gone but it looks like he's in here now too."

"Which one's your ex?" Sasha asks.

"The guy standing by the host stand."

With no discretion at all, we all crane our necks to see the host stand, and our collective jaws drop. Standing at the host stand is a tall drink of water. He's at least six feet tall with gorgeously tanned skin and dark shaggy hair. His broad shoulders are straining beneath his T-shirt. His confidence is clear as day.

"Okay, so is this the type of ex whose ass we need to beat? I would hate to mess up that pretty face, but I'll do it for you," Ciara offers.

"The breakup was just really embarrassing for me, so I'd rather not talk to him."

"Well, I hate to break it to you but you've been spotted." Her eyes fly upward to find the mystery ex walking toward us.

"Shit." She hops down to her knees under the table.

"Oh, honey. I feel like this has the potential to be more embarrassing than your breakup story," Sasha teases and I elbow her.

We pull our chairs in to cover Lindsay as best as we can right as the tall drink of water arrives at our table. Now that I see him up close, I see that he has piercing green eyes as well.

"Good afternoon, ladies."

"Hi there. Do we know you?" Ciara asks.

"I'm afraid not. My name is Wes. I came to say hello to Lindsay, but it's a pleasure to meet you as well." He holds his hand out to her.

She takes it. "Who? Never heard of her. I'm Ciara."

His eyes dance with amusement, and he bites his bottom lip. "Hi, Ciara. Ah I see. My mistake—I just assumed the woman hiding under your table was her."

Lindsay lets out a small groan. Sasha coughs to try to cover it up, but it obviously doesn't work.

I'm not letting my girl go out sad like this. "Oh, did you say Lindsay? I thought you said Rensley. She's not hiding; she's down there helping me. I can't really bend over anymore because I'm extremely pregnant, so she's searching for my earring. I'm Nina by the way." Not one to be left out, Sasha introduces herself as well.

He reaches his hand out to shake Sasha's, but when he grabs my hand, his eyes flick up to my ears. My ears that are each adorned with a hoop earring.

Lindsay takes her cue and pops up from the floor, pretending to hold something in her hand. "I found it, Nina! Told you I could find it no problem. Oh, Wes. Funny seeing you here. Do you know my friends?" If this whole situation wasn't obviously some bullshit, she'd be really convincing.

"Hi, Lindsay. No, I was just getting to know them. It's good to see you though. You look great."

"Oh, um. Yes. Thank you."

"We should talk."

"I don't think so."

He starts to say something else, but Ciara cuts him off. "Sorry, do you two know each other?"

"Unfortunately," says Lindsay.

"We used to date," says Wes.

"Oh really? She's never mentioned you. Was this before that hot Brazilian boxer you were dating, Lindsay? What's his name? Sergio?" Wes's lips part in shock, and surprise flashes across Lindsay's face for just a moment before she schools her lips into a smirk.

"Yep. Wes was just a footnote in my story." Ouch.

Wes nods slowly before looking around the table at us and clearing his throat. "Well, it was nice meeting you ladies. Congratulations, Nina. Take care, Lindsay." We all watch him walk to the host stand before turning back to Lindsay who releases a deep breath as she sits back down.

"Thank you, guys. Seriously, that was amazing. Sorry for making your lunch awkward."

"Are you kidding? That was better than TV. Consider myself subscribed to your season," Sasha announces.

We all fall into a fit of laughter. I'm so happy to have a distraction from my own drama that I don't even mind that I just peed a little more.

CHAPTER
Twenty-Three

Isaiah

THE NEXT AFTERNOON, I'M APPROACHING MONICA IN THE KITCHEN while Brandon is washing up for lunch.

"Do you want to stay for lunch?" Her voice is hopeful, and I start to decline because I just want to go back to my hotel and call Nina before I head to the airport, but then Brandon runs into the kitchen having heard his mother's request and asks me to stay. Damn, I'm a sucker.

Throughout lunch, I keep imagining Jada and Logan sitting there telling me about their days. They would love Brandon. I miss them. I wish we were all at a table together right now.

After lunch, Brandon gives me a high five and then runs to go play, and Monica immediately starts talking my ear off. *Remember when we got so drunk at the movie theater that one time and couldn't find our way out? Remember when we had that sexy night at the park? That was fun. Remember when we stayed at that hotel for the weekend just to get away, and we played ding-dong ditch for an hour?*

She's been trying to go down memory lane with me since Brandon left the table, and I'm trying to figure out her motivations. I don't care to talk about this shit.

"So what will you do if the results say you're the father? Will you move back to Arizona? I could help you look for places in this school district."

"No, I wouldn't move back here. I wouldn't leave Nina." I told her earlier in the week that my girlfriend is pregnant, and she seemed put off by that but congratulated me. I didn't mention Logan and Jada to her because I don't want her to know too much about my personal life. I only told her about Nina because I figured Alexis would tell her anyway.

A look of rage crosses her face at my comment about not leaving Nina. I don't know what she expected from me. If Brandon is mine I will of course be there for him, but I'm not uprooting Nina and the kids to do that.

"We'll have to figure out a joint custody arrangement, Monica. It'll be okay. We'll figure it out, but I'll be here for him." She starts fidgeting in her seat, and now I'm beyond suspicious.

"Monica." She finally meets my eyes. "Do you already have the results?" She averts her gaze again, and anger consumes me.

"Monica, what the fuck?" I shout. Suddenly, she lunges forward in an attempt to kiss me. At least I think she's trying to kiss me. She doesn't have a weapon so I don't think she's trying to kill me, but she lunges so aggressively, I can't be sure.

I jump up from the table. "What are you doing?"

"Kiss me, Isaiah." She closes her eyes and reaches for me again but I sidestep her. Jesus. This has to be a joke.

"You've lost your damn mind."

"No, I lost my mind when I let you go years ago. Come on, we were so good together. We had fun."

"Yeah, fun. And that's why you said I was a joke and couldn't be taken seriously as a partner, right?"

"I was just saying what Harris said. I didn't really think that. I miss you. Don't you miss me? We could be a real family." She reaches for me again and I sidestep her again, getting even angrier with every turn.

"Stop it. I'm not Harris. I'm not going to hook up with you. I'm sorry you're not happy in your relationship, but I am—and I'm not a cheater." Her eyes narrow at that and she scowls at me. She stomps over to the couch in the living room and sits down. I follow her but remain standing with my arms crossed.

"Let me see the results, Monica," I demand. She sucks her teeth but grabs her phone off the coffee table and pulls up the email. She tosses the phone in my face. I skim the entire email until I get to the bottom.

Probability of paternity: 0%.

I'm not Brandon's father. I can't deny the stab of sadness that cuts through my heart with that realization, but I'm back to feeling pure anger when I scroll back up to the top of the email and see that she got the results three days ago.

Three fucking days.

I look over at Monica, and her eyes are brimming with tears. I can't even look at her right now. I leave her sitting there and go to find Brandon playing in his room.

"Hey, buddy."

"Hey."

"I wanted to come say bye to you."

"You're leaving?"

"Yeah, I have to catch a plane back home."

He hangs his head for a moment but then looks back up at me. "You're not coming back, are you?"

I feel another piece of my heart crack. I'd love nothing more than to stay in touch with him, but I have no legal rights, and I know better than to think Monica and Harris will allow their son to spend time with me after this. "I wish things were different, buddy."

"Me too. It was cool having you to hang out with. My dad is gone a lot. He goes on trips for work." Fuck, as if I needed more reason to want to punch Harris in his goddamn face.

"He loves you though, buddy. Adulting is hard. You've got your mommy here all the time though, and she's fun, right?"

"Yeah." He looks somber. Shit. How can I leave him like this?

I take a look around his room until I see his tablet. I remember him telling me that Harris bought him the tablet to watch movies and YouTube videos on.

"Buddy, can you call people on your tablet?"

He nods. I walk over and grab his tablet and plug my number into it. I save myself under Buddy and hand it to him so he can see my contact.

"If you ever need anything. Anything at all. You call me. Okay?"

"You mean it?"

"Absolutely." His face lights up. He reaches up and gives me a huge hug. I pat the top of his head and leave before the tear falls down my cheek.

I walk right past Monica to the front door, but I stop at the last minute and turn to her. "That kid deserves the best of both of you. So you need to get your shit together. Goodbye, Monica." I turn around without waiting for her response and open the door.

How the hell did my life become this much of a clusterfuck?

I don't even call Nina when I get back to my hotel room. I just pack up my shit and head to the airport.

We made it to Denver with no problem, but when we landed the sky looked ominous. Almost like it was about to fuck up my entire life.

Everyone exits the plane, and I begin my three-hour layover before my flight home.

I turn my phone off of airplane mode to find three text messages. The first is from Monica.

Monica: I'm sorry it had to be like this.

I'm still shaking with rage at her. Three days she sat on those fucking results when she knew I had to be home. And then she tried to get me back? What a sick fucking joke. I don't even want to acknowledge her, but I feel the need to make one last plea for Brandon.

Me: I wish you and Harris the best. You raised an incredible kid. Put him first

I delete Monica from my contacts and move on to the next text. It's from an unknown number.

Unknown: *image*

Unknown: So u can have Blitz w u 2

It's Brandon. He sent me the picture of our giraffe, Blitz. This kid is too good for this world, or at least the parents he was given. I quickly save his contact information in my phone and respond.

Me: Thanks buddy. You're gonna have to take care of our guy with lots of visits, okay?

His response comes immediately.

Brandon: OK. I can get mom 2 take me

Me: Awesome. Tell him I said hi when you see him

Brandon: OK. Thank u

Me: You're welcome buddy.

I don't know how often I'll hear from him when Harris gets home and gets wind of what happened over this past week, but I'll always be on his side. The last text is from Nina.

Nina: Hey I know you're taking off soon. I'm on my way to Lamaze with Ci. LB's constant kicking right now tells me that she's vehemently against this class. That or she misses her papa. Be safe. Let me know when you land

I can barely contain the smile on my face. This woman is everything I've ever wanted and nothing I deserve. I can't wait to grab her, kiss her, and tell her I love her.

Me: She's a daddy's girl already. I'm in Denver for my layover now. I miss you all. See you soon

At least I thought I would.

But my three-hour layover turned into a nine-hour delay. Fucking Denver and its fucking snowstorms.

The airline has shuttled us all to a hotel close by to accommodate us for the inconvenience. I consider just getting a rental car and driving the fourteen hours to Austin, but the storm is really bad. I'd likely just get stuck and make everything worse.

As the hours tick away, I realize I'm not going to make it back in time for Jada's tournament. I'm going to have to call and break that little girl's heart and my own in the process.

CHAPTER
Twenty-Four

Nina

I SAIAH ISN'T GOING TO MAKE IT TO MY FIRST LAMAZE CLASS. I CAN'T deny that it hurts. It was his idea for us to sign up. I was planning on relying on Sasha, Reggie, Trinity, and Angela for their expertise, but he insisted that we'd both feel more confident going into the birth if we took these classes. Plus, it would probably be entertaining. So am I a little irritated and sad that he won't be here for the first one? Yes. But Ciara volunteered to be my baby daddy in his place so I plan to make the most of it.

I've been making the most of a lot of things over the last month. I've been supportive of Isaiah since he learned of Monica's potential betrayal. Second betrayal, I guess. When he came to me and said that he needed to fly to Phoenix and confront Monica in person, I supported that. Of course I did. If he's actually Brandon's father, they both deserve that truth. What I didn't expect was to feel like an afterthought the moment he landed. We've barely spoken since he's been there. A text conversation here and there. I've handed this man the power to completely break me, and he's doing just that.

He hasn't even checked in with Logan and Jada since that first day, and

I think that's what hurts the most. They've grown so attached to him, and the last thing they need is for another adult to abandon them.

"Knock, knock, bitch. You don't hear me?" Ciara is standing in the doorway of my bedroom. Shit, I really didn't hear her come in?

"You wanna put some pants on or is this the look you're going for? I'm all for it. If there's ever a time to dare society to say shit to you it's when you're seven months pregnant." I look down and realize I'm standing here in a T-shirt and panties. Okay, it is time to get my shit together. I laugh at Ciara and send her down to grab waters for us. I change into my T-shirt that has Logan deep in thought on it. It seems only fitting. I pull on a pair of sweatpants because even maternity jeans would be too much of a chore today. I step into my Adidas slides because I refuse to ask Ciara to tie my shoes for me, even though I know she would do it without a second thought.

Little Bean is kicking like crazy today. I texted Isaiah to check in even though I know he's boarding soon and let him know her kicking probably meant she misses him. When he finally got back to me with his flight information, I was so relieved to see he'd be coming home tonight so he'd be here for Jada tomorrow. I suck back the tear that threatens to fall down my face. No. An alien in the form of a sappy bitch is taking over all my emotions, and I'm not having it today.

I head downstairs, and Ciara ushers me out the door.

"You ready for some breathing exercises?" she asks once she pulls out of the driveway.

I chuckle. "If they show a birthing video I'm walking out."

"Hey, don't you wanna be prepared for what's gonna happen?"

"Nope. I'd rather be blissfully ignorant about that part."

"Yeah, I can't blame you. If I see some gross stuff today, I may just pull my birth control out of the trash when I get home today."

I turn as much as my belly will allow to face her. "You and Linc are trying?" I'm so excited right now.

"Not really trying, more like letting whatever happens happen. For now at least. But are we fucking like rabbits? Absolutely."

"I'm so happy for you guys. This is exciting! Little Bean really could have a little cousin close in age."

"Imagine all the trouble they would get into."

"We would need so much liquor to survive."

"Good thing you almost own a bar then. If a couple of cases go missing a month you won't even notice."

"Exactly. Man, I can't wait to be in the bar without judgment though."

"Judgment from what?"

"Our fucking patrons. Well, the college kids who come in couldn't give two shits, but the older crowd really have a problem with a pregnant woman being behind the bar. As if I'm drinking myself or like I can remove Little Bean from my womb during my shift and then put her back after."

She scoffs. "How have I missed this? People are so dumb. Point 'em out next time. I'll roast the fuck out of them." And she really would too. She may be a smartass, but she's usually not rude unless you fuck with someone she cares about. She lived her life in fear for two years, and she refuses to ever go back, so I would pity the fool who tried her next.

"No, it's okay. Fuck 'em. It's just the beginning of the mom shame that I'm sure is to come. I plan to bask in it. I think Chrissy Teigen has a recipe in her cookbook that calls for the tears of your haters, so I'll get to put that to use."

A burst of laughter falls out of Ciara. "Oh shit, I'm crying." I'm momentarily afraid for our lives when she laughs so hard she closes her eyes, but I can't help but laugh with her. I definitely needed her with me today.

We pull up to the Lamaze class, and there are seven other couples waiting for the class to start. The instructor walks in and greets everyone. She looks like a blonde Helena Bonham Carter. Something tells me this class is going to be wild.

For the next two hours, Ciara and I try and fail to contain our laughter. Between the couple who keep asking the instructor to slow down so they can take copious notes to the husband who threw up when the childbirth video was shown while his wife yelled at him that he better not do that in the delivery room, the entertainment was endless. I did learn a lot of useful information in the class though, and I managed to sit through the childbirth video without issue because I was so distracted by the other couple. When she drops me off at home, Ciara tells me that she reserves the right to attend any classes Isaiah has to miss. Honestly, right now I'm tempted to kick him to the side and have Ciara come to all of the classes with me.

As if he heard me talking about him, my phone rings and his number flashes across the screen.

"Hello?"

"I am so sorry."

I sigh. "You're not going to make it, are you?"

"There's a huge snowstorm happening here in Denver. They're saying we're definitely not flying out tonight. I might be able to still make it, but I'm just not sure."

I know he can't control the weather but, fuck, Jada is going to be crushed.

"Tell Jada I'm so sorry. I really am sorry. I'm trying my best." His voice is laced with desperation, but I can't find it in me to sympathize right now.

"I have to go."

"I'm sorry, Nina."

"I know. Just be safe." I hang up before he says another word.

I drag my feet to Jada's room to break the news to her.

"But he promised!" she yells.

"I know, Mini. He's trying his best, but the weather is causing problems with flights."

Her eyes widen in fear. "Is he going to make it back? Is something gonna happen to the plane?"

"He'll be okay. They won't let him get on the plane until it's safe to go in the air. He'll be back safe and sound." I make a mental vow to take Jada and Logan on a nice vacation one day after Little Bean is born. I don't want them associating trips and travel with abandonment and death their whole lives. I want them to fully experience life outside of the bubble of this state.

Jada calms down with my assurances and falls asleep in my arms. I slip out of her room as quietly as I can. When I'm back under my own covers, I let that sappy bitch alien take over, and I cry myself to sleep.

The following afternoon, we get to the tournament, and Jada's able to say a quick hi to everyone before she runs to join her team and coach.

Everyone is here. Logan, Isaiah's parents, Lincoln, Ciara, Sasha, Carter, Nevaeh, Reggie, Michael, Malcolm, Niecy, Dominic, Kai, and Shane. Everyone but Isaiah. No one asks me where he is, so I assume they already know, which is good because I don't have it in me to talk about it right now.

Jada does really well in her tournament. She wins first place in the balance beam event and second in the uneven bars event. She smiles at all of us as she's being given her award, but it falls a little when she sees that Isaiah didn't make it. That look of heartbreak in her eyes has me ready to fight the world.

Everyone comes back to the house with us to congratulate Jada. Jada beams at all the attention and she jumps at the chance to pull everyone in for a board game, but her eyes fall every time she looks toward the door.

A few hours later everyone is gone but Logan, Jada, and me. We've just finished our dinner when Isaiah walks in. Jada gasps but turns her head away from him. He walks right over and sinks down to his knees in front of her.

"Hi there, Flash, I'm so sorry. I know I disappointed you today."

She turns toward him and throws her finger in his face. "You promised. You promised you would be there."

"I know I did. I wish I could've been there."

"No you don't. You lie!" she screams. "You broke your promise, so you're not my friend anymore. You're just like them." She doesn't have to say who "them" is for us to know she means our parents, and I know that cuts Isaiah deep. She gets up from the table and runs to her room, slamming the door. Logan looks at Isaiah and follows her. I hear him gently knocking on her door before I turn my attention back to Isaiah.

"Fuck. I really fucked up."

"Yeah. You did." There's no sugarcoating that. Jada was counting on him, and he let her down. To a six-year-old, that's the end of the world.

"I can't believe I fucked up this badly. I was so busy freaking out about the delay that I didn't even tell you what happened." He proceeds to tell me how Brandon isn't his child and how Monica hid the results from him for days. While I feel bad for him that he basically lost Brandon for a second time, I can't help but be angry that we're sitting here having this conversation. He knew that he made a promise to Jada, and instead of leaving earlier to ensure he got back in time for her, he chose to stay until the last possible minute— just so that he could read the results off of Monica's phone instead of having her forward him the results or calling the fucking lab himself.

"I think you should leave," I tell him. He looks as though I've slapped him.

"You mean that?"

"Yeah. I think everyone needs some space."

"But I can't just leave Jada like this. And does this mean you need space from me too?" He looks so lost, but I can't be his life raft right now.

"Jada doesn't want to see you right now, and you need to be okay with that. And yes, we need a little space. Jada and Logan have been through enough disappointment for a lifetime, and I don't have the time or the energy to bring them back from you disappointing them too."

"Nina, you know I didn't do this on purpose."

"I know. But I think you need time for yourself too. To figure out what you really want."

"I want you. I want them."

"And I believed you at first. But this whole situation has opened my eyes. Whether subconsciously or not, Isaiah, you bumped us to second place when you thought the family you originally wanted might be within reach."

His eyebrows shoot up to his hairline. "That's bullshit, Nina. Don't do this."

"Don't do what?"

"Use this as an excuse to push me away."

"An excuse?"

"You've had one foot out the door this entire time."

And now I'm the one that looks shocked. "Now who's spewing bullshit?"

"Still you. Oh, come on, Nina. Not wanting me to move in with you. Wanting to 'wait and see where we're at when the baby comes'? Throwing in my face that the kids were your responsibility and not mine? You were never gonna let yourself fully trust me. You wanted me to fuck up so you could have an excuse to run from me."

Fuck this and fuck him.

"I did trust you, Isaiah, and I shouldn't have." I gesture toward the door. He looks like he wants to argue with me some more but then he just hangs his head and leaves.

I can't help but feel like we'll never recover from this.

CHAPTER
Twenty-Five

Nina

It's been two weeks since I've seen Isaiah. We had a doctor's appointment immediately after everything went down, but we didn't talk much and he didn't come back to the house with me after.

The kids are feeling his absence too. Logan is quiet again. He hasn't picked up one of his architecture books, and I think it's killing him. Jada hasn't been in the mood to play any sort of games. When I ask them if they want me to call Isaiah over, Logan defers to Jada and Jada insists she doesn't want to talk to him. I think Logan is denying the fact that he misses Isaiah out of loyalty to Jada, and Jada is too heartbroken and scared to forgive him right now.

I have no idea how to move forward. I've talked to the kids' therapist, and she says they're working through it but it may take some time.

Ciara and I are behind the bar, taking inventory and filling in order sheets. We've been fairly quiet all morning, so I'm waiting for the bubble to burst.

"Okay, I'm just gonna ask." That didn't take long.

"Have you talked to Isaiah since that night?" She knows the answer to that. I mean she's married to his brother, so I'm quite sure she's already spoken to him but I indulge the conversation.

"No. I haven't."

"Are you going to? I mean your next Lamaze class is coming up, and as much as I have thoroughly enjoyed the last two, don't you think he should be at the next one?"

"No one is stopping him from coming to those."

She tilts her head at me. "Okay, fine. So I'll tell him to go to the next one in my place."

"Fine."

"Break it down for me here. What exactly is going on here? Are you guys broken up? Is this just a fight? I don't understand." She's not the only one.

"I don't know. I don't know what I'm doing. And I don't mean about the baby. I would never keep him away from his child. I just mean about us."

She directs me to sit at one of the stools so I do. "Well, what do you want to do?"

"I don't know. I love him so much. He has the power to completely destroy me, and I just don't know if I can trust that power in his hands when I have three kids to think about who need me whole."

"But are you really whole without him?"

I scoff. "Are you saying I need a man to complete me?"

"Don't make me fight you. You know I'm not saying that. But the thing is a lot of us are walking around thinking we're whole until we meet the person who completes us and we realize we were never whole in the first place. It's okay to admit that." She pushes a glass of water in front of me, and I gulp it down.

"Well, I need to be whole on my own. For them."

"Nina, if you love him then you have to trust him. You have to trust that you can give him that power to destroy you and know that he won't abuse it because he's giving you the same power over him."

I know she's right, but I just don't know if I can do it. I don't know if I have it in me to hand him that trust.

"It didn't feel like I had that power over him when he was in Phoenix. I felt like I was his second choice. I don't want to be anybody's second choice, Ci. I don't even know if he loves me. He's never said it. He wanted me to take all these big steps like letting him move in, but he couldn't even tell me how he felt. I don't want to look back on our time and realize he was only with me out of obligation."

She gives me a sympathetic smile. "The words may not have been said but it's clear that he feels them. I know he handled it poorly. Believe me, I lit into his ass about this. But he needed that closure. It would've completely consumed him if he didn't get it, and no one understands that better than I do. All I'm saying is you should at least hear him out. I know for a fact he's miserable right now."

"I'll think about it," I relent. "I have more than myself to think about, and I don't want to put the kids in a position to get their hearts broken either."

"Okay. I respect that. Just remember that they are going to go through heartbreak in life no matter what. They've already been through so much. You can't shield them from that. All you can teach them is how to come out on the other side of it."

I'm trying to listen to my heart on this, but I have no idea what it's telling me.

I decide that the only thing I can do is hear Isaiah out before making any final decisions. It's Friday so the kids are at Sasha's. I take that opportunity to go over to Isaiah's house. I decide not to warn him I'm coming over because I want to hear what he has to say without time to rehearse.

I should've called first.

That's what I think to myself when I pull up to Isaiah's house and see Alexis strutting out of there to her car. She looks obnoxiously proud of herself, and my blood boils. Is this what he's going to do every time we have a fight or he gets his feelings hurt—call Alexis and have a drunken hookup? No. I'm not dealing with that.

I turn my car around and put Isaiah in my rearview mirror.

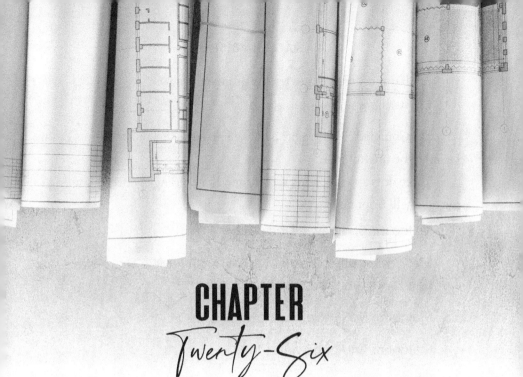

CHAPTER
Twenty-Six

Isaiah

D O YOU WANT TO KNOW HOW MANY GROOVES THERE ARE IN MY
kitchen's hardwood floors? I can tell you. I could probably tell you every
mundane detail about this house considering I've been doing nothing
but staring at it for the past two weeks.

I'm ignoring the guys. I'm ignoring my family. The only people I want
to talk to are the ones who aren't talking to me.

Nina only talks to me when she has something to tell me about LB.
Logan hasn't acknowledged any of my texts in the group chat with Malcolm
and Niecy. I have no way to reach Jada unless I show up at the house, which
is not welcome, or at her school, which will probably land me on some sort
of list.

I'm miserable. I want my family back. They were mine. I don't care that
those kids aren't my blood relation and Nina and I aren't married. I don't
care about any of that. They are my family and I want them back.

But they don't want me.

And fuck, does that hurt.

I pull out my phone and try the group chat again.

Me: What's everyone up to?

That sounded casual, right? Not like I'm desperate for a response. Damn, I used to be the fun one.

Three dots appear on my screen, and I'm holding my breath waiting to see who will respond.

Malcolm: Bad news, Uncle Zay

Me: You're up to bad news? Why say it like that? Have you been watching too much Golden Girls?

Malcolm: No I have bad news

Malcolm: And good news too

Oh shit.

Me: What's the bad news?

Malcolm: Mom found out Niecy went to the Post Malone concert. She took her phone away

Malcolm: So she's probably gonna call you

Fuck. It's a good thing I'm ignoring everyone then; hopefully I can wait her out.

Me: *inserts gif of Tony Stark sighing in frustration* And the good news?

Malcolm: She hasn't found out about me yet

Great, so I'll just keep avoiding her until that comes out.
There's a knock on my door, and I'm suddenly afraid for my life.

Me: Where's your mom now?

Malcolm: In the kitchen, why?

Okay, good. So at least I know she's not at my door prepared to kill me.

Me: No reason.

I walk toward my door, trying to think of a way I can get Logan to respond. He won't respond to my one-on-one texts, so the group chat is my only chance.

I look out of my window and see Lincoln and Kai standing at my front door. It's just the two of them. I don't see Shane or Dom anywhere, so it's not a complete ambush. They're probably here as the warm-up. To get me to open up and talk and then convince me to leave the house and meet up with everyone else. I'm not interested.

"Yo, jackass. Are you just gonna stare at us through your window or are you gonna open the door?" Lincoln waves his hand to get my attention. I flip him off and walk back over to my couch, using all my energy to flop down on it hard.

I hear a key turning in my doorknob, and I pull one of my throw pillows over my head. I forgot that fucker has a key.

"Damn, this is worse than we thought." I peek from under my pillow to find Kai sniffing the damn air.

"Fuck off."

"You need a damn shower. And how much takeout can one person eat?" Lincoln knocks over the tower of Chinese take-out containers I was building. I put a lot of effort into that tower.

"Hey, watch it. I don't come into your place knocking shit over."

"If I was living like this I would want you to."

"I'm living just fine," I lie.

"So if we told you we got Nina to agree to come talk to you and she was on her way right now, you'd be okay with her seeing your place like this? You'd be okay with smelling like that?" Kai asks. I jump up and look around my house. It's a fucking mess. There's take-out containers and beer bottles everywhere. I've taken off work for the last three days, so I've just been lying in my filth. It's embarrassing. Shit.

"Don't fuck with me. Did you?" I ask.

"Hell, no. Because we knew you'd look like this. You gotta get your shit together, man," Kai scolds.

"I don't know what to do. She won't talk to me unless it's about the baby. And the kids won't talk to me at all."

"So take what you can get. Whether or not you two are together, you still have a kid coming into this world in less than two months, so you need to pull it together." Now it's Lincoln's turn to scold me.

"I know that. I'm gonna be the best dad ever. But how do I fix what I broke with them?" It doesn't escape my notice that I said I'm gonna be the best dad ever. There was a time when I thought no kid needed me as a parent. That I wasn't worthy. But fuck that. There's no way I can be a bad dad when I love this kid as much as I do already. It's not possible.

Lincoln shrugs. "Beg."

Kai nods. "And you need to show her and the kids with your actions that they're your number one priority and you care about them."

"You gotta pull out all the stops," Lincoln adds.

"And take a fucking shower," they say at the same time. Assholes.

"Alright. I hear you."

"Good. Now we're going to meet up with Dom and Shane. Do you wanna join?"

"Nah, I gotta figure this out."

Lincoln puffs his chest out with pride. "Good answer. See ya later, little brother."

I don't follow them to the door. I'm too busy trying to figure out what I can do to show Nina, Jada, and Logan how sorry I am. I absently sniff my T-shirt and almost gag from the fumes. Okay, they had a good point; a shower is a must.

I'm fresh out of my shower when I hear a knock on my door. What the fuck is with all the unexpected visitors? I slip on a pair of sweats and a T-shirt before running downstairs to open my door.

Fuck. Why didn't I check to see who it was before I opened the door? I am not in the mood for Alexis tonight. Or ever, really.

"Alexis, it's not a good time." She ignores me and side steps her way into the house. Okay then.

"I thought I'd come check on you. I heard about your rough time at

Monica's." She rests her hand against my shoulder. I look at it then back to Alexis, and I let out a deep sigh. This needs to stop. Once and for all. I grab her hand and gently remove it.

"Sit down, Alexis." She practically skips over to the couch as if she's won a prize.

She starts to say something, but I just cut her off. "I'm sorry."

Her brows wrinkle in confusion. "Sorry for what?"

"That we ended up here. I never should have hooked up with you. Not because you're not great, but because I did it for the wrong reasons. I wanted to hurt Monica after she hurt me, and I used you to do that. You used me too for whatever toxic-ass competition you two have with each other, but I should've never let it get this far."

She sighs and hangs her head, but when she looks back up at me that confident smile is back in place. "We have fun together."

"Yes and no. It was great in the moment, but every time we hooked up we were drunk and I was fucked up over another woman. Don't you want more than that? Don't you want a guy who wants to be with you because he wants you? Not to get over someone else?"

Her smile falls at that, but she doesn't say anything.

"I'm done, Alexis. I don't want any part of this anymore."

"You love her, don't you? That girl?"

"Yes. I do," I say without hesitation.

She nods and stands up. "You know, I saw you first. Before Monica. I was the one who noticed you and wanted you, but Monica stepped right in and caught your attention. No one saw me when she was around." This is the first time I'm hearing this, and it makes me see her in a whole new light. "After a while, I realized that me pursuing you was more about getting the upper hand with Monica than about my feelings for you."

"It was about winning."

"Exactly. I'm sorry for the damage I caused."

"I forgive you, Alexis." A weight is lifted from my shoulders.

She gives me a small smile. It feels like the first honest smile she's ever given me. "For what it's worth, it seemed like she really loves you too." I can only hope that's still true. "She never for a second doubted you when I confronted her at that restaurant. She's a keeper." That she is.

I walk Alexis to the door. It's time to start working on my master plan.

The next morning, I decide to call Nina. I want to see if I can get her to meet up with me.

"Hello?"

"Hey, Nina. You answered—good."

"What do you need, Isaiah?" she asks in a clipped tone. She hasn't sounded angry with me in the few times we've talked since the night everything blew up so I'm wondering what's going on.

"Are you okay?"

"I'm fine."

"You don't sound fine. You want me to sing some Katy Perry? Lighten the mood?" My brain is screaming to shut up, but my mouth keeps running. Jesus.

She scoffs. "Listen, I think we need some boundaries."

"Boundaries?"

"Yeah, boundaries. I think we need to focus on co-parenting. Little Bean needs both of us, and it would be better if we could be cordial and co-parent in a positive way instead of trying to do whatever we were doing before and end up hating each other."

My heart takes a slash at that. "I could never hate you." She's silent for so long I think she hung up at first.

"I need you to agree to this, okay?"

No. Absolutely not okay. "Wildflower, I know I fucked up."

"No. Don't Wildflower me. We're Little Bean's parents and that's it. If you're looking for a hookup I'm sure Alexis can help you with that."

Alexis? Why would she bring her up?

Oh shit. Oh shit, shit, shit. She must've seen Alexis leaving my place last night.

"Wait, Nina. Listen to me. If you saw Alexis last night, it wasn't what you think."

"It's none of my business, Isaiah. You have your life, and I have mine. We should focus on living them." No. No. I want to live my life with her.

"Please just hear me out."

"I have to go." She hangs up and that's it.

This just keeps getting worse and worse. I have to fix this. I refuse to just be cordial with her. I can't go through life seeing her at LB's birthday parties, award ceremonies, graduations, and not be able to touch her. Hold her. Kiss her. I can't go back to Jada and Logan being Nina's sister and brother and nothing to me. I can't do it.

Kai says I need to show them I'm serious, and I plan to do just that.

I realize I've been fighting this battle with one hand tied behind my back. I need help to make this plan work. And to get that help, I'm going to have to come clean with my sisters.

I call Sasha and Reggie over to my house, and after Reggie reams me out for helping Niecy and Malcolm with their "dumbass kid behavior," I unload the story about Monica and the baby and what happened with Nina as a result.

Reggie looks pissed. Sasha looks hurt.

"Why didn't you tell us?" Sasha asks.

"I should've. But I didn't want to face you."

"Face us? What did you think we'd do? Laugh at you?" This from Reggie.

"I didn't want to be the failure of the family. You told me my whole life that I didn't take shit seriously, and I didn't want to hear you say I told you so when you found out that Monica cheated on me for that exact reason. I didn't want to hear you tell me that it was probably for the best that I wasn't having a kid then. You two didn't even want me watching your kids. You only called me when you had no other options."

"Are you serious? You actually think we—"

"Reggie, that's enough," Sasha demands. She puts one hand on Reggie's knee and reaches across the couch to grab my hand with her other. "I'm sorry."

What? "You're sorry?"

"I'm sorry that we made you feel like that's how we would react. We joke around that you're a big kid that we can't trust with our kids, but we don't mean it. I would put Nevaeh's life in your hands without question. Yeah, you're a jokester, but I'd never change that about you. You brighten everyone's day. The sun rises and sets with your laughter."

Reggie sighs. "What she said without the extra sappy shit. I may be incredibly angry with you for encouraging my kids to misbehave, but that's because I'm a mom and I don't like my authority being questioned. It's a power-trip thing. But I'm grateful that you take them on adventures. Lord knows they'd be the most boring, straitlaced kids without you. And I know I can trust you with their well-being." I didn't realize how much I needed to hear this from them. That they actually trust me and don't think I'm a total screwup. "Oh and also, fuck Monica. She's the joke, not you. If I ever see her I'm punching her right in her lady bits."

Now that gets me to laugh.

"Does that hurt as much as it does with guys?"

"How would I know? But it'll still hurt."

"Well, okay then."

"Now that that's settled, let's get you and my bestie back together, shall we?"

"Yes, please."

CHAPTER
Twenty-Seven

Nina

I WALK INTO NEON NIGHTS AND IT'S BEEN TRANSFORMED INTO THE perfect baby shower. Ciara and Sasha leaned into the movie theme that Isaiah used for the nursery. There's a huge clapboard that reads "Production: Little Bean, Director: Nina & Isaiah, Scene: Austin, Texas, Take: 1" hanging up so people can take pictures in front of it. The buffet is set up like a theater concession stand complete with must-have movie snacks and cupcakes. There are plenty of baby games, one of them being a baby movie quotes game where you have to match the movie title to the baby-related quote like "Mama always said life is like a box of chocolates" or "Hasta la vista, baby."

It's absolutely perfect. Brittany, Simone, and Sarah flew in for the weekend to be here, and I love them for that. Reggie's here. Trinity is here. Angela is here. Lindsay and Julie are here. Jada, Nevaeh, and Niecy are here too. All my favorite ladies.

"Aww, Boss Lady, you look so cute." Lindsay twirls me around in my "Mom, sister, all around badass" tee and maxi skirt.

I'm so happy to be here surrounded by these badass women who love me and Little Bean so much, but I can't stop missing Isaiah. I'm pissed as fuck. How dare he still be in my head like this? He needs to just get the fuck out of my head. I'm trying to enjoy my baby shower. But it's his as much as it is mine, and he's not here. Fuck.

"The testosterone has joined the party!" Shane yells as he walks in. He's followed by Dom, Lincoln, Kai, Michael, Carter, Malcolm, Isaiah's dad, David, and Logan.

"Oh wow, you guys actually came. Don't you dare think about eating all the damn cupcakes," Ciara scolds.

"We're here to play all the games. Take all the measurements of your belly, guess the movie quotes..." Lincoln lists in a singsong voice.

"Eat melted chocolate from a diaper," Ciara adds.

"I feel like that's supposed to scare me, but I'm all for it. Bring it on. I'm a chocolate connoisseur. I will smoke you guys in that game," Shane declares.

I hug all the guys and the baby games commence, but the whole time I'm thinking about the one guy who should be here and isn't.

The music on the speakers cuts off, and suddenly I hear what sounds kind of like a cat dying while singing "Can't Take My Eyes Off You." Isaiah comes around the corner with a mic in his hand and locks eyes with me. Then the band starts playing over the speakers and he continues singing—and I say that generously—the song. He's my very own Heath Ledger. I can't help the laugh that bursts out of me watching this performance. Everyone is hollering and cheering him on, and he marches right up to me and takes my hand with a wink.

He sings about loving me and needing me while looking right into my eyes. My eyes are brimming with tears, and Little Bean is kicking with excitement. I don't interrupt his singing, but I do take his hand and place it on my belly. His voice cracks when he feels her kick.

The song ends and everyone claps, but his eyes never leave mine.

"What are you doing?" I ask him.

"Co-parenting and nothing else is never gonna be good enough, Wildflower. I want you. I want our family. I'll do whatever it takes to prove that to you. I love you. I've loved you for a while. I don't know why I didn't say it before, but I'm saying it now and I'm gonna keep saying it for the rest of our lives." He takes a step away from me and looks around until his eyes land on Jada. She's on her tiptoes looking like she's champing at the bit to come over here. He motions for her to come over, and she runs right to my side. He looks and finds Logan and asks him to join us too.

"I have something I want to say to you three." He lines us up side by side and pulls a piece of paper out of his pocket.

He clears his throat and then gets on his knees in front of Jada.

"I love the way you sass at me,

And the way you make me tumble.

I love the way you always beat me at Uno,

And yet you're still so humble."

Holy shit. Holy fucking shit. This man remixed the poem Kat reads in *10 Things I Hate About You.* Cue the damn tears.

"I'm sorry that I let you down,

And that I made you cry.

I love you so much it hurts,

It even makes me rhyme."

He holds his hand out to her, and she hesitates for only a moment before diving into their special handshake and wrapping him up in a big hug. He stands up so that he's facing Logan before continuing his poem.

"I love you. I love the way you're always reading.

I love when we're on the same track.

I love the way you love your sisters,

Even more how you have their back."

He holds his hand out to Logan, and Logan smirks before giving him a bro hug. I can tell just by looking at him that he's impressed.

He moves over to stand face to face with me, and new tears form in the corner of my eyes but he catches them before they can fall.

"I love how you're carrying Little Bean,

And how you always make the right call.

But mostly I love the way I love you completely.

231

With my whole heart.

My whole soul.

I vow to give you my all."

I let out a half laugh, half cry and fall into his arms.

"I'm so sorry, Wildflower. I'm so sorry, guys. I know I messed up, and I'm sure I'll mess up again because I'm me, but I promise you no one is more important to me than you guys. I love you."

"I love you, ZayZay!" Jada yells.

"Good to have you back, man," Logan adds.

My turn. "I love you, KP. So much."

"Thank God." His lips crash into mine and I deepen the kiss before remembering where we are and pulling back.

"So where's my guitar?"

"Your what?"

"Well, you went all Patrick and Kat on me, but you missed one of the grand gestures. I'm gonna need my guitar now."

"Oh well, I gotta save something for the next time I mess up, don't I?"

"You know there's always drums, and bass, and maybe even one day a tambourine."

He throws his head back in laughter and rests his chin on top of my head. "Wildflower, I'll give you the world."

CHAPTER
Twenty-Eight

Isaiah

"WAKE UP! WAKE UP! IT'S SURPRISE DAY!" MY EYES FLUTTER OPEN to see Jada jumping up and down in front of me. I look over, and Nina is still dead to the world. Last night, she struggled to get to sleep so I know today is going to be rough on her on top of the obvious reason.

"Why don't you come with me to the kitchen? We'll make breakfast for Nina."

"Okay." She scurries into the kitchen, and I look again at Nina lying in our bed. And yes, I say our bed because I officially live here now. Two weeks after we got back together, Nina relented that she wanted me to be here with her and the kids, and I couldn't be happier. Waking up to her every morning is a dream come true.

I head out to the kitchen to find Jada pulling a pack of bacon out of the fridge. I ruffle the top of her head and pull out the stuff to make pancakes. Jada's favorite part is cracking the eggs, so I let her do that in a separate bowl and pick out the shells afterward. Logan comes in not too long after, so I put him to work cooking the bacon. We work together in perfect harmony until we have an impressive stack of pancakes, a mound of bacon, and some fresh strawberries. Logan and I carry all the plates up to the bedroom, and Nina is sitting up rubbing her eyes when we walk in.

"I thought I smelled bacon. I was about to come investigate. What's going on?"

"We wanted to have breakfast together but didn't want to make you get out of bed just yet, so here we are." Logan and Jada settle on the floor while I sit back on the bed next to Nina and hand her a plate.

"Mmm, delicious. Thank you, guys."

We eat our breakfast in comfortable silence. Nina finishes off her orange juice and then asks the kids, "So are you guys ready for today?"

Logan chimes in. "Yeah, I wanna know what you have up your sleeve, Zay. Just as long as it doesn't involve singing." I chuckle at the asshole. I've been getting shit nonstop from everyone since I sang "Can't Take My Eyes Off You" to win Nina back. I never said I was a good singer, but it got the job done so I can't be ashamed.

I'm honestly nervous about today, but I hope they like what I have planned. Today is the first anniversary of their parents' death. I know they have complicated feelings about their parents and their death is still hard on all of them, so I planned a surprise for them. I want to help them release a little bit of what I know they've been holding in and maybe associate today with healing instead of pain.

"Ha. Ha. Keep it up and I'm gonna sing the entire way there. Matter of fact, let me start my vocal warm-ups right now." I clear my throat and then begin "Mi mi mi mi. Do Re Mi Fa So La Ti Do." I start to do the run again but they all start yelling their objections.

"Please no more!"

"Make it stop!"

"Good God, please stop. That is not the voice Little Bean needs to associate with her daddy."

I shrug. "Listen, I can't have it all, you know? If I could sing I'd be just

234

a little too perfect." Jada fakes a gag, Logan throws a fork at me, and Nina rolls her eyes.

"Okay, Mr. Perfect. I'm gonna get dressed. You guys go too. Save yourselves." She whispers the last part and they leave laughing. I walk up behind her and wrap my arms around her belly and nuzzle my head in her neck.

"How are you doing today, Wildflower?"

She places her hands on top of mine. "I'm doing okay. I miss them. But I also love this family we've created, and I'm happy."

"Me too."

An hour later, we pull up to our destination—Lake Austin. The weather is gorgeous today which makes this even better. I lead them over to an empty spot I find close to the water. I pull out blankets for the kids and me to sit on and a maternity beach chair I found for Nina because I know if she sits on the ground it'll take all three of us to get her back up.

"Okay, are we ready?"

They all nod enthusiastically, and I pull out my project.

"Are those boats?" Logan asks.

"Yep. Wishboats."

"What do we do with them?"

"So we're going to write messages and then put them on the boats with lit candles and send them out into the water. You can write anything you want, but I thought you could write something to your parents. Tell them everything you wish you had a chance to tell them. Everything you want them to know. Get it all out. Let it go."

"Do you think they'll see what we write?" Jada asks, chewing on her fingernail.

"Do you want them to?"

She thinks for a moment and then nods.

"Then I think they will. Write what's in your heart. It's okay to be sad, angry, happy. Whatever you're feeling just feel it completely and let it go."

Jada's frown turns into a wide smile as she nods. Logan looks at the boats with apprehension.

"You don't have to let each other read what you wrote, but you can if you want. You're probably all feeling some of the same things, but it's up to you. When we're all done, we'll release them. And then we'll put this day behind us as best we can and move on."

Logan nods, and I hand him a stack of paper and a pen. Jada decides to write hers with a pencil. I turn to Nina to hand her a stack and a pen, and tears are rolling down her face.

"I'm sorry, was this not a good idea?"

"You're amazing." I take her hand in mine and kiss her knuckles with a smirk. "Are you gonna do one?" she asks.

"Yeah, I am."

"Who are you writing to? If you don't mind me asking."

"I've actually got some things I want to say to your parents." Her brow wrinkles but she just nods and starts writing.

Everyone focuses on writing their own messages, but I look around and see the emotions rolling off all of them. The words flow easily for me.

Dear Mr. and Mrs. Williams,

Thank you. Thank you for bringing three of the best human beings to ever exist into this world.

Nina describes her childhood as complicated. She always felt supported by you even if she felt she had to remind you to do so, but she grew up to be one of the most amazing, intelligent, compassionate, and driven women I've ever met. I have to believe that part of that is because of you, so you can rest easy knowing you did right by her.

I wish you had taken the time to get to know Logan and Jada. They are amazing kids and they're going to accomplish so much in life. I feel sorry for you that won't get to experience them here, but I'm hoping you're looking down on them now with pride.

I can make a few promises to you. I promise that I am going to love and care for them for the rest of my life.

I promise that I'm going to make Nina happy. I love her with every piece of me. I've taken my heart out and given it to her and yet I've never felt so whole. I will make sure she feels cherished every single day.

I promise that Logan and Jada will never again feel abandoned. I love them as if they're my own, and they will never spend a moment doubting how much I love and value them.

I promise that my daughter will know about her grandparents. We'll tell her and her future siblings about how their grandparents lived in the moment. We'll travel the world in your memory.

I promise that they're going to be okay.

-Isaiah

We decide not to read our messages to each other. There's no need to go through those emotions again. They've been released, and now it's time to let them go. We attach our messages to our boats and watch them sail away. Logan's shoulders relax more the farther out they get. Jada looks on excitedly. Nina looks completely at peace. I don't think I've ever seen her look so serene, and it lets me know I made the right decision.

Nina and I send the kids back to the car while we reel the boats back in to dispose of them. Nina chuckles to herself, and I raise my brows in question.

"I'm just laughing at how incredibly wrong I was about you."

"Oh yeah? What did you think of me?"

"Well, I thought you probably had a big dick, and I was definitely not wrong about that. But I also thought I'd never date you because you wouldn't commit. And yet here you are, loving me unconditionally. Being a pseudo-dad to my brother and sister. A real dad to Little Bean. I've just never been happier to be wrong. That's all."

I take her face in my hands. "I'll never be good enough for you, Wildflower. But I'll be damned if I let you go now."

She turns her face in my hand and kisses it. "Now let's get home so I can put this big dick to good use."

She laughs and smacks my hand away. "Nah-uh. Sorry, but you're officially cut off from action."

"What? Why?"

"Because Little Bean is a fully formed fetus now, and I'm lowkey scared your dick might actually poke her, and I don't wanna be the reason she needs therapy right out of the womb."

"Are you serious?" She just shrugs. Shrugs. I'm officially scarred for life and she just shrugs.

Her eyes twinkle with amusement before a deep laugh bursts from her lips. "I'm kidding, KP. I asked the doctor so we're all good. Take me home." She starts walking toward the car, but I'm still rooted in place.

I call out to her, "You actually asked the doctor this?"

She just looks back with a wink.

CHAPTER
Twenty-Nine

Nina

"OKAY, LISTEN HERE, LITTLE BEAN. I'VE ENJOYED CARRYING YOU these past nine months. It's been quite the bonding experience, but I would like my body back so I'm evicting you. You need to get out. Like now." I speak directly to my belly, but she doesn't even stir.

I'm six days past my due date, and I'm miserable. Pregnancy was rough in the beginning, but the last two trimesters weren't bad at all. But these last six days? No, actually, these past two weeks have been hell. At first I wasn't complaining because I could see the light at the end of the tunnel, but of course my daughter is stubborn and has decided she'll come out when she's good and goddamn ready.

The doctor said if I'm not in labor two weeks past my due date that they will induce. If Doctor Hunter and Little Bean think she's staying in here for eight more days, they're both crazy. She's out of here. Today.

"You know, we could try some vigorous activity to get her to come out." Isaiah wiggles his eyebrows at me, and I throw a pillow at him.

"Stay away from me." He laughs and calls Logan and Jada to our room.

"You guys wanna go for a family walk? We're trying to convince LB to exit Nina's body."

They agree and run to grab their shoes. Thirty minutes later, I'm completely over walking with my ankles swelling to the size of tennis balls, but my water hasn't broken. Damn stubborn child.

I blast "Can't Take My Eyes Off You," which has become our song, through the speakers. Our version is the Lauryn Hill cover though. I dance my little heart out and still this child sits. I'm personally offended. Does she enjoy her mother's suffering? Or should I feel honored that she doesn't want to leave my womb? I don't feel honored. Not one bit.

I call Ciara because I know she's probably writing at Sasha's so I can talk to both of them together.

"Is this the call that we need to head to the hospital?"

I scoff. "I wish. She won't get out. How do I get her out?"

"I gotta say you are not making a positive case for pregnancy at this time."

"Shut up. Little Bean needs a cousin her age so keep fucking like rabbits until it happens. But in the meantime, let's focus on getting this baby to exit my body."

Sasha jumps on the line at that point. "How's it going, babe?"

"This is trash."

She laughs like it's the funniest thing I've ever said, but I'm dead serious. "I know, being late sucks. But it happens a lot for your first pregnancy. I was three days late with Nevaeh. Reggie was a week late with Niecy but three days early for Malcolm."

"Don't even talk to me about second children right now."

"Did you try working out?"

"Yeah."

"Pineapple? Spicy food? Sex?"

"No, no, and yes. We had sex last night and here I am, not in labor. So he gets no more benefits until they're of use to me." I put the call on speaker so I can call out to Isaiah and ask him to run to the store for pineapple and spicy food.

"I'm not leaving because the minute I do will be the minute you go into labor. Then again, that would be great driving practice for Logan."

"He's only fourteen."

"Yeah, so he'll be ahead of the game."

"Good God, Izzy, I would not push her if I were you."

"You're right. I'll go cook up something spicy, okay?"

"Okay. Sasha, what else you got?"

"I got nothing. Maybe the spicy food will be the key."

"Ugh, fine. I'm gonna go. If I call you again, don't answer."

"What? Why?"

"KP will call you when it's actually go time, but if I call you it'll only be to cuss you out because the spicy food didn't work. But I'm not actually mad at you, I'm just highly irritable so it's best to just avoid me."

They both laugh. "Yes, ma'am. Hey, before you go, are you ever gonna tell us why you call him KP?"

"Sorry. I'm legally bound by the dick contract not to give you any more ammo against him."

"I'm gonna find out one day. Mark my words."

I hang up and let my nose lead me to the kitchen.

Surprise, surprise. The spicy food didn't work. When Little Bean gets here, she and I are gonna have a long discussion about boundaries.

"What do you wanna do now?" I hand him my phone and he laughs, having heard my comment to Sasha earlier.

"I give up. I can't try another thing. Let's just watch a movie." We settle on the couch and start watching *10 Things I Hate About You*.

We get all the way to the part where Bianca punches Joey when Little Bean decides it's time to get this show on the road. What an asshole. She really is her mother's daughter.

At the hospital, labor is agonizing. Now that she's on her way out I want her back in.

"I can't do this," I scream at Isaiah. He grabs my hand, and I squeeze as hard as I can.

"You can do this. You're a badass. There's nothing you can't do."

I start my breathing again. "Okay. Okay. Distract me. Talk to me about something else."

"Umm. Okay, yeah. Do you wanna know why I call you Wildflower?"

I never realized until this moment that I never asked him why he calls me that. He started calling me that when he brought wildflowers to our first date, but I didn't realize there was a deeper reason. "Yeah. Tell me."

"It's because a wildflower is a flower that grows in the wild."

What the fuck kind of shit is that? "Very observant."

He chuckles. "It grows in the wild because it wasn't intentionally seeded or planted. It grows where it shouldn't naturally. That's you. You've grown and flourished in spite of everything that's been stacked against you. You were never supposed to be a mom to your brother and sister, but you've taken that on and excelled at it. You were only supposed to manage Neon Nights, but you made it your own and turned it into the success it is today. You don't need someone to plant you; you grow on your own."

"Well, shit. That's incredibly sweet. I may just agree to have sex with you again one day."

"Thank fuck."

"Keep going. Distract me some more."

"Okay. How about a question?"

"Hit me."

"Will you marry me?"

Wait, what? "Huh?"

"Will you marry me?"

"Are you fucking serious?"

"Very."

"I'm a sweaty, nasty mess, pushing your big-headed baby out of my vagina, and you're proposing?"

"You're bringing our daughter into this world. You have never looked more beautiful to me."

Alright, he's getting major swoon points for that. If he's not careful we're going to end up with Irish twins, and that sounds like a nightmare to me. "You and I are gonna work on timing for big moments later, but are you serious? You actually want to get married? I don't want you to propose because you think it's the right thing to do."

He takes one of his hands off of mine to reach into his pocket and pull out a gorgeous cushion-cut engagement ring.

"I've actually been carrying this around for a while, trying to find the perfect moment. Now feels like that moment."

"Holy shit. I love you."

"So is that a yes?"

"Yes, yes, yes." He leans down and lays a sweet kiss on my lips.

"I'll put this on you when your fingers aren't the size of sausages."

I narrow my eyes at him but laugh anyway. "Put my damn ring on."

He laughs and slides it onto my finger. It fits perfectly. Just like us together.

"Okay, Mommy, it's time to push again," Dr. Hunter announces.

Four pushes later, Little Bean enters the world.

She's absolutely perfect. Isaiah cuts the umbilical cord and the nurses clean her off before laying her on my chest. I literally can't take my eyes off of her. Every time I look at her I notice something new that I adore. We made her.

"Look what we did, KP."

"She's perfect just like her mama."

"Hi, Little Bean. It's your mommy and daddy. We love you so much. Your daddy is pretty amazing. And I ain't half bad so I think you're gonna be just fine. What do you think?" She just coos in response, and I may be biased, but it's the cutest coo I've ever heard in my life.

"You know we never decided on a name."

"You have any ideas?" I still don't take my eyes off of her.

"How about Bianca?"

I mull that over until recognition hits me. "Bianca like the younger sister in *10 Things I Hate About You*?"

"The very same. It's kinda cute that she decided to enter the world when we were watching your favorite movie. I imagine you two bonding over that and so many other movies, forcing me to watch them every damn weekend."

"It is pretty cute. I like it. That's funny that you picked the first name because I've been thinking about middle names."

"Are they Nigerian?"

"Of course. I don't wanna face your mother's wrath."

"I'm impressed. What did you come up with?"

"I was thinking either Sade, who not only is one of my favorite singers, but it means honor earns a crown. That or Adamma, which I learned means beautiful daughter. You pick."

"I say Adamma."

"Bianca Adamma Cole. I like it."

"Welcome to the world, Bianca."

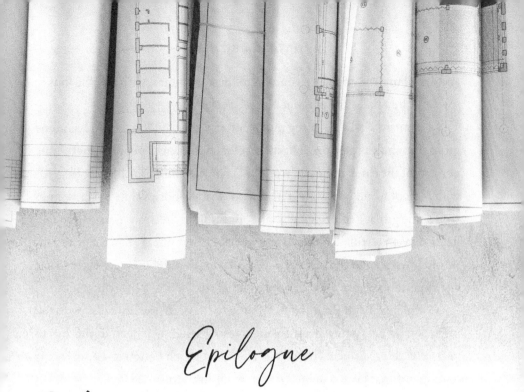

Epilogue

Isaiah

Five months later

"**THIS PLACE IS FUCKING PACKED**," DOM GRUMBLES.

"Well yeah, it's Movie Night. Even though it doesn't start for another hour you know people start piling in early." Nina rolled out her monthly movie idea the minute the bar was officially hers. It's been a huge success. Who doesn't like playing drinking games along with their favorite movies? Doing it in a bar full of people who love the same movie is the ultimate bonding experience.

Nina insisted I come tonight because I need a guys' night and tonight's movie is *Die Hard*, one of my favorites. I know the real reason she wanted me to come tonight is because she wanted me out of her hair. I've been a little annoying but I can't help it—I'm kind of obsessed with my wife and my daughter.

Yeah, you heard me right, my wife. Nina and I got married two months ago. We decided that if we waited to plan a big wedding we'd never do it because life is crazy enough with two careers, raising a teenager, an adolescent, and an infant. We ended up running to the courthouse with just the kids in tow and then had a big party at Neon to celebrate.

Logan and Jada are doing much better these days too. Logan has come out of his shell a lot more. He still prefers books over people ninety-nine percent of the time, but most weekends you can find him either at Reggie's with Malcolm and Niecy, with his friends from robotics club, or sometimes with some girl he's tutoring that Nina always sighs dreamily at when she sees her. Jada isn't terrified at the idea of traveling anymore. When Bianca's a little older we plan to start taking weekend trips to different places just so she can experience more and get used to it before we take a big trip.

I still hear from Brandon from time to time. He mostly calls me to tell me when he gets a new Transformers toy or when he's been to the zoo to visit Blitz. He, Monica, and Harris are doing much better. It seems Harris finding out that he is one hundred percent Brandon's dad kicked his ass in gear to do better by him.

Ciara comes over to take our drink orders. We all order beer except for Kai because he's too busy watching the women's soccer game that's on.

"Oh sorry, Ci. I'll just take a Speedway."

She nods and starts to turn away, but Lincoln grabs her wrist and starts rubbing circles on her pulse point.

"You doing okay tonight?"

She rolls her eyes and laughs. "Yes, Papa. Me and your seed are just fine." Ciara is four months pregnant. Nina about died when they announced it, but I can't lie—I'm excited my brother is having a kid around the same time as me. He's going to be way worse than me when the baby comes. He can't stop fussing over Ciara now and she is sick of it which cracks me up.

"I'm just making sure you're okay on your feet."

"You're so annoying, I love you. Now let me go pour these drinks before you cost me my tips."

"These assholes better tip you." He points to all of us.

"Not them. All the hungry *Die Hard* assholes in this camp." She presses her breasts together in her shirt and Shane coughs a laugh. "How are the tits looking? Pregnancy is working wonders for them, so I plan to use this advantage to rake the tips in."

Lincoln's eyes bug out of his head before he glares at her. "You think you're so funny."

She throws her head back in laughter. "I don't think. I know." She gives him a quick kiss on the lips before rushing away to pour our beers.

I shake my head before pulling my phone out to find a text from Nina. It's a picture of her sitting in front of Jada while she holds Bianca in her lap. Jada's favorite things in this world are gymnastics and board games, but holding Bianca now tops both of those things. She loves the fact that at seven years old she's an auntie, and she takes the role very seriously. No one can mess with her precious niece.

Me: My three favorite girls

Nina: Aren't we cute?

Me: Cute doesn't do you justice

Nina: So remember how I kicked you out of the house because you were on my nerves with your constant hovering?

Me: LOL hmm I thought it was because you thought I needed a guys night and Neon is playing Die Hard tonight?

Nina: Right...that. That's what I meant. Anyway, can I change my mind?

Me: You want me to come home?

Nina: I kinda miss your annoying ass tonight. Plus Jada has demanded that Bianca sleep in her room tonight so umm mommy and daddy could have some alone time *wink wink nudge nudge*

Nina: Unless you're having too much fun with the guys

Me: Fuck the guys! On my way

Nina: LOL *inserts gif of Cardi B with her tongue out*

Jesus. I need to pay my tab and get the fuck out of here. When the wife says it's time to fuck, you fuck. We're in a weird in-between place—in the horny newlywed stage on one hand and raising three kids on another. Privacy doesn't exist anymore, but that just means we've gotten really good at sneaking around and being creative with our alone time. If you've never had sex in your SUV during your lunch break or taken a sick day from work and begged your parents to watch your baby so you can fuck like rabbits while the kids are in school then you wouldn't understand.

Kai's gasp pulls my attention to him. I see he's caught up in the TV again. Ciara notices his freak-out and turns the volume up.

The announcer speaks. "US midfielder, Olivia Harding, went down and it looks bad. Her upper body went one way and her knee went the other. The team medics just carried her off the field. I think it's safe to say she won't be returning for the rest of the game. She might be out for the rest of the season, if not longer."

I look over at Kai, and he's just staring slack-jawed. He looks like his heart has been torn out of his chest. Kai never gave me details about the woman from his past—the one who got away. I think this Olivia woman holds the key. Before I get a chance to ask, Kai throws some cash on the bar for his tab and takes off.

Something tells me that he's starting to plan for that second chance he said he'd never give up if it came his way.

The end

Want more of Isaiah & Nina?
Sign up for my Mailing List to get this exclusive Bonus Epilogue of them two years in the future!

Go here for the Bonus Epilogue:
https://dl.bookfunnel.com/nqscs1gg0v

Also by

NATASHA BISHOP

The Lost & Found Series

Acknowledgements

Wow, is this really my second published book? If this is a dream, don't wake me up. I'm so humbled and honored that you decided to pick up my second book baby and actually read it. Thank you! It means the world to me.

Mom—Mama we made it! I don't know if I'll ever reach your level of style, grace, and badassery but I continue to strive for it every day. Love you to the moon and back!

Brad—Please accept this as your Executive Producer credit. Now will you please stop crying about it?! Also, thank you for being my photographer and begrudgingly teaching me how to edit Tik Toks. Next step is getting you to be in Tik Toks with me.

Kim & Chula!!!—My BABWKAs for life. I honestly can't even put into words how grateful I am that we connected and became besties! Thank goodness for Kim's thirstiness over firefighters. You two are always there for me no matter what and I don't know where I'd be without you. Our brainstorming sessions and story times are *chef's kiss*. I love you both with my whole heart and I can't wait until the world gets to see your talents.

Jerrica—I'm so thankful we were put in each other's path. You're stuck with me now! Your feedback on Isaiah and Nina's story gave me the push I needed to move forward. I appreciate you so much and whenever you need me, I'm here for you. No matter what.

Andrea & Eve—I love you both so hard. You're always down to let me bounce ideas off of you and for that I'm so grateful. You're both badasses and I admire the hell out of you!

Tricia—Thank you for sticking with me through books one and two. Your feedback is so helpful every single time!

Stacey—This cover is insane! Thank you so much for all that you do. Everything you put into this series has been a labor of love and I couldn't imagine doing this series without you.

Linda & Alissa—You guys are truly the best. I'm pretty sure my mind would've already exploded into a million pieces if it weren't for you two keeping me together. Words can't express how hard I appreciate you. Thank you!

Bish Brigade—To all the bloggers, bookstagrammers, readers, etc. who read this book, share it, leave reviews and ratings, and just continue on this journey with me, thank you! The Romance community is truly amazing and I'm so blessed to be here. Thank you for giving me a chance. From the bottom of my heart.

ABOUT
the Author

Natasha is an indie contemporary romance author living in Baltimore, MD with her family and fur baby.

She likes to write about everyday heroes who are a bit haunted and heroines who are sweet, sassy, and a little badass-y.

When she's not writing, she's usually reading, obsessively binge-watching TV, playing with her adorable dog, or hunting down delicious gluten free snacks.

Stay Connected!

Newsletter Sign Up (https://geni.us/NBNewsletterSignUp)
Goodreads (https://geni.us/GoodreadsNatashaBishop)
Instagram (Natasha Bishop (@natashabishopwrites))
Tik Tok (https://geni.us/NBTikTok)
Facebook Reader Group (https://geni.us/BishBrigade)
Facebook Author Page (https://geni.us/NBAuthorPage)
Amazon (https://geni.us/NBAmazonAuthorPage)
Linktr.ee (https://linktr.ee/NatashaBishop)
Website (Authornatashabishop.com)

Made in the USA
Las Vegas, NV
30 December 2023

83723407R00152